A DARKNESS OVER COVENANT

*To Rev/Chief Gary Hall
God Bless You,
WJ Eyer*

A DARKNESS OVER COVENANT

WILLIAM J. EYER

Bridge Publishing
South Plainfield, NJ

The Scripture quotations in this publication are from the King James Version of the Bible.

A Darkness Over Covenant by William J. Eyer
ISBN 0-88270-722-1
Library of Congress Catalog Card Number 95-77899
Copyright © 1995 by Bridge Publishing, Inc.

Published by:
Bridge Publishing Inc.
2500 Hamilton Blvd.
South Plainfield, NJ 07080

Printed in the United States of America.
All rights reserved under International Copyright Law. Contents and/or cover may not be reproduced in whole or in part in any form without the express written consent of the Publisher.

Dedicated to . . .

my mother and father, who by their own choice
brought me into their lives—and gave me hope.

my wife, Jan, my daughter, Terra, and my son, Jarrett—my reasons for living.

all Christians who are presently fighting for Jesus on the front lines of life.

TABLE OF CONTENTS

1. THE AMBUSH 1
2. MEMORIES 15
3. AARON'S PROMOTION 27
4. HOLDING ON BY A THREAD 33
5. HEAVENLY VISIT 47
6. PRAYERS VS. MURDEROUS THOUGHTS 53
7. THE SIEGE BEGINS 73
8. EVIL DOCTOR—SWEET WIFE 83
9. TUMULT DECLARES WAR 91
10. THE HEAVENLY LIFE 113
11. DEMONIC BOMBS—ANGELIC SHIELDS 119
12. THE TEMPLE 139
13. THE ANGELS FLEE 153
14. UNTHINKABLE ACTS 161
15. CODE BLUE 173
16. DR. WHITE IS APPREHENDED 179
17. A MIRACLE FOR THE PRESIDENT 191
18. CONVERT AND MURDER 199
19. A DEFECTOR'S HELP 207
20. WITCH OR CHRISTIAN 221
21. THE TROUBLE WITH TAPES 231
22. CASUALTY OF WAR 239
23. THE BATTLE OF COVENANT 249
24. THE STATE OF THE UNION 259

Acknowledgments

I would like to express my appreciation to my good friend, Debbie Fritchley, for telling me to put more meat on the skeleton of my story.

My heartfelt thanks to Father Hayes for giving me the computer on which to work.

Thank you Gene Brown, Rev. Beyers, Mary Esker, Rev. Meyers, and Darla Loos for reading the first drafts of this novel.

I am also grateful to my publisher, Guy J. Morrell, to Catherine J. Barrier, and to my editor, Hollee Chadwick-Loney, as well as all the other wonderful people at Bridge Publishing who have made this work a reality.

And finally, to my Lord and Savior, Jesus Christ, who through the Holy Spirit has brought to life a wonderful gift in me—I am eternally grateful.

Chapter 1
The Ambush

The demon streaked across the night sky amid flashes of unnatural lightning. He landed on the roof of the building and hunkered there like a gruesome gargoyle on an ancient temple. Beside him knelt a human sniper, carefully wiping his weapon with a thick, soft cloth. The apparition reached over and buried the slime-coated yellow claws of his twisted right hand deep into the man's skull.

The sniper put his arm through the sling of his rifle and placed the butt-end against his right shoulder, looking through the night scope which provided an illuminated though dull, green overcast view. He scanned the alley below, his heart racing with anticipation like a predator with the scent of his prey burning in his nostrils. He smiled and whispered, "This is much too easy!"

He placed the cross hairs of the 30-30 caliber rifle square on his target and slowly squeezed the trigger.

*   *   *

"C-4, this is Central."

The static of the police radio broke the stillness in the squad car.

"Central, this is C-4. Go ahead."

"C-4, we have a 101 in the alley between 22nd and Olive streets."

The officer chuckled as he answered the dispatcher.

"Central, I've never seen a suspicious vehicle yet, only the people who drive them, but I'll check it out,"

"Cute, Josh. You're a real funny guy. Central out."

This Sunday night was like countless others. The air was cool and crisp, just perfect for taking a brisk walk. The moon and stars shone with such brilliance that it made him want to reach up and pull them down from their place in the heavens. A gentle breeze, wafting through the leaves on the trees, brought with it the fresh smell of newly-mown lawns from the nearby residential area.

The officer driving the squad car was Joshua White. He was a six foot-three inch, muscular, two-hundred pound bear of a man. His crisply-pressed, dark blue uniform was decorated with an abundance of ribbons, medals, and his gleaming silver badge. Joshua's still jet-black hair was barber-cut in a neat, no-nonsense style. His only indulgence in vanity was the blue contact lenses that deepened his already deep, blue eyes. His thin face and square jaw gave him a stern and determined look that was softened only by his radiant smile At forty-one years old, he was a twenty year veteran of the Covenant police force

It was still early in Joshua's midnight shift—1:20, according to his watch. The streets were quiet. Occasionally a stray cat would scamper across the street or a dog would bark at some unseen intruder. The late night strollers had long since returned to their homes, most of which were already totally dark.

It had been a slow evening, for which he was thankful. He'd had to remind a few under-aged teenagers of the 11:00 P.M. curfew and had checked on an alleged prowler, which turned out to be a raccoon rummaging through some garbage cans outside a local restaurant. Other than that, the night had been uneventful.

He wished that he hadn't agreed to work Wilks' shift back to back with his own; he was feeling a little worn around the edges. *Ah well, that's police work for you*, he thought to himself. As Joshua cruised up and down the streets of Covenant, he hummed his favorite praise choruses and talked to God about things he couldn't share with his fellow officers.

He thought about the report he'd given to Chief Wilson, wondering how the chief was going to react to the conspiracy that he'd uncovered. He was afraid that his superior officer would react the same way that Marla Brinkle had.

Ms. Brinkle, an action reporter for the News Channel, had listened patiently as Joshua told her what his investigation had uncovered. He'd discovered that Governor Bradley was a warlock and headed the largest coven in the state. Bradley was planning to use the National Guard to invade Covenant, and strip the Christians living there of their citizenship.

Ms. Brinkle had thanked him for coming and then summarily thrown him out of her office. Well, maybe the chief would listen. Either way, he'd know soon enough—he was due to meet with him at 8:00 A.M.

This call from central wasn't out of the ordinary. In all these years he'd followed up on reports of hundreds of suspicious vehicles. *Probably just another false alarm*, he told himself. *Teenage parkers again*. The thought brought a smile to Joshua's face. *Boy, the stories I could tell some parents about their kids!*

Twenty-second and Olive streets were on the other side of town—the typical other side of the tracks—and embodied every implication in that term. It was a run-down, shabby neighborhood. Many of the buildings had windows boarded up with large sheets of graffiti-covered plywood. The original signs over the storefronts were faded by the weather and the ravages of time. The few windows that remained intact were filthy, with iron or steel bars protecting whatever, or whoever, was hidden by the greasy glass.

The sooty streetlights dimly exposed an equally deteriorated state of affairs on the streets and sidewalks of this section of the city. There was trash everywhere. Broken glass, beer cans, half-smoked cigarettes, crumpled newspaper; floating in the gutters, or strewn on the sidewalks, or hugging some light pole. The whole atmosphere screamed neglect and despair.

A shiver of revulsion crawled down Joshua's spine. The only sound he heard through the open window of his squad car was that of a beer can being tossed along the street by the brisk breeze that was picking up out of the west. He found the intersection indicated by the dispatcher.

As he turned his squad car into the alley between the two run-down buildings, his nose wrinkled involuntarily in distaste at the evidence of how low and uncaring people could become. He tried, unsuccessfully, to ignore the stench as he turned his spotlight on and shined it into the alley. His stomach turned at the sight of the filth everywhere.

The dumpsters behind the buildings were completely full, overflowing with slop and who knows what else. Wine, whiskey, and beer bottles lined the alley, shining in his spotlight like discarded gems.

He couldn't see into the dark shadows--his imagination ran wild with thoughts of the rats who were probably feasting on the rotted garbage which had been haphazardly thrown in the general direction of the dumpsters.

The Ambush

Then he saw the "suspicious vehicle" parked a bit further into the alley, just beyond the dumpsters. He called in his position.

"Central from C-4, I've arrived."

"Go ahead. C-4."

"Sure looks like parkers to me, Mandy. Go figure why anyone would park in this dump. We got one white male on the driver's side, and one white female in the front passenger's seat. I'll stop and have a chat with the lovebirds."

"Lucky you!"

"I'll be out on pack radio, Central."

"10-4, Central out."

Joshua had lived in Covenant all of his life and loved this city of thirty-thousand-plus people. Except for the recent upsurge in illegal drug business and the signs of occult activity, this was a peaceful, non-violent community. The youth still tested the limits of their parent's endurance, as they did anywhere, but they were, for the most part, good kids.

That's why Joshua wasn't too concerned as he marked the 1:30 A.M. time on his field report, turned on his pack radio and removed the flashlight from its charger, located just under the dash by his right knee.

Nor was he concerned when he stepped out of his squad car and noted the night sky rapidly turning overcast. The wind had a chilly bite to it that hadn't been there just an hour ago. As Joshua approached the vehicle, which was lit up by both the spotlight on his squad car and the flashlight in his hand, another shiver ran down his spine.

* * *

A seven-foot tall, translucent figure glowed a pure white in the chilly, overcast night. His nearly-transparent wings unfolded from their neat, flat position on the angel's back as he jumped down from the squad car on which he'd been riding.

Aaron had been assigned to protect Joshua White by Michael the Archangel himself, over forty years ago. He'd gotten him through many dangerous situations and had helped him overcome many trials over the past forty years. He really liked this man of God.

The hedge of protection around Joshua was a strong one—he was a praying man. Aaron had very little trouble getting Joshua's prayers up to God or bringing God's answers back down again.

Aaron's job, however, required caution, so he advanced on the parked car just ahead of Joshua. He had a nagging, uneasy feeling, and he didn't like it. Aaron searched deeper into the alley and spotted the source of his uneasiness thirty yards beyond the vehicle he and Joshua were approaching, on the roof of the building to their left. Aaron whispered in disbelief, "Cono!"

Cono, a hideous, high-ranking demon, one of Satan's best, was looking down at Aaron and Joshua, and an evil smile formed on his lips like a mad dog baring his teeth. He dug his yellow claws into the skull of the sniper who was lining up the cross hairs in the sight of his weapon on Joshua's forehead.

Aaron saw the flash from the muzzle of the powerful 30-30 rifle. He drew his sword, which illuminated the night with its fire and, almost too late, deflected the bullet. Instead of hitting Joshua squarely in the forehead, the bullet grazed his right temple. Aaron let out such a high-pitched scream of rage, that it sent fear into the hearts of all the minor demons that accompanied Cono like leaches wherever he went. Cono just laughed all the more with demonic glee at seeing Aaron's bewildered pain and loss, as Joshua's limp form slumped to the ground of the filthy alleyway.

Joshua had seen a flash, but before he'd even heard the report, he felt the impact of the bullet, as it kissed his right temple. He didn't even remember hitting the ground. He shook his head to clear his rattled brain. *Whoa! I won't do that again!* His head exploded with pain and he splattered himself with his own blood. He felt dizzy and nauseated.

He groped for the mike on his pack radio and called in, "White to Central, 10-32, officer down, need back-up."

Too dazed to say anything else, he just managed to clip the mike back onto his shoulder.

Nothing strikes fear into the heart of a dispatcher faster than those words do.

"C-4 . . . Josh! Respond, C-4."

No response.

Mandy called for back-up.

"All units, proceed to Twenty-second and Olive streets. Shots fired. Officer down."

She dispatched the ambulance and then as she picked up the phone to call Chief Wilson at home, she whispered through her tears, "They said they would just scare him a little."

Joshua drew his 9mm Beretta from its holster and rolled over onto his stomach. Another wave of nausea and dizziness washed over his body. *Look at the bright side*, he thought, *at least you can still feel something.* Using the back of his gun hand to wipe the blood from his eyes, he saw the man get out of the driver's side of the car, followed closely by the woman. He immediately recognized the 9mm automatic rifles they each carried. He couldn't see the demon that rode on each of their shoulders--demons who dug their claws deeply into their skulls and whispered viciously, "Kill him! Kill him! Kill him!"

Aaron saw the man and woman get out of the car accompanied by their tormenting companions and with his flaming sword drawn, he attacked with all the force of an angry and avenging angel. When the demons saw Aaron advancing on their position, they were forced to let go of their slaves and defend themselves. They drew their own swords and with their venom-filled eyes glowing fiercely red, attacked Aaron.

Joshua noted the sudden look of confusion on the faces of his attackers. Taking the advantage, he took aim and fired twice at the man and then twice again at the woman. The first bullet out of his Beretta hit its mark and Joshua heard the man's right shoulder shatter. The second hit the man in the chest, driving two ribs deeply into his lungs. The man dropped his weapon and fell to the ground, blood foaming from his mouth.

Both shots fired at the woman missed their target, giving her a chance to get off one short burst just before Joshua fired again. Two bullets hit home--one burrowing deep into Joshua's bullet-proof vest, breaking three of his ribs, the other passing cleanly through his left arm, embedding in the ground behind him. He fired again, cutting a deep groove through the top of the woman's skull, taking her down.

He got to his hands and knees and began to crawl toward the man and woman.

Aaron ducked and whirled, swinging his blade and cutting deep into the chest of the demon on the right. He saw the familiar puff of red smoke and smelled the noxious odor of sulfur, as the demon traveled back to the abyss. With his blade free, Aaron faced the remaining demon, but instead of finding a fierce warrior, he faced a pathetic, terrified creature who was looking first at him and then to the dying body he used to possess. Aaron lunged toward the panic-stricken demon and bellowed, "Boo!" The demon turned and fled down the alley in terror. Before it disappeared into the dark recesses of the alleyway, Cono stepped out, drew his sword and struck the retreating little coward down. There was another puff of sulfuric smoke and the demon was gone.

Cono stepped forward and with arrogant disdain, snorted at the heavenly being, "You don't even have enough rank for me to bother with you. What do you want here?" Without waiting for an answer, Cono continued, "Why don't you just collect the man's soul and take him to that foul place you call home. Do it quick, angel, before I lose my patience with you!"

The deep voice rumbled and though a weaker being may have been tempted to run, Aaron held his ground. He stood straight and tall and without fear as he looked Cono right in the eye and said, "His soul is not for me to take--the man lives."

Cono watched in amazement as Joshua struggled to his feet again.

"Let him rise, angel. My man, Lt. Poe, is now controlling that sniper up there and he'll soon end this pathetic little dance."

With a loud demonic laugh, Cono flew off into the darkness.

Joshua could definitely remember having better days than this one. He got up cautiously. His ribs were hurting terribly; the pain so great it took his breath away. His arm was throbbing and he could feel blood running down and pooling at his feet. He felt his body trembling uncontrollably--he realized he was going into shock.

He closed the distance between himself and the man who lay silent, the woman only a few feet away. From the time that he had called this in until now was only about a minute and a half, but it seemed like an eternity;

everything was moving in slow motion. He kicked the rifles away. He knelt down by the man and after finding a weak pulse, began to pray fervently, "In the name of the Lord Jesus, I claim victory over this man's soul!"

Cono froze in flight, paralyzed by this man's powerful prayer. He began to shake with fear and rage.

Aaron also stood still, not in fear and anger, but with reverence and worship for the name of Jesus.

The man moaned with pain, but he tried to open his eyes. Joshua lifted the man and held him with great compassion.

"Young man, do you want to know Jesus Christ?"

The man started to let loose with some vile expletives, as was his habit, but something in the cop's eyes stopped him.

Jake had been raised in a Christian home by Godly parents. He had even been baptized as a young man and had tried to lead a good life. Somewhere along the way, however, he'd gotten mixed up with the wrong crowd and had turned his back on the teachings of his parents, the church, and God. The look that he saw in the cop's eyes, was the same look he'd seen in the eyes of his dying mother, when she had pleaded with him to turn back to God. He hadn't been able to hold his mother's gaze that day because of the shame he felt.

But somehow, today, perhaps because he was so close to death, he could see a love and compassion that he wanted to share with his mother and the God he had turned his back on.

Tears welled up in Jake's eyes and Joshua's face blurred. Jake's sin-hardened soul began to soften. Death scared him. He whispered, "Yes, please."

"Do you reject Satan and all of his works?" Joshua persisted.

"Yes!" Jake answered with conviction.

"Then accept the life that Jesus died for on the Cross, and announce that you believe and accept the Lord Jesus Christ as your Lord and Savior!"

Jake smiled and said, "I do accept Jesus Christ as my Lord and Savior, even though I ain't good enough."

Peace came over the young man's features as he kept whispering, "Jesus is Lord! Jesus is my Lord!"

Immediately a streak of white light shot out of the sky, and an angel appeared next to Aaron, who had been watching the exchange with pleasure. Because of Joshua's prayer and Jake's repentance and acceptance of Christ, an angel had been dispatched to protect Jake and his soul.

Cono had heard Joshua's prayer and Jake's acceptance of salvation, and had seen the arrival of yet another angel. He knew too well what his master would do to him when he found out that yet another soul was lost to the enemy. This soul, that they had toiled over and invested a lot of man hours in, had succumbed to the gentle pleadings of this bleeding heart cop, and now, he, the great Cono, was in terrible trouble.

He screamed at Lt. Poe, "What are you waiting for, you fool, kill him, now!"

The sniper, who didn't understand how he had missed with his first shot, took careful aim, and fired a second time. Joshua was looking into the face of this new Christian, when Jake's face exploded from the impact of another 30-30 bullet.

"Not that one you idiot, kill the cop!" Cono shrieked.

The new angel's job had been short. He gave Aaron a salute and then collected Jake's soul and they departed for heaven and the loving arms of Christ.

Aaron was watching their departure when he heard yet another shot ring out and saw the high velocity bullet speeding toward Joshua's head. This time it was right on target.

Joshua jumped, not from the deadly bullet speeding towards him, but rather from the knife that was suddenly and viciously thrust into his side from behind. As he turned toward his attacker and fell forward, Joshua felt the woman withdraw the bloody knife, heard a bullet scream past his ear, and then watched as it tore open the woman's chest, killing her instantly.

Cono's first thought was to kill the sniper for his incompetence, but instead he just stood there, clenching and unclenching his claw-like hands, in impotent fury. His bulbous eyes glowed red as his sulfuric breath spewed out one obscenity after another.

As the woman's soul began to separate from her body, Cono ceased his ranting, and pulling rank on all present, dove down and claimed his prize. He fervently hoped that by taking this soul to Satan personally, it might lessen his punishment. Cono hungrily yanked the soul out of the dead body, locked her under his arm and then dove into the deep, dark abyss from which he had risen.

The last thing that Aaron heard was the blood-chilling pleadings from the woman's terrified soul to a God who could not hear her. She had waited too long. Seeing his chance, Aaron stretched out his wings and flew to the rooftop where Lt. Poe was ripping at the sniper's brain while yelling, "Kill him, you moron! Hurry!"

Lt. Poe was afraid. He saw the look Cono had given him when he flew away. Cono was going to hold him personally responsible for the killing of this cop, and he couldn't get this fool to fire again. Out of the corner of his eye, Poe saw the white blade coming down on his neck. He barely got his own sword out in time to block it.

Their swords clashed, and Aaron followed through with a kick to the midsection, causing Poe to stagger backward. As he fell, Poe struck the angel in the right arm with his sword and was delighted to see the large red gash appear on Aaron's arm.

The Ambush

As Joshua stood, he saw a flash and heard the report. His feet flew out from under him and he felt the death blow hit his already injured chest. He squeezed the trigger of the rifle as he flew through the air, firing in the general direction of the sniper's roof. Miraculously, he hit the sniper in the head and shoulders, toppling him headlong into the alley below.

Lt. Poe looked from the wounded Aaron to the falling sniper and greed made his decision for him. After all, he could always kill an angel, but he wanted to get credit for this soul.

As the sniper hit the ground, Poe was already pulling the screaming soul from his body and was gone in a puff of smoke.

Aaron, though wounded, still found the strength to fly down to where Joshua lay in the filthy refuse of the alley. What he saw made him cry out to God for assistance, guidance, and miracles.

Chapter 2

Memories

Chief of Police Andrew Wilson arrived at the scene shortly after the sniper had fallen from the rooftop. He pulled his car in behind Joshua's and the scene from his worst nightmare unfolded before his eyes.

The red and blue glow from Joshua's police lights were dancing on the early morning mist and the sightless open eyes of the dead. The spotlight was focused on the back window of the suspect vehicle which was parked a short distance away.

Wilson saw the limp form of the police officer and fear seized his heart. He had not yet lost one of his men and he never thought Joshua would be the first. The chief didn't like the incredible amount of blood that was pooling around Joshua's body, but before he could check on him, he had to check the suspects that lay about four feet farther down the alley.

Before he approached the bodies he called into Central.

"Central, C-1."

"Go ahead C-1," Mandy replied.

"What's the E.T.A. on that ambulance?"

"Should be any time, Chief!"

"Well, tell them to hurry up, this is serious."

"10-4, Chief!"

Wilson pulled his 9mm out of its holster and approached the suspects. He could hear Mandy on the radio.

"I don't care how foggy it is, get to that scene! We have an officer down! Move it!"

Go get 'em, Mandy! Wilson thought to himself.

After verifying that the two suspects were dead, Wilson noticed another body sprawled a few yards past the first two bodies. He approached with caution. The man was dressed in a black jumpsuit, boots and a pullover with a black hood. Next to his body was a badly-bent 30-30 rifle. Wilson quickly verified that this guy was dead also.

He hurried over to where Joshua lay. At closer scrutiny, he looked even worse than the chief had first anticipated. Joshua had sustained multiple hits, some of which still oozed blood. The rough gash on his right temple seemed to be clotting. The hole in Joshua's left arm, and the hole in his side were still spilling blood onto the ground. Surprisingly, the chief was still able to find a weak, erratic pulse.

Joshua was in trouble, but alive.

Wilson took off his coat, twirled it between his hands to make it thick and then wrapped one end of it around the wound on Joshua's arm and held it tight. The other end he stuffed into the hole in Joshua's side and applied pressure to it. As he prayed for God to help Joshua, he recalled how Joshua had, at one time, been the target of his wrath and jealousy.

* * *

Andrew Wilson looked every bit the twenty-five year veteran that he was. His body bore the many scars that attested to the wounds he'd received during his tour of duty. The only visible scar stretched across his right cheek, pulling his eye down slightly. His salt and pepper hair was worn in a military butch-cut--"I don't have to comb it in the morning!" he would tell his friends who poked fun at his lack of style. He had dark, nearly black eyes that could make the calmest man uncomfortable when pinned with a stare. His large nose was covered with a spidery web of blue veins—he had the nervous habit of squeezing and pulling on it when he was thinking. His barely-contained temper caused a permanent flush on his face—a flush that deepened when he exerted his heavy-set form beyond its usual sedentary limits.

Wilson had been with the LA. Police Force for most of his tour. As he got closer to retirement, however, he'd decided that he wanted to be somewhere where the pace was a little slower. He'd called in some favors owed him by a couple of senators and judges and got connected with the city of Covenant, which was looking for a new Chief of Police. The city council had wanted to hire him right away, but the people were backing a man named Joshua White. He'd thought he was going to lose the position, but instead, White had announced that he wouldn't accept the position. He'd said, "The Lord has other plans for me and I'll trust in Him."

Wilson was appointed that very day, and from that day, he'd looked at Joshua White as a weak-minded fool, lacking in ambition. He even ridiculed him in front of the other officers for being a religious fanatic. Wilson had made life pretty hard for Officer White.

Even so, Joshua never reacted in less than a respectful manner and took the abuse with grace, which really unsettled Wilson. As time went by, the chief found Joshua White to be one of his best officers. The sense of peace that surrounded this officer still rankled him, though.

One morning, about five years after Wilson had taken over as Chief of Police, Joshua came into his office and said, "Chief, as you know, we're having a marked increase in the drug use, gang activity, and violent crime here in Covenant."

"Yeah, White. What about it?"

"There's a new program available that teaches our children how to avoid all of these things, and I'd like to volunteer to teach it in our schools. I would teach Junior High and High school students how to deal with the pressures they're under and teach them how to deal with conflict in a non-violent way. It..."

The chief interrupted. "Look, Officer White, I appreciate your concerns, but I have a budget to maintain and can't afford to pull officers off the street to re-assign them to the school. *Not for you anyway, White, no matter how much merit the plan has*, the chief thought to himself. "So I want you to leave my office, get in your squad car and just do your job, is that clear?"

Joshua looked at the chief for a moment with those peace-filled eyes and then said, "Yes, of course, Chief."

Without another word, he walked out of the office.

Wilson had put White in his place, yet somehow, it didn't feel like a victory to him.

About three months later, Wilson started receiving phone calls from concerned citizens, asking about the new program that they'd heard would help their children. When was the chief going to start it in the schools?

Wilson finally asked one of the concerned parents how they had heard of the program. "Oh, Officer White told me all about it..." Wilson hung up on the parent and sent word for White to report to his office immediately.

Agitated, Wilson paced back and forth until Joshua arrived. Joshua figured something was up; everyone in the room had stopped what they were doing and looked at him with sympathetic eyes like he was a condemned man approaching the gallows. He walked into Chief Wilson's office and quietly closed the door. He watched the chief pace back and forth; his naturally florid face getting redder with each turn.

Finally Wilson stopped and loosed the storm that had been raging inside him.

"White! What is this I hear about you telling everyone about this new program for the schools? I thought I'd made it quite clear that I would have none of it. Now I find out that you've been telling hundreds of parents to call me about it. My phone's been ringing off the hook and I can't get anything done." He'd continued his tirade for a few more minutes and then asked, "Well, what do you have to say for yourself?"

Joshua answered, calmly and confidently, "Chief, I only spoke of the program after people asked me, point blank, what the best way was to handle our current problems. I gave them my honest opinion. When they asked how we could get it, I told them that you make all of those decisions. That's all I said, the rest—well, that's the parents' doing."

Wilson, angrier than ever, yelled, "Get out and tell them that we won't do it! Do you hear? We'll never do it!"

By the end of the month, however, the City Council held a special meeting to address the issue and, to their surprise, three thousand parents attended to show their support of the program. Wilson had no choice; the Council voted unanimously to implement the program and allotted the necessary money for it from the city budget. Knowing when to fight and when to give in, Wilson agreed to oversee and man the program. White was not among the officer's appointed to the program, which raised a cry of objection from the parents. He was finally forced to allow White to run the program. Wilson was furious, but then it occurred to him that this might be a blessing in disguise. *White will be so busy with his pet program that he'll be outta my hair,* he thought to himself.

Shortly after this meeting, however, Wilson's wife joined the same church White attended, so all he heard was "Joshua this and Joshua that" from her. "Joshua helped a drug dealer come to the Lord. Joshua befriended a lost youth and brought him back to the fold today. Joshua helped a young prostitute leave her pimp, find a job, and join the church."

Everyday she had a new story of what White had done. To make it worse, Wilson had to admit, however reluctantly, that the man was having equal success in the schools.

Wilson thought that all this God stuff was for women and old people. He didn't believe what White was always saying about criminals being victims of evil spirits and that they needed to be saved and brought back to Jesus. Wilson had seen the way White seemed to light up when he talked about the Lord with the prisoners, leading them in a prayer of repentance.

He endured this for nearly a year, until one day he had an opportunity to see what a Bible-believing, Holy Spirit-filled man could do.

The day had been a busy one for Wilson, so it was no wonder that his temper flared when he heard the crash from outside his office. He threw open his office door with every intention of chewing out the idiot responsible, but what he saw left him standing with his mouth hanging open.

Two of his strongest men were being held in the air by their shirtfronts by the largest man Wilson had ever seen. The man threw the two officers across the room like they were nothing. He easily swatted away every effort to restrain him and then threw a chair through the plate-glass window that separated the waiting area from the desks in the squad room. People scattered as the glass exploded onto their desks, cutting faces, and filling hair with glass fragments.

Amid the screams and shouts of protest, this giant of a man suddenly, and with lightning speed, jumped over a desk, grabbed Wilson by the throat with one hand and pulled Wilson's 9mm from his holster with the other hand. He held the gun to the chief's head. Everyone froze.

As long as he lived, Wilson would never forget the feeling of the cold steel of his own weapon pressed against his temple, or for that matter, how menacing the weapons of his own men looked, aimed at him and this big rage-filled man.

The man's fist tightened around Wilson's throat, and he dragged him toward his office, shrieking obscenities, threatening to blow away the chief and anyone who tried to stop him.

The man's murderous grip cut off his air, causing Wilson to drift into unconsciousness. Just like he'd always heard, he began to see flashes of his life.

He knew he was about to die. Desperately, he wished that he'd listened to Margie and White when they had talked about Jesus, but he knew that now it was too late. Frantic with fear, he cried out in his heart, *Jesus, have mercy on me! I'm not ready to die. Help me!*

At that moment, Officer White came through the door carrying his anti-drug books in one hand and a Teddy Bear in the other. Joshua took in the scene in a flash, put the books and bear down and started walking towards the chief and the crazed man that was squeezing the life out of him. Though he appeared to be talking to himself, Joshua's eyes never left those of the crazed man; he looked so calm and reassuring that he even calmed Wilson down. White apparently hadn't noticed that the maniac had a gun pointed at his superior officer's temple!

When White was only a few feet away, the crazed giant began to tremble violently. He yelled, "You cursed man of God, what do you want with us? We have nothing to do with you, leave us alone!"

Joshua spoke calmly, and without raising his voice, said, "Demons of hell, leave this man immediately, in the name of Jesus Christ! You must obey that name. Now go!"

White's last two words were loud and sharp and rang with authority.

The big man dropped the gun, shoved Wilson away from him, grabbed his own head, and fell to the floor, writhing in agony.

Immediately the other officers rushed to the chief's side but stood gaping as Joshua continued to minister to the crazed man.

Soon the man's moans quieted. Now Joshua spoke to him in a soothing voice.

"What's your name?"

"Killer."

"No, not your nickname, your real name, what is it?"

"It's Harold Barber. I think I done bad again."

"No, Harold," Joshua said, "you've just been influenced by evil demons, but they're gone now. You'll have to go with these men. I'll come and talk to you later, okay?"

The man nodded and the other officers came and took charge of him.

Officer White turned, picked up his books and bear, and walked out of the room and down the hall to his own office. The remaining officers let out their breaths in a collective sigh of relief. Everyone began to speak at once.

"What happened?"
"White saved the chief!"
"He saved all of us!"

Now, no matter what Wilson had thought in the past, White was a hero, to both himself and his men.

Sometime later, Wilson learned from his wife that Joshua had visited the detox tank every day to talk to the big man, Harold Barber. Once the man had realized that Officer White really cared about him and his salvation, he finally began to truly listen to his words and was eventually led to the Lord.

Barber explained how he had been in a motorcycle gang and had gotten hooked on crack, marijuana, and alcohol. Now, however, he promised to stay off of the drugs and when he went to prison, he promised to bring others to the Lord.

Joshua had followed Harold's prison career and even went to visit him when he could. He was there when Harold got out a year later, on good behavior. That was the last contact the two men had, but Harold told Joshua that he wanted to start a Christian motorcycle gang and spread the gospel as far as he could.

Wilson's thoughts were suddenly interrupted by the screams of sirens and the squealing of tires as ambulances and squad cars fishtailed around the corner.

Yeah, Wilson thought with a smile, *it only took Joshua another two months after that incident to get me into that church of his for the first time, and I'll always be grateful to him for that.*

He hastily wiped his tears away and again became the tough police chief that his reputation demanded.

When the first officers arrived on the scene they were ordered to move both the chief's squad car and Joshua's. The paramedics quickly took charge of Joshua.

Wilson directed his men with skill and determination. He had them block off the entire alley and ordered that no one was to come in or out withoutauthorization from him personally. He wanted this scene secured when the coroner, crime scene reconstructionist, and the crime scene technicians arrived. Wilson saw Officer Grady arrive and waved him over.

"How is Josh, sir?"

Wilson's expression grew somber. "It doesn't look real good, Grady. I think this was a professional hit—they may try to finish the job. I want you to take two of our best officers and go with Josh to the hospital. Stay with him at all times. You, inside the room, the other two outside the door with radio checks periodically. You get all that?"

"Yes, sir! I won't let him out my sight!" Grady turned to go when Wilson called him back.

"Something else, sir?"

"Don't let anyone near Josh unless you know personally that they're medical staff."

"Yes, sir."

Grady hopped into the ambulance just as it was pulling away.

Wilson knew he could trust Grady; he and Josh were best friends.

He saw Assistant Chief Anderson drive up, noticing as he checked his watch that it had been twenty minutes since Anderson had been called. The assistant police chief lived close and should've arrived a long time ago. He walked over to Anderson's car.

"Where've you been, Anderson, I expected you to be the first officer here?"

Anderson just shrugged his shoulders, "Sorry Chief, but when I got out to my squad car, I noticed that one of the tires was flat. Had to change it."

Wilson thought there was something missing here but he had other questions to ask.

"Another thing, Anderson, why was White working alone on the midnight shift?"

"Since the budget cuts, I had to cut back on our less busy shifts. This was one of `em. By the way, how is White?"

"Not good, but at least he's still alive. Let's just pray that God will watch over him tonight."

Wilson turned his back on Anderson and walked back into the alley. He didn't see the fear that passed quickly over Anderson's face, nor did he see the hatred in the man's eyes as Anderson glared at his back.

Anderson gritted his teeth and tried to quell the panic that rose in his chest.

Chapter 3

Aaron's Promotion

Michael, the Archangel, left the presence of the Almighty God, glowing a brilliant white from the contact. This wasn't as joyous a visit as it usually was—the Lord had shared some disturbing news.

Aaron, an angel in Michael's legion, had just been wounded, and Joshua White, his earthly charge, was precariously clinging to life, after a vicious attack by the enemy forces. The Lord ordered Michael to send his very best captain to handle the situation in Covenant. After searching his memory of all his most capable captains, Michael made his decision. He sent for Capt. Worl. Worl had proven himself in many important battles, including battles with the very demon he would face in this mission. His experience with Cono and other high ranking demons could be the difference between success and failure in this mission. Michael turned when he heard a flutter of wings.

"Ah, Capt. Worl, we must talk."

He dispensed with the formal salutes and chose the more personal touch with Capt. Worl. He put his muscular arm around Worl's shoulders and, in a conspiratorial tone, began to inform him of his mission.

Aaron watched as the ambulance crew carefully placed Joshua on the table and started the difficult and tedious task of removing his bloodied and torn uniform. What he saw didn't look good.

They couldn't remove the bullet-proof vest; the 30-30 slug had pinned it to Joshua's body. The fabric around the knife wound was already stuck to his skin with dried blood. As they pulled the uniform off, it tore the wound open again, causing it to bleed profusely.

Aaron winced when he saw the small entry hole in Joshua's arm, the larger exit hole, and the gaping wound in his side. A sudden memory flooded in on Aaron of another gaping wound, this one in the side of the Lord, from which the last of His blood and water flowed. *Ah, who among the angels could ever forget that day?*

Aaron frowned as he began to feel dizzy and weak and then he remembered his own wounded arm. As he fell to the ground, the room was filled with a dazzling light and the sound of wings. Confused, Aaron thought he was in the presence of the great Captain Worl, and that the captain was now kneeling on the floor supporting Aaron's head and shoulders. He struggled to get up but Worl restrained him, saying, "Rest a moment, soldier, you've earned it."

Aaron nodded but still managed to give the customary right arm to left shoulder salute, causing pain to ripple through his body.

Worl smiled at Aaron's determination, feeling great love for him as the wounded angel spoke.

"Capt. Worl, I have failed in my mission. I was to protect Joshua and now look at him."

Capt. Worl glanced at the human and said, "Yes, Aaron, he is badly wounded but he is alive, and the Lord has great plans for him. You have saved his life. Don't be so hard on yourself. You couldn't have foreseen that Cono would attack your charge himself.

"Aaron, I've been sent here by Michael himself, to handle this operation, and to put you in charge of all of our protective forces around this hospital. You are hereby promoted to the rank of lieutenant."

Before Aaron could object, the room was filled with the flutter of more wings—those of the angels who accompanied the police officers sent to protect Joshua. The angels saluted Capt. Worl, who returned the gesture with mutual respect.

"Ah, Warren, Adam, Brock—how have you been since we last met—at the battle in Germany, wasn't it?"

"Yes, Captain," Warren answered, "we fought at your side with constant attention."

Aaron realized that he had been staring at Worl's guards and he forced himself to look away. He listened as Worl explained the situation to the three other angels.

"Lt. Aaron will be in charge of setting up the defenses around Joshua and this hospital. Now, here is what you four must do . . ."

When Capt. Worl finished briefing them, he simply turned, and along with his two guards on either side, spread his wings and made a very impressive exit.

* * *

Cono's dark form came into the room and landed on the human's shoulder. He sank his long sharp claws into the human's skull. He was a huge creature, with large pointed teeth and claws. His right ear was missing its pointed tip—his boss had just bitten it off in his anger. His right eye was swollen shut and his lips were also bruised and swollen. He'd taken quite a beating. His master hadn't liked the news that Joshua White was still alive.

The soul he'd delivered had saved him from suffering in the torture pits for a few millennia, but that was about all. The boss had threatened just that fate if Cono didn't get Joshua killed and stop these souls from being saved.

Cono's human host was Theodore Connelly of Connelly Shipping, a very prosperous and ruthless businessman. Connelly was just about to develop a pounding headache.

There was a knock at the door. Connelly yelled, "Come in!", and then winced with the pain that washed over his brain.

As the door opened Cono saw Lt. Poe skulking behind his human host, Assistant Police Chief Alex Anderson. In a deceptively calm voice, Cono asked, "Is he dead yet?"

Poe shrank back a bit and hesitated before sputtering in fear, "N-n-no, he was t-t-taken to the hospital and is st-st-still alive."

Cono broke out in a violent fit of rage, and with his teeth bared and his claws spread he coiled for the attack. His sulfuric breath filled the room with a yellowish haze as he spewed forth threats and curses, and then chased the retreating Lt. Poe into the darkness beyond the door.

Connelly's headache was suddenly gone. Nevertheless, he was still in a deadly mood. As Anderson entered the room, Connelly snapped, "Is he dead yet, Anderson?"

"I don't know how, boss, but White lived through the ambush."

When he saw Connelly's expression, he sheepishly whined, "The man has more lives than a cat."

Connelly rose to his full height of five feet-five inches and ground out through clenched teeth, "We paid those fools good money to kill him, and you're going to stand there and tell me that a sniper and two people armed with assault rifles couldn't kill one lousy cop?"

"Uh . . . well, it seems that White has killed all three of them somehow. He . . ."

"They outnumbered him three to one, and outgunned him by more than that. What is this guy, super cop or something? Never mind! I want him dead! Now!"

Anderson couldn't believe what he was hearing. "Are you out of your mind, Connelly? That's impossible! Wilson just put round-the-clock double guards on him, with no one in or out, but medical personnel. Besides, I hear he might die . . ."

Anderson stopped when he saw the sinister smile spreading across Connelly's face.

"What is it, boss? What are you thinking?"

Connelly, his anger forgotten, whispered as if he were deep in a dream, "This could work, Anderson. This could work."

He returned his focus to Anderson's face.

"Do you remember the doctor that we set up with Becky? We videotaped them together, and then invited him to join the coven."

"Yeah, I remember all right. Man, those were some tapes. I still think we should've sold them."

"That's why I'm in charge, Anderson. I think further ahead than you do. Now is the time to cash in the favor he owes us."

"What favor is that?"

"Why, the fact that we didn't send the tapes to, oh . . . let's say, his boss, or the press, or his wife, for that matter."

Anderson still didn't get it. "But how can he help us with White, boss?"

"Anderson, you don't remember the doctor's name, do you? It's Chad White. Dr. Chad White. Joshua White's brother."

Anderson's blank look was slowly replaced with a look of comprehension. "Oh, I get it! Dr. White is his brother, he's on medical staff and we own his soul. Oh, this is rich, really rich!"

"And what makes it even richer is Dr. White hates his super cop brother. Some kind of family falling-out, I think."

Both men were soon doubled over with laughter as they reveled in the sheer genius of their plan.

Chapter 4

Holding On By a Thread

Lt. Aaron was still having a hard time believing that he had been promoted. He looked his defenses over and thought, *These orders did indeed come from the top.* He counted over five thousand angelic beings—all under his command. He had worked with many of these angels on numerous occasions, and they were all very good warriors. Each window, door, and access hole leading into the hospital had an angelic guard standing with sword drawn, ready to cut down any demon stupid enough to try to get in. Every angel here was prepared to stand at their post for eons, if necessary, to fulfill their assigned task.

Each angel stood at least seven feet tall, carried a blazing sword, and had the knowledge and skill to wield that sword with great effectiveness. The Lord was taking no chances with Joshua's life.

Word had spread of the attack on Joshua, and the Christians in Covenant were on their knees asking God to protect him. These prayers added to the strength of Aaron's forces. Aaron let the power of the prayers wash over his own body, allowing his confidence and courage to increase with every passing moment.

Capt. Worl, accompanied as always by Left and Right, landed next to Aaron.

"Report, Lieutenant!"

Lt. Aaron snapped to attention and gave the right hand to left shoulder salute.

"Captain, all sentries are posted. The humans can pass freely into and out of the hospital, but any demons they carry with them will not enter. The Saints are praying with reassuring power, and the angelic reinforcements are ready and standing by."

"Excellent, Lt. Aaron! You are already proving to be the leader that Michael said you would be. Dr. White will be arriving soon and you know the importance of making sure that he enters the hospital alone, don't you?"

"Yes sir, I do."

"Fine then. I'll leave the battle to you, Aaron, and may the Lord bless your efforts."

With that the trio, as if one creation, took flight, leaving a brilliant trail of light that slowly faded. Aaron watched in awe until the entire trail was gone and then he returned to the duties at hand.

*   *   *

Lt. Poe cautiously peeked in at Cono and asked if he could enter Cono's chamber. Poe's eyes were blackened and he had several deep lacerations on his face and back, put there by Cono's claws. He was grateful to be alive and still in the battle.

Cono looked up and growled, "Enter, you fool!"

Poe entered, hesitantly, expecting an ambush by some demons waiting in the corners, but the chamber seemed clear.

"Report, you worthless cretin," Cono barked impatiently.

"Yes, sir! Uh, I'm afraid there is yet more bad news, sir."

Poe spoke quickly trying to stay ahead of the new storm that he saw brewing in Cono's face.

"You see, sir, somehow, five thousand angels have infiltrated our territory and have attacked our forces at the hospital in Covenant. They've killed over a thousand of our warriors. They've totally cleaned out and sealed off the hospital, and aren't allowing any of our kind to enter. They even promoted Aaron to Lieutenant, and placed him in charge."

As Poe finished his report, he stepped back and braced himself for the beating that was sure to follow.

At first his rage had built to a dangerous level, as Cono listened to Poe's report. He wasn't pleased that so many of the enemy had entered his territory, but when he heard that Aaron was in charge, he couldn't contain his laughter, and it rocked his frame.

Poe looked on in confusion, thinking that his superior had finally cracked under the pressure.

Cono, seeing Poe's confusion, said, "Aaron in charge? What idiot would put him in charge of even one squad of angels, let alone several squads? You must be exaggerating their numbers!"

"Honest, sir, I'm not! They . . ."

"Oh shut up!", Cono interrupted, "This is getting serious, no matter how many angels there are. Who would've thought that the enemy would get so upset about one, worthless little Christian."

Capt. Worl appeared seemingly out of nowhere. "Not so worthless, Cono!"

Poe went for his sword, but thought better of it when the intimidating duo, Left and Right, appeared with their swords already drawn.

Capt. Worl continued, "That 'worthless Christian', as you called him, has been directly or indirectly responsible for the salvation of three thousand, two hundred and thirty souls; no, make that thirty-one souls, counting the one that Joshua led to our Lord in between being shot and stabbed by your people this morning."

Cono started to speak, but Worl laughed him into silence.

"Don't try my patience, Cono, with worthless denials and vain threats. I don't have the time or the desire to listen to you. Understand this! I am in control of this town now, and even though you started this evil plot, I'm here to make it crumble around your evil ears. Speaking of ears, Cono, did your master have yours for lunch?"

Cono involuntarily reached for his half-chewed ear, but quickly stopped himself. Inwardly he seethed with anger and vowed to rid this world of this angelic being. He decided it was better to wait until another time; a time of his own choosing.

Worl taunted him as he turned to leave, "I hope your master doesn't punish you as severely as the last time I sent you back in defeat."

As the angel's laughter filled the room, Cono, forgetting himself, charged Worl, but was restrained by Lt. Poe.

Cono screamed at the fading angel, "You, you . . . I . . . !"

As Poe let go of Cono, he asked, "When did you meet Capt. Worl in battle? What happened?"

Cono turned on Poe with such rage, that Poe fled, again.

As Dr. Chad White drove up, he noticed the police swarming around New Hope Memorial Hospital. There must have been thirty officers and all the auxiliary officers as well, guarding the entrance, searching people, checking bags. He could feel a headache starting behind his eyes.

"All I need is this aggravation!" He spoke in anger, pushing his glasses up on his head and rubbing his left eye.

As he walked up to the emergency room entrance, Dr. White was unaware of the two creatures who were sitting, one on each shoulder, with their claws dug deeply into his skull.

Lt. Aaron stood in Dr. White's way, and behind him stood one hundred and fifty very determined angels. The demon named Envy, who sat on the doctor's right shoulder and the demon named Jealousy, who sat on his left shoulder, puffed themselves up to their entire three feet of height, and screeched in unison, "Let us pass!"

Not intimidated in the least by the puny pair, Aaron drew his sword, and stepped toward them with a menacing look in his eye.

The twins, without even trying to save face, fled for their lives.

Dr. White entered the hospital, oblivious to the confrontation which had just occurred, noticing that his throbbing headache was suddenly gone.

Over his protests, Chad was patted down inside the hospital lobby. He was checked again by the two guards that stood just outside of the emergency room doors. Once inside the emergency room, Officer Grady O'Leary checked the doctor's ID badge as he brushed past him.

Chad approached the examination table and stopped and stared with his mouth open. The color drained from his face when he saw his brother, Joshua, lying on the table. Checking the extent of his injuries, he almost felt sorry for Joshua, but then the long years of hate and envy flooded his heart, and it was all he could do not to just turn around and walk out.

* * *

Chad White was five years old when his little brother was brought home from the hospital. From day one, Chad had been jealous of this little bundle of joy that got all of the attention from the adults that Chad was accustomed to getting. Up to now, Chad had been the little darling of the family, but now there was sweet, adorable Joshua.

When Chad was the only child and the only grandchild, he was completely spoiled by both sides of the family. Whenever he wanted to play a game, someone would drop everything and play with him. Now, however, when he wanted to play, he heard, "Not now, Chad, Joshua needs to eat." "Joshua needs changing." "Don't wake up Joshua."

Chad felt left out, and when he tried to tell the adults how he felt, they would say, "You're a big boy now, and Joshua is just a baby. He needs our help now."

Chad didn't feel like a big boy. He felt like a lonely five-year-old who had been deserted by his parents.

Within a year of his brother's birth, Chad had developed a surly expression and attitude and became more demanding with every passing day. When people commented on how sweet Joshua's nature was, or how cute his dimples were, or how beautiful his blue eyes were, Chad would dream of the day he would poke those eyes out. He would amuse himself by pinching the baby when no one was looking. When the baby cried, he hoped that people would get irritated at the little brat. Instead, they would rush to Joshua to see what was wrong, and when they saw the red marks on his arms or legs, they would yell at Chad, "What did you do to your brother? Go to your room right now, little man."

As the boys grew older, Chad's jealousy and envy of his little brother grew as well. All he heard was, "Joshua did this and Joshua did that, and why aren't you more like Joshua?"

To make matters worse, the "little brat", as Chad called him all the time, adored Chad and was always hanging around him. Chad would ignore him, punch him, yell at him; but no matter what he did, Joshua would always come back for more.

Although his parents were good Christians who went to church on Wednesday nights, twice on Sunday, and all church functions, Chad never really participated much. He would do what he was made to do, but no more. When he did hear God calling out to his heart, he turned a deaf ear and a cold shoulder to Him. Then Chad began to run with boys who would smoke, drink, and occasionally take drugs.

Little Joshua, on the other hand, heard the Lord calling him and he got up right in front of everyone, went down to the altar, and received Jesus into his heart. If people liked Joshua before, now it was like he'd sprouted wings and became an angel himself. People would ask Chad, "When are you going to give your heart to Jesus, Chad? You really need it more than Joshua does, so don't wait."

After these comments, Chad knew that he would never give himself to this Jesus.

The one thing that Chad could do better than his brother was to handle dead things. Blood didn't bother him either, whereas, it would make Joshua sick as a dog. That's why Chad became a doctor and then a surgeon, because he knew that Joshua would never be able to do that, and he wouldn't have to compete with his brother anymore. People even commented, "Chad is just a genius when it comes to fixing injured animals or giving first aid."

Things smoothed out a bit, until eleven years ago.

Joshua's wife, Patricia, died of cancer. All the attention and sympathy his brother received brought all the pain and hurt back into Chad's heart and he refused to go to the funeral. Then three years ago when his parents were killed in a car crash, it was Joshua that was called. It was Joshua who was asked to make arrangements. It was Joshua who people came to comfort. Chad fled back to his hospital and his patients as soon as the funeral was over.

The last straw was last Thanksgiving, when his wife Ellen had insisted that they invite Joshua over to eat dinner with them. When the big day arrived, Susie, Chad and Ellen's daughter, ran to meet her uncle at the door. He picked her up and was rewarded with a big hug. Susie loved Joshua far too much for Chad's taste. Ellen seemed far too happy to see him herself.

Suddenly, with eyes ablaze, Chad yelled, "Why don't you get your own family, Joshua? Leave mine alone! You're trying to steal my wife and my child, just like you've taken everything else that belongs to me."

"Chad!" Ellen exclaimed, mortified.

"No, Ellen, I've had enough! Joshua has gotten you to love him more than me, and you three are always together in that church you go to. You don't have any time for me or my problems, but you can run off to church anytime he calls. God only knows what you two do behind my back. I bet . . ."

Joshua interrupted him, "Chad, you're way out of line! I think you'd better apologize to Ellen right now!"

With eyes full of hatred, Chad stood up and with both hands on the table in front of him, he said in a deceptively calm voice, "You get out of my house, right now, and don't ever come back!"

Joshua tried to calm Chad, "Ah, come on Chad, I know you're upset, but you can't mean . . ."

Before his brother could finish, Chad surprised him with a quick uppercut to the jaw, which staggered Joshua. He stood there in stunned silence with a tear running down his cheek and a trickle of blood running from the corner of his mouth.

Chad ground out between clenched teeth, "You make me sick!" and stomped out of the room.

Ellen rushed over to Joshua and wiped the blood from the corner of his mouth. She apologized for her husband's behavior, but Joshua insisted on leaving anyway. He picked up his jacket, gave Ellen and Susie a quick hug, and then left the house.

After Joshua left, Ellen found Chad in his den, staring out the window.

"I think you at least owe me an explanation, Chad."

"I don't think anything needs to be explained. It's all too evident how you feel about my brother."

"You must be out of your mind!"

"You will never again have anything to do with Joshua, is that understood?"

"No, it is not understood! What has gotten into you, Chad?"

Chad got up and grabbed Ellen by the shoulders and shook her as he screamed into her face, "You're not to go back to that church or see that brother of mine again! I forbid it!" Then he threw her to the floor.

Ellen got up and tried to reason with Chad, but he slapped her face in rage.

"I'm your husband and you'll do what I say, woman! Now do you understand?"

Ellen, pushed herself away, and slammed her knee into Chad's groin, bringing him to his knees. As he groaned and tried in vain to keep from throwing up, Ellen spoke in a surprisingly calm voice.

"You may be my husband, but you will never hit me again, do <u>you</u> understand? As for never going to church again, you have no right to stop me, for God has given us a free will. I can't make you go with me, but neither can you stop me. As for your jealousy toward Joshua, it is totally unfounded. I have never hidden the fact that I loved Joshua first, before I knew you, but when I fell in love with you, any feeling I had for Joshua became history."

Ellen turned to leave, but stopped and looked down at Chad and said, "You clean up that mess before you go to sleep. This has just become your bedroom for tonight. Tomorrow you can stay at the hospital until you come to your senses."

In a weak voice Chad said, "You go back to that church, Ellen, and we're finished! You hear me, Ellen, finished!"

Ellen didn't turn around, but walked out of the room. She had meant every word she'd said.

Chad and Ellen separated for a few days, but Chad cooled down after staying in a hotel room for a week, eating out every night. He begged Ellen to take him back, apologizing for his brutishness. Ellen agreed, on the condition that he apologize to Joshua. He agreed to do so. But later on, he lied to her, saying that he had apologized. He had not seen or spoken to Joshua since that Thanksgiving day.

Now I got you where I want you, baby brother, Chad thought smugly.

It just took a few seconds for all the memories to rekindle the spark that flared into full-blown hatred in Chad's heart. It took all his professional training to approach the table as a doctor and do his job. Chad put on his professional face, hid his feelings, and allowed the nurse to put a sterile gown, mask, and gloves on him.

Blood was still frothing out of the patient's mouth and nose, indicating lung damage. Chad said, "Let's get this man to surgery, shall we?"

Grady followed, but Chad stopped him. "You can't come into surgery!" The doctor turned, expecting to be obeyed. However, Grady still followed.

Dr. White turned back again and spoke sharply, "Didn't you hear me? You can't come in!" Grady spoke with equal force. "I have orders not to leave his side."

Dr. White practically yelled this time. "You can go to hell with him, but you will not enter my surgery! That's final, Officer O'Leary!"

As Dr. White turned, sure that he had put this ingrate cop in his place, Grady grabbed his shoulder, turned him, and slammed him against the wall. He put his face directly into the doctor's face and pressed his 9mm against his temple. In a voice filled with deadly calm, he said, "Listen Doc! I've discussed this as much as I intend to. I've heard you hate your brother's guts, but I warn you not to slip even one time. Someone has shot your brother down in cold blood and it's now up to you to make sure that they haven't succeeded in killing him. Get in there and do your job and let's not hear any more about me doing mine!"

Grady pulled Dr. White off of the wall and straightened his white jacket. Chad glared at Grady, who was putting his 9mm back into its holster, but he told the nurse to get the officer a fresh gown, shoes, and gloves. As they entered surgery, Chad ground out through gritted teeth, "You stand over there and stay out of my way."

Suddenly, Joshua went into convulsions.

* * *

Chief Wilson approached Rev. Smith who was in the waiting room of Covenant's New Hope Memorial Hospital. They shook hands, then hugged, and the tears fell without shame from both men's eyes.

"Chief, this is a sad day for Covenant. Joshua was a good man. Who would want to kill him?"

"Remember, Pastor, Joshua isn't dead yet. As to who did it, I intend to find out. Look, Pastor, could you do me a favor?"

"You know I'll do anything to help."

"This story will be hitting the media soon, and this place will fill up with well-wishers, news people, and the just plain curious. Would you try to get some people together, organize a prayer meeting, and hold it out in front of the hospital? Explain to them that for security reasons we need to keep the lobby area clear of a lot of people. Whoever did this may try again, and we got to be ready."

Rev. Smith answered quickly, "I'll do my best, Chief, but don't you think we should take a moment and ask for God's guidance and direction in all this first?"

The Chief nodded his agreement, bowed his head, and agreed in his heart as Rev. Smith prayed.

*   *   *

Joshua looked up through the fog and he could swear that he saw the shimmering form of an angel, but his mind told him it was just the lights reflecting off of the misty fog hovering above him. He felt numb and couldn't move, nor did he want to.

Joshua prayed, "Lord, thank You for the peace I feel in my soul. I always wondered when You would bring me home and I guess this is it. I'm ready, Lord. I miss Patty so much; I can't wait to see her again. Your will be done, Lord, as always, Your will be do . . ." Joshua slipped into unconsciousness again.

Enroute to the hospital, Joshua had slipped in and out of consciousness, giving the trip a dream-like quality.

"His pressure is dropping again, Hank. We better step on it or we'll lose him for sure." Joe let the pressure off the cup and then began to pump it up again for another reading.

Hank was driving with his nose practically pressed against the windshield, trying to see through the fog. "I'm going as fast as I can in this soup, Joe. It won't do us or the cop any good if we hit a telephone pole."

Joe took a deep, slow breath and then said, "Okay Hank! Hand me the mike and I'll call us in." "New Hope this is AS-12, come in, please."

All they heard in reply was static. He repeated his call two more times, and finally a tired and irritated voice answered, "Traffic for New Hope?"

"Yeah, New Hope, this is AS-12. We're on the way in with one white male patient—age 41 years, 190-200 pounds, with multiple gunshot and stab wounds. He's a police officer. His vitals are..."

Joshua drifted off again into blackness.

When he drifted into consciousness again, he heard, "... not to slip even one time. Someone has shot your brother down in cold blood ..." Joshua turned his head and through blurred and tearing eyes, he thought he saw Grady pressing his 9mm against a doctor's head—no—Chad's head! He tried to tell Grady to stop being such a hothead, but when he attempted to speak he coughed blood instead.

Suddenly he felt a crushing pain in his chest.

Joshua White went into full cardiac arrest.

Chapter 5

Heavenly Visit

When Joshua emerged from the tunnel of light, he noticed that there was an angel holding him. As he watched, the angel's wings unfurled, and their speed increased. He felt as though he was aboard a jet fighter, yet no wind buffeted his face.

Joshua could see very clearly as his eyes drank in the beautifully lush forest which spread out below him. It was broken only by rolling green meadows filled with wildflowers of all colors and types. The fragrance of the flowers combined with the woodsy scent of the forest filled Joshua with a beautiful sense of peace.

On a distant hilltop he could see a magnificent city, which shimmered and sparkled as though it were built of gold, silver, and gems of every hue. *It shines like the glory of God*, thought Joshua.

It was not to the city that they headed, however, but towards a solitary figure who walked along the shore of a clear blue lake, below the city's wall. They slowed, descended, and then with stilled wings the angel gently set Joshua down right in front of the lone man.

Jesus addressed the angel, who bowed low before Him.

"Fine work, Aaron! Now I want you to return to your men and plan for the next phase of our operation."

A DARKNESS OVER COVENANT

Jesus blessed Aaron, and the angel departed, without saying a word.

The Lord turned to Joshua, who was standing dumbfounded. This was all too much for him. Jesus embraced Joshua, "Welcome home, faithful servant."

Joshua had truly come home.

As they walked along the beach, Joshua's joy overflowed. With tears and laughter, he praised Jesus for all of the things He had done for him in his lifetime. Most of all, he praised Jesus for taking his place on the Cross. Jesus allowed Joshua to continue talking for awhile, for He understood the need in the man's heart to express his love for his Lord.

Soon, He laid a hand on Joshua's arm and interrupted him.

"Joshua, our time together is short, and we have to prepare for the battle to come."

"A battle, Lord? I don't understand."

"As you know we are constantly at war with Satan. Yes, it is a war we have already won, but the question is, how many human souls will Satan take with him to hell? Are you willing to serve Me even if it means returning to earth?"

Joshua had listened intently, and now answered, a little confused, "Well, yes, of course, Lord, but what would I do?"

"Joshua, the things I am about to tell you and show you, are for the benefit of all humans on earth. You will remember all of your experiences here as the need arises. For the most part, however, like everyone else, I want you to rely on faith and the Holy Spirit to guide you along the right path.

"Joshua, what I am about to show you is not pleasant and it is not what I want for the human soul. You must see it and then go back and convince the others of the dangerous game they are playing with their eternal future. Convince them that they will share the future I am about to show you if they do not turn from their wickedness."

Joshua screamed as they suddenly appeared on the rim of a huge crater, white hot and filled with boiling tar. No—it had more than just tar in it . . .

Jesus supported Joshua as he stumbled backwards in horror. He had seen the poor inhabitants of the steaming tar pit only dimly at first, but then his vision cleared. He held onto the Lord with all his failing strength and forced himself to look into the pit again. Terror threatened to overwhelm him.

On the surface of the tar pit were flames. They skipped across the bubbling muck and licked at the exposed flesh of the poor souls that were caught there. Waist-deep in this boiling tar were the most pitiful creatures that Joshua had ever seen. As they brushed their hands across their faces, the skin would stick to their hands, stretching and pulling it into a distorted mask. When the flesh was released, it retained its new and hideous form.

Agonizing moans reached Joshua's ears, "Please Lord, just let us die."

"If only we had listened to those who tried to tell us, Oh, why, why, didn't we listen?"

These mournful statements were punctuated by the screams of the lost. The screams were only silenced as the hideous figures would sink out of sight under the surface of the boiling tar.

Some creatures were coming up from the depths, but all they did was stare at the radiant city at the top of the hill.

"Who are these, Lord?"

"They are the ones who have been released from the torture chambers that Satan has deep below this pit. Satan drains the life-substance out of a soul, while he makes sure that they know that their loss is for eternity. Then he allows them to rise to the top of this pit, so they can look upon, but never enter, the Eternal City."

Jesus bowed his head and as the scene faded, Joshua heard the desperate souls call out again to the Lord for help, but He could not. Jesus explained that He could only save those who choose Him as their Savior, but they could only do that while their mortal bodies yet lived. Once dead, there was no redemption. These souls must live for eternity with the decision they made while on earth.

Joshua wept bitterly as the Lord held him to His chest. When he finally looked up, he said, "Lord this is too horrible to accept; how can God allow this?"

"Joshua, We are a Triune God, and in Our wisdom, We created a garden in which men and women could have shared Our glory. Adam and Eve, however, chose to listen to Satan, who made them desire to be gods themselves. When they broke Our relationship, they gave Satan the power to enter their lives and they were cut off from Us. We will not force anyone to love Us, or serve Us, but if they don't, they automatically choose to follow Satan and receive his rewards, which I have shown you.

"Of course, the lost souls are always crying out, 'If we had known what would happen, we would have chosen You, Lord!' They heard, but they did not listen to the prophets I sent to warn them. They did not listen to Me when I put on human flesh and walked among them, nor did they believe My Word which I gave them as a map to the eternal.

"No, Joshua, I have given them all they need to learn the truth, yet they shut their eyes to that truth. Not only did I die for their sins, but I sent the Holy Spirit to guide them, and I even sent angels to help and protect them.

Yet they chose to worship the gods of their own making: greed, envy, adultery, murder.

"We do not send them there; they chose this way of eternal life for themselves. All must repent, turn from their wickedness, and obey the Word in order to share in Our kingdom."

"Lord, tell me what You would have me do."

"You have been fighting on the front lines for years and are to become the leader of an army that will lead the frontal assault against the enemy forces."

Jesus studied Joshua's face for a moment, and then laughed, saying, "What! Is that doubt I see on your face, Joshua? Come, I will explain further as we walk."

As they walked, Jesus showed Joshua all the lives he had already affected while on earth. He introduced him to several souls who were in heaven because of Joshua's testimony to the truth. Perhaps the happiest of the group was the young man who had tried to kill Joshua not too long ago in a dark alley. Jake hugged Joshua, thanking him for taking time to minister to him before it was too late. Jake's mother also came and thanked Joshua for his love and the care he showed for her son. Joshua watched as the happy mother, who had just kissed him on the cheek, and her son walked back toward the Eternal City on the hill.

When he and Jesus were alone again, Joshua said, "Lord, I didn't realize just how many lives I have touched. I helped people that I had never even met or talked to. I helped one person, then they, as a result, helped someone else; so I have indirectly helped that person. Wow! That is neat!" Sadness, however, soon fell over Joshua's face.

"I know your thoughts, Joshua. Please speak freely."

Joshua looked into the Lord's eyes with tears running from his own. "I want to share in this life so badly, Lord, and yet I think of all those poor souls that still need saving. I keep seeing all those new arrivals at the pit and the lost desperate souls that have been sucked dry, and I feel the urgency in helping everyone I can. Lord, whatever you want me to do, I will gladly do it."

Jesus smiled, put his arm back around Joshua's shoulders, and said, "Come, let me finish showing you around. We will talk later about the details of your assignment. First, however, there are a set of parents that want very much to speak to you, and I believe a certain Patricia would like to spend some time with you before you go back."

Jesus led Joshua along the path through the great forest which led to the Eternal City. Along the way, he instructed Joshua in all of the wonders on this side of the Eternal City's wall. There were many.

Chapter 6

Prayers Vs. Murderous Thoughts

Wilson had spent the bulk of the early morning hours personally supervising all aspects of the crime scene investigation. There were the drawings to make; placing each spent cartridge where it landed, showing the positions of the bodies, as well as a detailed layout of the alley. Bullet holes had to be marked, photos of the entire scene had to be taken and processed and any evidence that could possibly be helpful to the investigation had to be collected, logged and tagged. All of this had to take place before the bodies could be removed to the morgue. An autopsy would be performed on each body to determine not only the cause of death, but also to study the direction from which the bullet entered each body. This information would help determine what had actually happened in the alley. The officers on the scene had collected everything from the suspects' pockets and were trying to piece together an identification for each.

Now, Wilson was mulling over the information that had been collected so far. The young man that had been laying closest to Joshua in the alley turned out to be Jake Roberts, according to the driver's license in his wallet. Also found in his wallet was a check stub from Connelly Shipping. The only other item found in Jake's wallet was twenty-one dollars in cash.

The young woman found at the scene had no identification on her at all. A fingerprint check identified her as Martha Peek, a local prostitute, who's current address had her living with Jake Roberts.

The man in black was a little harder to identify. By using the FBI records faxed to his office, Wilson was finally able to identify him as Clyde Barton, lately from Chicago, a known professional hit man wanted for at least fifteen murders. It crossed his mind when he read the fax that at least Joshua had closed the case on Clyde Barton. He also lost any doubt that he might have had that this was anything but a professional hit.

The chief was infuriated over the ambush of one of his officers; the cowardly way in which it was done added to his anger. They had phoned in a false police call which lead Joshua right into the ambush and then they cut him down in cold blood. The car they had used turned out to be stolen. When Mandy called the owner listed on the registration she listened as the phone was dropped on the table, and then heard the man running out the door and then running back and picking up the phone. Out of breath, he had exclaimed, "My car is gone, do you have it? Is it all right? Where is it?"

Wilson had received the report from the reconstruction team just five minutes ago and now he was ready for the morning news conference, scheduled to begin in a few minutes at 7:00. He would withhold the names of the attackers until the next of kin were notified. He hoped that when he found the next of kin it would bring him closer to finding out who had hired these people. He'd left word for his men to hit the streets and shake down every source they could find. He wanted answers and he wanted them yesterday. These cop killers would be brought to justice.

When Wilson returned to the hospital, he found that a number of people from several different churches had congregated in the lobby of the hospital to pray for Joshua, and await news of his condition.

As he moved through the lobby Wilson heard a news report on one of the television sets and paused to listen, "Special Bulletin, just in from the city of Covenant. Covenant police officer, Joshua White, was cut down in a pre-dawn ambush. It is reported that a fierce gun battle ensued earlier this morning, leaving three suspects dead and Officer White critically wounded. In a few minutes, we will hear from Chief Wilson, who . . ."

The chief turned and left. Walking toward the nurses station, he found Grady O'Leary drinking coffee and talking to a nurse. When Grady looked up and noticed the chief coming toward them, he poured another cup of black coffee, handing it to him as he arrived.

"You look like you could use one of these."

"Sure could. Thanks Grady!" He took a sip. "How's Josh doing?"

Grady's concerned look spoke volumes. "He's still in surgery, Chief, but they're just sewing him up and sticking tubes everywhere. I just had to get out of there for a couple of minutes. Martins is in there with him, until I relieve him."

The chief gave Grady an understanding nod and continued, "Yeah, I'm sure that was terrible to watch, but please catch me up on any events that might help us. Did Josh say anything? Anything that could possibly help us?"

Grady's anger flared at the memory of Dr. Chad White.

"The first thing that happened was that creep brother of Josh's, Dr. White, tried to throw me out of the operating room, and then stood there arguing with me while Josh went into full cardiac arrest. Thank God, we were already on our way to the operating room. When they finally got started on him, they had to bring Josh back twice before they could get him stabilized. It was touch and go for a while during the actual surgery. I headed up to the OR observation room so I could keep an eye on the good doctor. Chief, y'know I've seen my share of autopsies over the years, but none of them prepared me for what I saw them do to that man in there.

"To answer your other question, Josh didn't say anything during the ambulance ride. Oh, and uh, Dr. White may complain about the fact that I had to draw my 9mm to prove to him that I had the authority to stay."

With raised eyebrows, the chief looked up from his cup of steaming coffee.

He shrugged. "Well, I did tell you to stay at his side no matter what, and that is <u>exactly</u> what I meant." He swallowed the last of his coffee, put the cup in the garbage and said, as he straightened his uniform, "Well, Grady, I have to do this news conference in a couple of minutes, so why don't you assign some guards, and then go home and get some rest."

Grady began to object, but Wilson insisted, "I want you in my office rested and ready to work this afternoon. I'll have a job for you to do tonight."

Grady understood and accepted. "Anything you say, Chief."

As an afterthought, Wilson added, "I'll call you when it's about time for us to meet, I'm not sure just yet what time that will be."

Grady nodded and left.

Wilson entered the chapel to find Rev. Smith sitting in a pew with his head buried in his hands. There were tears running down his face.

He looked up as Wilson placed a hand on his thin shoulder.

"I've gotten hold of the other pastors and we'll meet shortly out in front of the hospital to begin our prayer service. We wanted to wait until after your news conference. When you clear the lobby, send the crowd to us."

Rev. Smith wiped his eyes with a handkerchief, and continued, "I was just thinking of how Joshua shamed me when I first arrived here to take over the church. That was seven years ago, wasn't it?"

The chief smiled at the memory. "Yes, Pastor, I believe that's correct. I've had similar thoughts this morning myself."

* * *

Rev. Jonathon Smith was twenty-five years old and fresh out of the seminary when he arrived at his first church--The Church of Grace, located on the square in Covenant. The church already had one hundred-fifty families and a lot of potential for growth. One of the six elders who had hired Rev. Smith was a police officer named Joshua White. From their very first meeting, Rev. Smith felt intimidated by this man of God and was therefore never very friendly toward him. He had barely been at his new church for a year when Joshua came to inform him that an abortion clinic was opening up very soon. It was to be right down the road from the church and Joshua wanted the Pastor's advise on how to stop it.

Rev. Smith told him, "I'm against abortion, of course. I'll speak against it from the pulpit."

"Pastor, we need to stop it from opening at all. We can't let it open just two doors from this church. We shouldn't let it open anywhere in Covenant at all!"

Rev. Smith bristled with indignation, "It's my responsibility to preach the Word of God, not . . ."

"No, Pastor! It's your job to live the Word of God and put it into action to stop the slaughter of the innocent children!"

Rev. Smith looked over his glasses at Joshua, and then in a condescending tone, he said, "Mr. White! As I was saying, it is my job to preach, not to walk picket lines. That brands one as a radical, a troublemaker."

Rev. Smith sat back satisfied, but Joshua came back with growing anger, "I thought being a Christian meant being a radical, a troublemaker. You don't think Jesus was considered a troublemaker when he cleared the Temple of money changers, or when he called the Pharisees 'a brood of vipers'? We can't sit back and let these people move in here and start the wholesale slaughter of innocent children. It's our duty to stop them with any legal means at our disposal."

Rev. Smith jumped up, leaned over his desk and spoke forcefully. "Mr. White, you have asked for my opinion and I gave it. Now listen to me as your pastor. I forbid you or any member of my church to participate in any foolish demonstration which would in the end make Jesus look foolish to the world and bring shame on my church. Besides, these people are too powerful! You can't stop them!"

Now it was Joshua's turn to jump up, but with a disciplined control and in an even voice, he said, "I believe in your authority over the flock, Pastor; however, your stand in this matter is based on worldly values, not God's. The order you just gave is contrary to what God has instructed us to do in this world, which we learned from Jesus' example. I feel the Holy Spirit is guiding me in this matter and I must follow His lead."

Rev. Smith looked down at his feet and said quietly, "If you do this, Mr. White, you will not be allowed to attend church here. It's up to you, but I've given my final word on this subject. Good day, sir!"

These words that Rev. Smith had spoken so emphatically and with such conviction would soon be words that he would regret. Seventy-five families left the church with Joshua. Joined by over a hundred families from the Catholic church and another three hundred from the rest of the churches in the area, the protesters set up a twenty-four hour picket line around the clinic building. The signs carried by the picketers left no doubt that they would settle for nothing less than total closure of the clinic. They demanded that the doctors and nurses go back to healing people instead of killing them off.

Every minute of Joshua's off-duty time was spent marching around the clinic. He was ridiculed by his fellow officers, and was even threatened by Chief Wilson, who told him to stop this protest or he would fire him. The pro-abortion people threatened violence and set up counter-demonstrations. The number of pro-life demonstrators continued to grow until more than nine hundred were involved in the protest, with more people from the surrounding counties and states volunteering to march everyday.

The day the clinic opened, the only people to enter it were Dr. Chad White, its new administrator, and his doctors and nurses. The medical staff sat like the proverbial spiders in their parlors, waiting for their first victim. Outside the building half of the nine hundred people knelt and prayed, while the other half marched and sang hymns.

As the end of the first day came to a close and the doctors and nurses were leaving the building, a man wearing a sign which read, "Jesus for Life!" approached one of the doctors. Joshua looked up from where he was kneeling just as the man pulled a revolver from under his jacket and aimed it at the doctor. The man yelled, "Death to the killers!" Joshua drew his 9mm Beretta and shouted, "Police, freeze!"

The man turned his gun toward Joshua.

"Lay down your weapon, slowly!"

It could have been the man's body language, the way he was holding his gun, or Joshua's years of experience, but Joshua knew that he wasn't going to have to shoot this man. The man dropped his weapon and was arrested by the officers who had watched the whole scene from their assigned posts. It was later revealed that the man was a gay rights activist who had been hired by unknown parties to create an incident and make the Christians look bad.

After this occurred, Joshua decided to take his entire one month vacation and camp out at the picket site. He ate there, slept there, and prayed there. He would talk to the crowd and keep their spirits up and did his share of marching around that building.

Father Jerry Powell, from Covenant's Catholic church, also conducted some of the prayer services and led in the singing. There were now people representing nearly every denomination present and they all agreed to put aside their differences for this important task. They recognized the fact that they were all members of the Body of Christ, and as such should be able to work together. The number of pickets continued to grow but still there were only two ministers and one priest in the entire number. The rest were the Christians who made up the various congregations.

The administrator of the clinic—a clinic which had seen absolutely no clients for three weeks now—decided he'd had enough. Chad called Chief Wilson and demanded that he "stop this madness." The chief reminded him that he could do nothing without a court order. Chad secured a court order and had the county's Sheriff Ricker serve it on Joshua personally. The order limited the picket line to three people.

It was ignored.

Chad filed another complaint with the courts and the judge issued a warrant for Joshua's arrest for contempt of court.

None of Joshua's fellow officers would arrest him.

Sheriff Ricker and seven deputies pushed their way through the crowd and ambushed Joshua as he knelt in prayer. They threw him face down on the ground, handcuffed him behind his back and hauled him off to the county jail. Even as he was being dragged through the angry mob, Joshua kept urging them to continue their work, but to remain peaceful.

The next day, a bruised, black-eyed Joshua, was dragged into county court and flopped into a chair. His cracked ribs made it hard to breath, but he managed to stand when the judge entered the court room. In front of a packed courtroom, the judge asked the sheriff what had happened to his prisoner.

"He slipped in the shower, Your Honor!"

The judge looked uncomfortable in front of this angry mob of Christians and said, "I've warned you before about this rough handling of your prisoners. This type of thing must stop! Do you hear me, Sheriff?"

The sheriff, hanging his head in mock repentance, said, "Yes, Your Honor. I am sorry."

The judge said, "Yes, well then, all right!"

He turned to Joshua and continued, "You, Officer White, should know, as a police officer especially, that you cannot ignore a court order. You were ordered by the law of the land to disperse your mob, and yet you ignored my order. What do you have to say for yourself?"

Joshua raised both blackened eyes to the judge and said, "Your Honor! I will obey the laws of the land when they don't condone the murder of innocent children. Until then, I must follow God's law which states, 'Thou shall not kill'. If you force me to choose between following man's law, which is upholding the death of innocent children and God's law of love, I will have to choose God's law."

The court room exploded with applause and a very fearful judge rapped his gavel and said, "$100.00 fine, and I warn you, White, to limit that picket line."

Joshua walked out of the courtroom and straight back to the picket line, ignoring the warning of the judge. He was surprised to find that the number of picketers had now grown to over two thousand people.

That night, Sheriff Ricker came back and arrested Joshua again on new charges. At the jail, after the deputies were done having their fun, they threw Joshua into a cell with twenty hard-core criminals. Joshua wiped the blood from his mouth and started singing some of his favorite hymns. The criminals, who looked at Joshua as a kindred spirit due to the beating he'd just received from the hands of their common enemy, listened with respect. Joshua then knelt and began to share the love of God and the plan of salvation with his cell mates. By morning he had led nearly all twenty of them to salvation.

Half of the crowd left the picket line at the clinic and came to the jail to sing and pray. A delegation of selected men, who carried with them a collection taken up for Joshua's bond, entered the jail. They paid his bond and brought him out. The crowd cheered and led him to the city square, just opposite the abortion clinic. Some of the Christians had set up large trailer-type barbecue grills in the adjacent park and were in the process of cooking what looked like the entire cattle population of Covenant's surrounding farm lands. The aroma was mouthwatering, and the other dishes which were spread on the many tables were equally tempting—casseroles, corn on the cob, fresh bread, pies, cakes—it was truly a feast.

Father Powell drove up in a large pickup truck, then jumped out, all smiles. He went to the back of the truck and pulled a tarp off the bed, exposing a mountain of iced-down soda. The cold beverage hit the spot.

Not since anyone could remember had the Christians of Covenant fellowshiped like this. No divisions, no titles other than Christian—they all worked together. Their differences set aside; they all enjoyed a common meal, common song, and common prayer.

There was one tense moment. Chief Wilson, several police officers, and three county deputies walked up to the food table. They'd been attracted by the sights and sounds of this Godly fellowship, but everyone was nervous. Then little one hundred-year-old Granny Girard, feeble of body but mighty in the Spirit, wheeled her chair up to the chief and handed him a plate, saying, "What you waiting for Sonny, you ain't getting no younger." With that said, she turned and wheeled away. The tension lifted and they were all accepted into the fellowship.

When everyone had eaten their fill, Joshua jumped up onto the top of one of the picnic tables. After a moment to collect his thoughts and a couple of deep breaths to control the pain in his ribs, he spoke in a loud clear voice, pointing toward the city square where a large replica of Moses' stone tablets heralded the founding fathers' ethics.

"Our city was founded over one hundred years ago by people who sincerely believed in the Ten Commandments. They called this city Covenant, in honor of the original Covenant between God and Moses, and the New Covenant between Jesus Christ and His people. One of the commandments is, 'Thou Shall Not Kill', and I believe that this refers most certainly to the murder of the innocent. Who is more innocent than the baby in the womb? These murders will not go unpunished by God!

"I for one, am willing to picket this clinic until it crumbles to dust, or they lock me up, or they close it! Is anyone with me?"

Cheers and applause started from the front and rippled like a wave all the way to the back of the crowd. Even Rev. Smith could not hide his admiration at such conviction and dedication, and joined in the applause, knowing in his heart that Joshua was correct. The cheers and applause of over five thousand Christians was a frightening sound for the clinic personnel to hear. As the voices of the Christians lifted in song, it felt as though the very foundation of the abortion clinic shook.

The fervor not only lasted for the next three days, but it spread to such proportions that businesses had to shut down for lack of workers—or customers. Over fifteen thousand people stayed away from work, refused to shop, and joined the pickets at the clinic.

Theodore Connelly, being a businessman above all else, called the clinic administrator, Chad White.

"Look, Chad, this has gone too far! It's affecting every business in town, and the owners are very upset. The members of the Chamber of Commerce have met and agreed that the clinic has to go. These people aren't going to stop and we can't afford another business day to go by with no sales. I've made arrangements for you to take over as chief surgeon at the hospital. You'll receive a generous salary, minus my ten percent, of course, and any money you make on any secret operations you do, well, you can keep that yourself."

Chad walked out the front door of the clinic, carrying in his hands a sign which read, "Closed - Sale Pending." He drove the stake into the ground, glared at the silent mob and then turned and walked down the street toward the hospital. All the clinic personnel left the clinic, heads hung low, out of work.

A mighty cheer from the huge crowd resounded through the empty stores and businesses of Covenant. Songs and shouts of praise to God were carried on joyous angel's wings to the throne room of God.

Later, as the crowd began to disperse and people began to return to their homes and jobs, plans for building more day-care centers, homes for unwed mothers, and other support groups were in the works. Covenant would not leave these girls without loving support and a means to keep their babies if they chose to, or assist them in finding loving homes if they chose adoption.

Looking back, Chief Wilson felt the same shame that Rev. Smith did, but he also realized that he hadn't been saved then and that he had since been forgiven, by Joshua, and most importantly, by the Lord.

"Well, Pastor, I'm not proud of what I did during that time either, but I know that Jesus, and Joshua, have forgiven me—and they've forgiven you as well. After all, that was a turning point for us both. I started believing that there was something to this Christianity thing and you became a much better minister for the Lord. Look, Pastor, just keep praying for us all, but especially for Joshua.

"Well, if you'll excuse me, Pastor, I have to give a news conference in . . ." He glanced at his watch, "Oh, no! Right now!"

Rev. Smith bowed his head again and realizing that the chief was right, felt a renewal in his spirit and continued in fervent prayer.

As Chief Wilson left the chapel, he saw Dr. White coming out of the operating room, pulling off his green surgical cap and running a weary hand through his prematurely gray hair. *He looks beat,* Wilson thought, but said, "How's Joshua, Doctor?"

An irritated Dr. White answered, "Not bad for a man who's been shot three times, stabbed with a razor sharp knife, and then suffered an acute coronary. He's alive, but I don't know how he survived it." Chad removed a report from the clipboard he'd carried with him from the operating room and handed it to Chief Wilson.

"I've written everything down just like you asked. Officially, he's in critical condition and the next twenty-four hours will tell us if he'll pull through or not. Now, if you'll excuse me, Chief, I'm late for breakfast."

The doctor walked off toward the cafeteria, and Wilson headed back toward the lobby and the waiting reporters.

As Wilson stepped up to the microphone, he noted that the lobby was full of reporters and well-wishers. A hush fell on the room as the chief organized his thoughts and made eye contact with the waiting crowd.

He took a deep breath and motioned for the crowd to sit as he said, "Please, have a seat if you can find one, ladies and gentleman. I'll make a brief statement of the facts as I know them, but I'll not take questions at this time."

There were loud protests from the reporters, but he waited them out.

"I don't want to jeopardize this investigation or the life of my officer by giving out too much information. I will not, therefore, divulge either the names of the attackers or the evidence that we've found to date. As soon as I can tell you—I will, I assure you."

More protests erupted, but he continued, "We know that Officer White had responded to a 1:30 A.M. call which sent him to the alley between Twenty-second and Olive streets. Seconds later, Dispatcher Mandy Miller heard the 'Shots fired' warning from Officer White and according to procedure, she called for back-up, and then phoned me and, of course, the ambulance service. "I was the first officer on the scene. I secured it, and then called in the reconstruction team. Their preliminary report reads as follows: Officer White got out of his squad car and was immediately shot in the right temple by a 30-30 high-powered rifle shell. Though wounded superficially, the force of the bullet was significant enough to knock him down. There were two attackers, a white male and white female, who were on ground level with him. It appears that Officer White shot the male attacker first, because he was hit in the right shoulder, which caused him to drop his unfired weapon. The second shot from Officer White's firearm hit the man in the chest, puncturing the right lung. The fatal shot, which hit the man in the head, did not come from Officer White's gun, but from the same 30-30 rifle that had shot Officer White earlier. This leads us to believe that the third attacker was a sniper on a nearby building, who in attempting to shoot the officer, instead shot one of his partners.

"Two bullets from the officer's weapon were found just beyond the body of the female assailant, leading us to assume that he fired upon her twice, and missed. At this time the woman apparently fired several shots at Officer White, hitting him once in his bullet-proof vest, and once in the left arm.

"The second attacker, as I've already said, was a white female. According to the autopsy, she was shot twice. A third of the three bullets fired at the female from the officer's gun creased the top of her scalp, which we believe may have knocked her out.

"Officer White, while apparently checking on the male attackers condition, was then stabbed in the back by the female, who was still holding the switch blade when we found her. The second bullet found in the woman's chest, came from the same 30-30 rifle that shot first Officer White, and then the male attacker. Again, we believe that the sniper was aiming for the police officer and not the female assailant. She died instantly, according to the autopsy report.

"Judging from the position of Joshua White's body and the proximity of one of his assailant's rifles, it has been determined that the officer had finally spotted the sniper and had managed to rise to his feet with a rifle in hand. He was then shot in the chest by the sniper. Officer White fired upon the sniper as he fell, fatally wounding him in the head and shoulders and causing him to fall from the rooftop to the ground below.

"Now, the shot that causes us the greatest concern is the 30-30 hit that Officer White took to the chest. The vest was quite strong enough to stop this bullet; however, half of the 30-30 shell passed through the vest and punctured the officer's chest, driving his broken ribs into his lungs. The stab wound, that I mentioned earlier, was to the right lower back. The knife did not hit any vital organs, but did cause a large loss of blood."

The chief took a breath, while he looked over Dr. White's report. Then he reported, "According to Dr. Chad White, head surgeon here at the hospital, and also the officer's brother, Officer White remains in critical condition. He's in shock and has suffered an acute heart attack, which they don't believe at this time has caused any permanent damage. He reports that the next twenty-four hours will be the critical test as to whether or not Officer White will survive."

The chief folded the papers before him and said, "That's all for now ladies and gentleman. I'll keep you informed." With that, he walked out of the hospital, amid the barrage of inevitable questions, all of which went unanswered. Chief Wilson had done his duty to the public, but now he had an investigation to conduct.

* * *

Chad put his breakfast tray down on the cafeteria table and sat down. He felt terrible; his stomach hurt, his throat was scorched from belching bile, and he hadn't slept well lately. This surgery had further exhausted him. He had done his best for Joshua and had hated every minute of it. Except for eagle-eyed O'Leary watching his every move, he could have killed Joshua at any time. A slip of the knife here, the wrong medicine there—nothing to it. But the one thing that Chad had done right in his life was to become a good surgeon. It was a habit that was hard to break, even for a chance to kill his brother. Well, at least it was over for now. He would eat breakfast, go home and take a shower and hopefully get some much needed rest.

Assistant Chief Anderson carried his own breakfast tray toward Dr. White's table. Chad was nodding off with his fork only halfway to his mouth. He nearly jumped out of his skin when Anderson dropped his tray onto the table with a deliberate crash. Chad's fork flipped up and onto the floor, scattering the scrambled eggs.

Anderson asked in a deceptively polite voice, "Mind if I join you, Doc?"

Chad, glaring at Anderson, asked, in an irritated, raspy voice, "What do you want, Anderson?"

Feigning concern, Anderson said, "Ah, I was just worried about you, 'cause I heard just how hard you've been working lately."

"Well, thanks, but I don't need your concern."

Chad began to rise.

In a suddenly malicious voice, Anderson said, "Sit down, Doctor! We have business to discuss."

The doctor sat and watched Anderson, like a mouse watches a cat.

"That's better. Oh, by the way, I ran into a friend of yours this morning. Do you remember Becky?"

Chad glared at Anderson again.

"No? Well, she sure remembers you! Think about it. You must remember something. How can anyone forget a night like that? That was some night, wasn't it, Doc?"

"What's your point, Anderson?"

"The point is, my friend, that if necessary, we could jog your memory with a video tape recording we made of your little tryst with Becky."

Chad jumped across the table trying to grab Anderson's throat. Anderson just slapped his hands away, laughing.

"Calm down, Doc, you're making a scene."

With a little push from Anderson, Chad flopped back into his chair with a thud. With the same malicious smile, Anderson continued, "Look Doc, out of the kindness of his heart, Connelly is going to give you a way to be free of that tape—forever. Interested?"

"Go on." With seeming lack of concern, Chad picked up his half-full coffee cup and took a sip, eyeing Anderson over the rim.

"All you have to do is make sure that your brother does not recover." Anderson sat back to watch, as the implications crashed in on the good doctor. Chad nearly choked as he swallowed his coffee. Anderson laughed as he continued, "Oh, come on, Doc, it shouldn't be hard for a man with your talents."

Chad shot back, "I won't kill my brother for you!" However, even as he said the words, the familiar feelings of envy and jealousy of Joshua came flooding back into his heart.

Anderson didn't miss the change. "Look, Doc, it's no worse than all those babies you kill in that secret surgery of yours. Joshua is no more human than they are in his condition, so sometime in the next forty-eight hours, you just make sure he dies. If he's still alive after that, the tape will find its way to both the press and your wife."

Chad clenched his fists on the table, his face becoming a mask of pure rage.

Anderson put up his hands in mock defense and said, "Don't hurt me, Doc!" With a broad grin, he repeated the doctor's options.

"Remember, Doc, forty-eight hours."

As Anderson rose to leave, Chad whispered, "Why do you fear Joshua so much?"

Through clenched teeth, Anderson replied, "I'm not afraid of anyone, least of all Joshua White!"

"Then why not wait for him to die? Why take a chance of getting caught killing someone, who will, more than likely, die before the forty-eight hours is up anyway?"

Anderson put both his hands on the table and leaned close to Chad. "Well Doc, it's like this. Idealistic people like Joshua just won't ever see the reality of life. They always tend to stand in the way of progress by forcing an ancient code of morals down our throats—a far too restrictive code. It's almost impossible to make any money in this world if your only option is the ethical approach. Joshua is hurting business with all of this anti-drug and anti-violence teaching that he's exposing our children to. He even tells them the dangers of joining the occult, which, as you know, we can't allow to continue.

"So you see, Doc, Joshua just has to go, and Mr. Connelly has picked you to do the honors. Nothing bloody; do it quietly but effectively."

Anderson stood up and stretched, then continued, "Now you go home and have a nice rest today, Doc. But remember, get it done in forty-eight hours; then you're a free man."

Chad watched as Anderson turned and walked out of the cafeteria, leaving his untouched food tray laying on the table where he had dropped it. He rubbed his throbbing temples.

As Chad returned his tray and left the cafeteria, he began to see the advantage of having Joshua out of the way. It would be like reclaiming his own life.

Passing through the lobby, he saw the television crews tearing down their equipment. He exited through the main doors of the hospital and into the warm sunshine, ignoring the police officers who were still checking everyone. He paused to take a deep breath and felt a strange peace settle over him. He stood for a moment and enjoyed what he had so rarely felt before. He walked to his car, got in, and headed for home.

Yes, he would go home to his wife, Ellen, get some sleep, and when he awoke, he would make everything up to her. With Joshua out of the way, Ellen would, once and for all, have only him to love.

With a smile on his face and an evil plot in his heart, Chad turned his car onto the highway that would lead him to his home.

Chapter 7
The Siege Begins

Cono pierced the twin demons with his scowl. Jealousy and Envy were fat blobs of overlapping flesh whose eyes peeked out from between drooping eyelids. They stood before Cono and shook from their ugly heads to their contorted oversized toes.

When Cono spoke, his voice rolled forth from somewhere deep within his belly and he sounded like an angry bear awakened early from hibernation.

"You ran away without even a fight?"

The force of his words hurled the twins backward and when they hit the floor of Cono's chamber, they curled up in little quivering balls of flesh, doing their best to hide from the worst of his wrath.

Cono continued, "Answer me! Is what Poe tells me correct or did he lie to me?" The twins shook in terror and could not answer.

With a sneer, Cono finally hissed, "Get up, you fools!"

Both demons unrolled enough to peek out, but were still afraid to come out, though more afraid not to. They finally stood up, clinging to each other for support.

Cono leaned in and spoke in a whisper, forced between clenched teeth.

"You two will go back to the hospital with Lt. Poe and you'll do whatever he tells you to do. Is that clear?"

The twins nodded in unison.

"Good!" Cono launched the word in a sarcastic sneer and then bellowed, "Get out of my sight!"

Lt. Poe, who was standing behind the twins watching the entire exchange with mirth, picked them up by the scruff of their necks and flung them in the general direction of the chamber door, yelling as he did so, "Wait outside for me!"

The twins scurried like rats to escape the presence of their angered superior. Poe turned to face Cono. After a moment of tense silence in which Poe wondered about his own fate, Cono finally sat down and motioned for Poe to sit.

He leaned forward and with an evil glint in his eye, he said, "Poe, here's what I want you to do . . . ."

Aaron stood on the roof of the hospital where he could observe the battlegrounds. He was gratified thus far. There had only been a few minor skirmishes with demons who refused to leave their human slaves. Some of these fought fiercely and were dispatched back to the abyss in short order, while others were scared off by the mere sight of the advancing angelic forces. Thus far, Aaron had lost none of his forces to the enemy and he was now praising his Creator for this.

Aaron thought about what it means to be "killed" or "dispatched," whether demon or angel. When the demons were dispatched they appeared before their master, Satan. The demon would then throw himself at the feet of Satan and beg and plead in vain for forgiveness while Satan stripped him of his rank, title, and sword. Satan would then hand him over to the demons in charge of the torture chamber. After these "jailors" were finished biting, kicking, clawing, and

The Siege Begins

humiliating the fallen demon, he was returned to the ranks, a broken spirit. He was then doomed to work his way back up the ladder of power.

Angels, on the other hand, were sent to the feet of Jesus when they were "killed" by the enemy. God, and His Son, Jesus, praised the angel for his valor, healed his wounds, and then gave him the choice of rejoining the battle or doing some other duty, which was just as important and rewarding. The angels generally chose to return to the fight.

What gave Aaron pause now, however, was the fact that all the demons, who, though cowardly, were usually very greedy, and would therefore fight viciously for their territory. But this time, most of the demons were practically volunteering to give up their human host. They flew into the darkening sky and, there, in a growing dark cloud, hovered and taunted the angelic forces, who held a firm grip on the New Hope hospital. Occasionally, the demons would attack the angels, but for the most part, they just taunted them.

Aaron had seen this before, and he didn't much like its meaning. He could feel the saints of God praying, which made his forces stronger, and he took heart in that. Yet, he couldn't shake the feeling of dread that was growing as fast as the churning, black cloud of demons overhead. Aaron knew that the news conference, called by Chief Wilson for this morning, was about to begin. Chief Wilson would report that Joshua was in trouble. This, Aaron hoped, would cause the saints to pray all the harder, thus reinforcing his already strong positions.

Suddenly Aaron felt disoriented, dizzy, and weak. He nearly dropped the sword which he held in his right hand, but recovered it and steeled himself for the attack that was now imminent. A moment later, he was dealt a blow to the chest that knocked the wind out of him, bringing him to his knees. Aaron turned to look for his unseen attacker. What he saw shocked and dismayed him. Half of his army were being forced to their knees while the other half looked on in disbelief. Aaron began to pray. "God, our Creator, we are under attack, and the lack of prayers from the saints has brought us to our knees...."

As Aaron prayed, unashamed, Lt. Poe began to jeer in a loud voice, "Look at the almighty angels now! They can't even hold their swords by themselves! Perhaps we should help them, what do you think, my friends?"

This brought laughter and cheers from the churning, vile cloud of demons which circled the hospital. Lt. Poe was thoroughly enjoying himself, but he knew that he had very little time to bask in the glory of this moment. Poe took a deep breath and ordered in a loud, foul smelling yell, "Now! Move in! Now!"

Aaron watched as the churning horde turned into a twirling, twisting, demonic tornado. The bottom of the cloud began to descend toward the hospital building. As it approached, the cloud expanded and began to engulf the entire hospital with shrieking, jeering demons, and in just a few short minutes, the entire five-story hospital building was completely swallowed up by the evil creatures. Their red eyes glowing, they spewed their foul, sulfuric breath and acid-rich spittle, at the brave angelic guards who were determined to hold their posts.

Aaron struggled to his feet, raised his sword with great difficulty, and yelled, "Defend yourselves, brothers, as best you can, for the saints have failed us. May the praise, glory, and honor be to our great God, in Whom all things exist."

Lt. Poe descended upon Aaron and swung his wickedly curved sword with such ferocious power that, when it connected with Aaron's sword, knocked Aaron off the roof of the hospital. Poe laughed as he killed two angels who had come, too late, to help Aaron. He then took up Aaron's former post and watched the battle with satisfaction.

As Aaron plummeted toward the earth, he mentally kicked himself for not being ready for this. He and his forces had been counting too heavily on the saints' prayers. When the news conference began, virtually every Christian had ceased praying at the same time in order to watch it on television. Aaron hadn't experienced prayer of this magnitude for a long time and he had carelessly forgotten just how big a blow it was when it all ceased at once.

He slowly unfolded his bruised wings. As they reached their full ten-foot span, they filled with air like a billowing sail. He came out of his dive and began to gain altitude again. He took a deep breath and rallied his angelic forces, "Remember the empty tomb!"

Aaron's strength returned, as well as the strength of his angels, and the war raged on. He impaled a demon warrior, and then raced ahead to assist a soldier who was being attacked by three demons. Catching them off-guard, he held one demon in a head lock, and shoved the blade of his sword through the other, causing a foul puff of smoke. Aaron swiftly broke the neck of the trapped demon, while his soldier cut the throat of the third. The soldier nodded his thanks, but as he did so his head came off and he faded out of existence.

A shocked and angry Aaron stood facing four demons who had come out of the darkness of the cloud to attack the angel from behind. The four attackers didn't want anything to do with an angry angel who was ready for battle. They bolted like wild horses with Aaron in hot pursuit. The four demons were flying in single file, so as Aaron caught up with the last one in line, he swung his large sword and separated the demons head from its shoulders. He flew through the red smoke caused by the demon's demise to find that the three demons whom he had been chasing had stopped, turned, and now attacked him with furor.

Aaron struck at the demon on his right and their swords clashed, causing bright red and white flashes against the dark evil cloud which churned all around them. Aaron quickly kicked the demon on his left, breaking the demons knobby kneecap, wrenching a shriek of pain from him as he beat a hasty retreat. Aaron grabbed the wrist of the demon whose sword he had just blocked and butted heads with him. The demon staggered, trying to clear his vision. The third demon, who had worked his way in behind Aaron, brought his sword down toward the middle of Aaron's back. Aaron, alert now, felt his approach, and somersaulted backwards over the demon's head, landing behind him. The demon's blade came down upon his staggering cohort, sending him on his way to the abyss and his audience with Satan. As the demon turned to defend himself, Aaron's blade sliced through him from his left shoulder to his right hip, sending him trailing after his evil companion.

Aaron didn't even stop to watch the demon vanish, but instead flew off to help an angel who was being tortured by a small cloud of the vile creatures. They were holding him down and biting his wings off. Aaron screamed in rage, and raced toward his comrade. As he came near, Aaron heard the valiant angel pray, "My Creator, I come to you in the way you deem fit for an angel in battle."

The light around the angel began to pulsate and the surprised and suddenly frightened demons tried to get away, but they were much too slow. The blinding light

The Siege Begins

dissolved not only the small group of demons, but also nearly three thousand of the other hideous creatures who were caught in the blast.

Aaron bid farewell to his warrior and friend. He was grateful for this secret weapon—an angel, who knows he is about to be dispatched, can cause a large power output which, though it destroys the angel, also has devastating effects on any demon within a mile of the angel. The "fallout" had no ill effects on his fellow angels who could go on fighting as if nothing at all had occurred.

Fighting is exactly what Aaron was prepared to do when he saw Lt. Devok, one of his division leaders, coming his way. Unknown to Devok, there was a demon closing fast on his back. Aaron gave Devok a hand signal. Devok ducked just as Aaron's sword blade spun past him, bare inches above Devok's head. The smirk on the big demon's face turned to painful rage as Aaron's sword blade dug deep into his chest. As the demon evaporated, Devok caught Aaron's sword and returned it to him with a grateful smile.

Devok saluted, "I've come to report that the demons are now retreating just as quickly as they attacked. The saints of God have begun their prayers anew and our strength is increasing past our normal boundaries again."

Aaron let the feeling wash over him, but reminded himself, this time, not to count too heavily on it. When he opened his eyes, he saw that the demon cloud had dissipated and he could again breathe fresh air. He thanked Devok, who returned to his post, and Aaron collected the reports of all his leaders. This battle had temporarily cost him a few thousand angels, but the demon losses were even greater and longer lasting. He had retained control of the hospital and had kept it, and Joshua, safe.

Lt. Poe had kept an eye on Aaron all through the battle. He used the distraction of the dispatched angel blasting three thousand of his demons to sneak the whining twins into the basement of the hospital building through a window which had been left temporarily unguarded. Poe turned to the twins and made sure that they understood what fate awaited them, if they should fail him.

Lt. Poe went back to the battle to find that he had already lost over ten thousand of his troops, but he didn't care. He had accomplished his actual objective—he had gotten the twins started on their quest. Poe ordered his troops to pull back and took a position high above the hospital where he could watch the fun.

Jealousy and Envy found Dr. Chad White in the cafeteria sitting across from Asst. Chief Anderson. Dr. White was saying, "I won't kill my brother for you!"

The twins smiled at each other, and raced to do their jobs. Jealousy took one side of Dr. White's head and Envy took the other. When they were in position, they nodded and then simultaneously dug there claws deep into the doctor's skull. They began to whisper their poison into the doctor's ears, sending their messages of hate deep into his soul.

The demons, except for a few sentries and their leader, Poe, had all pulled back behind their lines. Aaron made his rounds, congratulating his warriors. When he was finished, he stood before them, about to speak, but had to stop when they each, one by one, unsheathed their swords and held them across their chests, with the points resting on their left shoulders. This was a recognition of Aaron's worthy leadership. Tears welled up in his eyes; he was deeply touched by their gratitude, and raised his own sword in a return gesture to their own worthiness. This brought a loud cheer from the ranks.

The Siege Begins

After a short time they sheathed their swords, bowed their heads, and Aaron began the victory prayer, "God, our Creator and Master, we thank You for Your power and Your love. We have victory because of Your might and all the earth should praise Your name! We . . . ." Aaron gasped for breath, eyes wide with shock, then disappeared. Lt. Devok drew his sword and screamed in rage at the enemies' cowardice, but there was little he could do, for the twins scurried out of his reach as they resheathed their daggers.

An ominous black force snaked into view on the distant horizon, stopping just short of the angel's hedge of protection which had been placed around Covenant.

Captain Tumult looked at his horde of demons and then looked at the last haven of God's peace, the City of Covenant. He licked his lips at the knowledge that this holy city would soon be his to destroy. Tumult's evil smile was almost as cold as the evil which was about to descend on Covenant.

Jesus turned away from the battlefield and left to prepare for the next stage of the war.

Chapter 8

Evil Doctor—Sweet Wife

By the time Dr. Chad White had turned onto the street where he lived, he had become a new man. For the first time in years he knew that Joshua was out of his life, and it was as if a mighty weight had been lifted from his shoulders. Chad was a happy man and it showed in his face.

He no longer cared whether or not Ellen and Joshua had ever had an affair. With his brother dead, Ellen would have to turn to him and he would be there for her this time. He had been a little cold and distant lately with Ellen, but he could see clearly now, and he knew that it was not her fault. She had just fallen under his brother's spell like everyone else had. He felt a brief surge of anger when he thought of Ellen in Joshua's arms, or worse, the possibility that she thought of Joshua when she was in Chad's arms.

But even with these thoughts going through his mind, he began to smile again, because in a very short time he would end his brother's life and in so doing, he would resurrect his own.

The twins, Jealousy and Envy, were digging and twisting their claws deep into Chad's brain. They smiled at each other as the last barrier in the doctor's conscience crumbled and they took complete control of Chad's mind.

Chad looked out of the window of his large and very expensive sedan and took note of his surroundings—the sunshine, the lush green lawns and elaborate landscaping of the estates in his neighborhood. It was a beautiful day, a fact that usually escaped the good doctor.

He purposely looked around him as if seeing these sights for the first time. He liked to put himself in the place of the middle-income sightseer out on a Sunday drive, dreaming of one day living in a home like these.

Each estate house was centered on five acres of gently rolling hills. Each house was surrounded by tall, stately trees that provided an abundance of shade and kept the yards pleasantly cool. The winding driveways were also lined with trees or fragrant flower borders.

Some estates had swimming pools, tennis courts, hot tubs, sauna bathhouses, and some had entire greenhouses, just for the owner's pleasure.

None of the estates fortunate residents took care of the grounds solely on their own. That job belonged to old man Pulky, and his three sons, who made up Pulky Landscape and Horticultural Hospital, Inc. Pulky had really lucked out when he secured a monopoly on this neighborhood. *Just goes to show how far hard work and a little bit of talent can take you, as long as you have the right connections,* Chad thought with a smile.

Though each house was similar to Chad's own; each a three-story wooden, stone, and brick frame with a full basement, six bedrooms, a large master suite with its own private bath suite, two extra bathrooms upstairs and one down, a den or library, a kitchen, formal dining room and some with the optional servants' wing, Chad was extremely proud of the fact that his home was one of the most magnificent. Chad and Ellen's home had been featured in *Beautiful Home* magazine twice already. He'd had the magazine cover photographs framed, and displayed them ostentatiously in the entry foyer.

Chad punched in the code which opened his gate as he pulled into his own drive. When he got out of the car, his step was a little lighter and he still wore a self-satisfied smile.

Ellen had been in the den staring at some Sunday School papers that needed grading, when she heard the car drive up. She stood up, stretched, wiped away her tears, and then walked to the window to see what Chad looked like this afternoon.

Her tears of worry for Joshua were still forcing themselves from her eyes as she spread the blinds apart. She had to look twice to convince herself that it really was Chad. He had been so irritable and surly for the past few years that she barely recognized this man. He was smiling, and though she couldn't hear anything through the closed window, she could swear that he was even whistling.

Ellen had been doing a lot of crying lately. She wasn't used to this lifestyle and never would be. Her tastes were on the simple side. A nice house would have done just fine and she felt guilty spending all this money on an estate, just for them. She did her best to help the poor and needy, but she just couldn't get used to this opulence. Chad, however, insisted that they deserved this kind of lifestyle and that was that.

Ellen thought how out of place Chad's smile and light steps looked. Not because he had been so depressed, but because Joshua was in critical condition. Yet his own brother seemed to be happy!

She knew that they had their differences, but this would be cold, even for Chad. Ellen opened the front door for him.

As he walked up the front porch steps she started to comment on his inappropriate happiness when Chad interrupted. "Ellen, everything is going to be fine."

He smiled and held his arms out to her. She ran to him and they hugged in earnest for several minutes. Ellen could feel the warmth and love that was in the hug and she gladly returned them. To her, Chad's statement meant that Joshua would live, and that Chad had finally gotten over his jealousy. Ellen thought when Joshua recovered, everything would be good again.

Chad could feel Ellen's enthusiastic response to his hug and he knew that his plan to rekindle his marriage would work. He took Ellen by the hand and like two happy lovers, they entered their home.

As Ellen and Chad embraced, the twins tried to sink their claws and fangs into Ellen's head. Oath threateningly poked them with his bright sword. They pulled back quickly, helpless and unable to hurt this saint of God. Many demons had tried to attack this Godly woman, but they had met Oath, and for most that was the last thing they did on this earth.

Still holding hands and walking through their living room, Ellen felt that this was again the man she had married. This was the father of their daughter Susie and the man Ellen had dedicated her life to.

Chad had not been a happy man for a few years now, but the last year had grown even worse. He had joined a strange club which met once a week, but he never told her what they did there. She felt very uneasy about this club. She didn't know why, of course, but it just felt evil somehow. She had said this to Chad once, but he had just laughed nervously and changed the subject. Ellen shook off these thoughts about the past that threatened to disturb her enjoyment of the present.

She had let the maid off early today, so as they entered the kitchen, Ellen poured a cup of coffee for Chad, and they went out onto the patio to talk. Chad told Ellen all about his long hours at the hospital, the ever-present police, the crowd and, of course, how he had saved his brother's life.

He told Ellen how unfortunate it was that it took something like this to make you realize just how much you care about someone. He apologized for the way he'd been acting and promised that it would be much better from now on.

Ellen innocently thought that Chad was talking about Joshua. Chad fully intended to give her that impression even though he was really talking about how he and Ellen would love each other once Joshua was eliminated. He even went so far as to comfort Ellen, telling her that there was nothing to worry about; Joshua was strong and would pull through.

Ellen looked deep into Chad's eyes and saw love looking back. She felt reassured by their conversation.

After Chad's coffee was gone, Ellen suggested that he go up and take a nice hot shower. She would be along shortly to give him a rub down to relax his tense muscles. Chad got up, kissed Ellen, and then headed inside.

He was a happy man.

While Chad and Ellen chatted amicably, the demon, Deceit, wove his tangled web around Chad. He had arrived as they entered the kitchen, but Oath couldn't stop him unless he tried to harm Ellen. Deceit, shoving aside Jealousy and Envy, perched on Chad's shoulders, and slipped his dagger blade deep into Chad's spine.

He controlled Chad's every emotion. For now, he was allowing him to be happy and loving. Deceit knew that women fall for that every time. It was important that he be successful in this, for his own life depended on it. He must make Chad believe that he was not only happy, and doing the right thing, but he must also make him believe that Ellen was on his side. He had just accomplished both.

The twins, Jealousy and Envy, had scampered out of the way and only tried to touch Ellen once, which resulted in Envy losing a knotted finger to Oath's great sword for his trouble. Neither of the twins tried again. Oath stood near Ellen, sword drawn, and very alert.

When Chad was done with his shower, he laid on the bed while Ellen rubbed his sore back. Chad, caught up in the peace and relaxation of the moment, began to fall into a deep sleep. As he drifted off, he thought to himself, *I knew it! Ellen is already mine again. She is showing me more attention already, because she knows that Joshua will soon be out of the picture.* He drifted into a contented sleep.

Deceit sat back, rubbed his own aching back, and smiled at a job well done. The three demons, keeping their distance from Ellen, and, of course, Oath, sat and talked about how easy this assignment had turned out to be. They were dreaming of their promotions and the large swords they would receive as reward for their hard work.

Ellen covered Chad up and kissed his cheek. She then knelt by the bed, lifted her blue eyes and loving heart heavenward, and prayed softly, "Thank You, God, for giving me the strength to stay with Chad during this year of mood swings and pain. I also thank You for bringing him back to me, his old self. He may even be able to turn to You, Lord, and that would be great. Thank You for sending your Son, Jesus Christ, to save us from our sins." Ellen knelt there awhile and enjoyed God's presence.

The three demons stopped talking at the name of Jesus Christ, and snarled. Oath yelled, "Get on your knees—you know the rules. Every knee must bend at the mention of that Name." Oath was already on his knees, and the three demons reluctantly did the same. When Ellen stopped praying they all got up and raising his sword, Oath said, "Get out! Your slave is asleep and you have no claim here." The three demons didn't move. Oath flew at them with the resolve to dispatch each of them to hell and they all left the house screaming in fear.

Oath returned to where Ellen knelt and put a sympathetic hand on Ellen's shoulder. He prayed his own prayer to the Lord asking that Ellen be given the strength to endure what must surely come next.

Ellen completed her prayer by asking that the Lord lead Chad away from that "club" that she so feared. She hoped, and prayed, that Chad would sleep right through the dinner meeting that was planned for tonight at Mr. Connelly's Estate. Chad had tried to get her to go, but she just couldn't do it.

She had Oath to thank for that.

Chapter 9
Tumult Declares War

"And this is the condemnation, that light is come into the world, and men loved darkness rather than light, because their deeds were evil. For every one that doeth evil hateth the light, neither cometh to the light, lest his deeds should be reproved.
But he that doeth truth cometh to the light, that his deeds may be made manifest, that they are wrought in God."
John 3:19-21 (KJV)

The demon called Captain Tumult stood on a hill and looked down with disgust on Covenant. He looked over at Crygen, his Lieutenant and bodyguard.

"You see this city laying bare before us? This is the largest stronghold left to the enemy and the one that pushes all those outdated values on the rest of the country. Once we wipe out this nest of vile Christians, we'll be able to rule the world. We'll leave nothing standing in this place as an example to any who would dare to stand in our way."

Crygen just nodded, knowing that Tumult wanted agreement, not conversation. He contemplated his leader for a moment. Tumult was tall for a demon, standing a full six feet. He was heavily muscled and had the strong forceful features of a leader. He wore loose pants, a wide cloth cummerbund around his waist. His chest was bare and his massive arms sported red bands which displayed his rank insignia.

Crygen could see the muscles of Tumult's chest rippling with tension, as if he couldn't wait for the war to begin. Crygen knew from experience, however, that Tumult was a dangerously patient warrior, and he would do whatever it took to win.

Tumult turned again to Crygen and issued the expected order, "Set up camp here and dig in, the war will soon begin. Until then, I want this city surrounded by a circle of demon warriors, just outside that hideous border of light that marks their territory—at least it's theirs for now. No one is to leave their post for any reason, and Crygen . . . make that last order understood!"

"Yes sir!" Crygen began to fly away to carry out his orders, when Tumult called out to him. He stopped and faced Tumult.

"Yes, Commander!"

"Send a scout to tell that worthless Cono that I have arrived and that I expect him to meet me at the earliest opportunity."

"Yes sir! Right away sir!"

As Crygen left to carry out his task, Tumult followed him with his eyes. As much as Tumult could trust anyone, he trusted Crygen. Crygen had served him well in many battles. They'd had some glorious times, collecting souls for their lord.

Tumult saw a scout soar out of the camp, into the sky, and then race toward the city. He would have loved to go with him. To scout the front lines of the enemy, that was the real fun, but his rank forbade him that pleasure.

His hand rested on the hilt of the sword that Satan had given to him personally as a reward for services rendered. The sword hilt and scabbard were embedded with precious jewels of all kinds: diamonds, rubies, and emeralds. Each one represented a battle won or a hundred souls stolen from the enemy. There were two spots left to fill on his scabbard—one for when he won Covenant and the other for when he turned America into a socialist state. He would then be able to stamp out God completely from the earth.

Tumult raised his eyes from his sword which he still rubbed lovingly, to his troops who were preparing the camp. He thought to himself, *How wonderful are the sights, sounds, and odors of an army preparing for battle.* He had brought over fifty thousand troops and he knew that this time he outnumbered Worl, five to one. Worl, his arch enemy, who had embarrassed Tumult in front of his men and the lord Satan himself.

Tumult just knew he had won on that long-ago day, by turning all of the apostles against Jesus at the Cross. They were discredited. No one should have listened to them, let alone followed them. Somehow, Worl managed to get people to forgive them and the apostles had continued their warfare against Tumult and his dark lord.

As he watched the dark line of demons crawl around either side of Covenant, he thought, *Not this time, Worl, not this time!* As his army enclosed Covenant like invading ants, Tumult began to laugh—a deep, guttural laugh, which sent fingers of fear crawling up the spine of the demon who had just arrived at Tumult's newly-raised tent. It was this demon's misfortune to be Tumult's entertainment for the evening.

A large, unmarked semi-truck pulled into the local motel's parking lot, just outside of Covenant. The driver, Butch, got out of the truck and walked over to the nearby phone booth. He dialed the number he'd been given, and when the party answered, said, "The package has arrived!" He hung up the phone and walked into the cafe, which was attached to the motel. He ordered a cup of coffee and then sat and waited. He hoped the wait would be short. His boss was in a foul mood.

* * *

Grady jumped! Suddenly wide awake, he reached for the 9mm Berretta that he kept in his nightstand. Had he heard a noise? He wasn't sure, since he'd been in that place somewhere between this world and the world of dreams. It could've been nothing more than the echo from a lost dream.

He climbed out of bed with the pistol in his right hand and ready. He searched his bedroom. Nothing. He entered the hall which led to the other three rooms of his small apartment. The first door on the right was his bathroom and he found it empty as well. Grady then inched his way into the living room. To the left was his entertainment center, which held his television, stereo, speakers, and books. He looked behind his couch and chairs. Nothing. He entered his kitchen/dining area. He felt foolish but he checked under the sink and in the broom closet anyway. He found no intruder lurking anywhere in his apartment. Even the door in the kitchen that led to the outside hallway was locked.

Just as Grady relaxed the phone rang. Startled, he raised his pistol in an instant and was only a fraction of a second away from pulling the trigger when he realized what it was. The phone rang again. Grady threw the gun on the couch, plopped down and picked up the phone.

He said, a little more irritably than he intended, "What do you want?"

A hesitant voice on the other end said, "Boy, did you get up on the wrong side of the bed!"

Grady sat up, "Chief! I'm sorry, I, I . . ."

The Chief laughed. "Don't worry about it. I was worried about you. I just called not two minutes ago and there was no answer. I guess you were in the shower?"

"Well, no, I was just in a deep sleep. I must have heard part of the last ring." Grady laughed, "As a matter of fact I was . . . uh . . . well, never mind."

He didn't want to tell the chief that he had just made a fool of himself by searching the apartment, and then almost blowing his own phone apart. He asked instead, "What time do you want to meet, Chief?"

"Meet me in my office at 4:00 P.M."

Grady agreed and hung up. He looked at his kitchen clock—2:30, just enough time to shower and shave.

Grady was anxious to get started on this case. He wouldn't rest until the people responsible for shooting Josh were behind bars.

After Grady had entered the bathroom and turned on the shower, the tall angel, Warren, sat back down on the bed, resheathing his sword. He hadn't sensed any danger, but when Grady bolted out of bed with his gun, he drew his own sword, just in case. He had watched Grady search his apartment in this fashion many times, but for the last couple of weeks he'd been especially edgy. Even Warren could feel the impending doom that was creeping into and around Covenant.

Warren, like all the other angels had been given specific orders from Worl himself, not to do anything until the evil one made his first move.

Grady let the hot water run over his aching muscles. When he was finished, Grady turned the water off, opened the shower curtain and felt the suddenly cool air brush against him raising "goose bumps" on his wet skin. He dried off quickly and then donned his undergarments and uniform pants. He wiped the mirror clean of the fog that had formed on it, and lathered his face.

Grady looked at himself between the water beads which were reforming on the mirror and reassured himself that he still had a young-looking face, even for twenty-nine. His damp red hair was sticking out everywhere, giving him the look of an Irish Medusa, and his green eyes were bloodshot from lack of sleep.

Grady's thoughts shifted as he remembered the first time he'd shaved in this bathroom. It had been eight years ago and he looked much like he did today, except that his thoughts were very different.

Grady O'Leary was fresh out of the police academy and was shaving for the first time in his new apartment. He was preparing for the first day of his new job as a full-time Covenant Police Officer. He would've been totally thrilled too, if it weren't for the bad news he'd received from one of his friends on the force.

He'd learned that his field training officer was to be Joshua White, a well-known Jesus freak. Grady was a Catholic, and went to Mass on Christmas and Easter. As far as he was concerned, that was all he needed to know about Jesus. Now he found that he was to be coached by a Bible-thumping, hell-fire preaching, training officer.

This guy was said to be a good police officer, but some of the newer officer's had their doubts. They figured that any man that would go around talking about Jesus in public had to be a wimp. Grady had learned about men like that in the academy. Men who, when you got in a pinch, became more of a problem than a help. He looked at the bathroom clock and noted that he only had ten minutes before White would be there to pick him up.

He rushed into the bedroom and put his bullet-proof vest on and then his brand new, crisply-pressed, uniform shirt. After tucking in his shirt, he strapped on his duty belt, which held his night stick, bullet reloaders, handcuffs and a sparkling new, stainless steel .357 magnum pistol.

Grady stood in front of his full-length mirror and placed the police cap on his head, being careful to wipe the fingerprints off the bill of the hat with his handkerchief. He stood there and admired himself, a six-foot, 198 pound, blue-eyed police officer. A child-like smile creeped into Grady's features and he drawled to the figure in the mirror, "Draw, you sidewinder, if you got the guts!"

The "men" stared each other down for a moment and then the man in the mirror went for his gun as Grady drew his.

Grady laughed out loud and said, "You're fast, partner, I'll let you live this time."

The two men blew on the barrels of their guns to disperse the imaginary smoke that was coiling out of them and reholstered their weapons.

Grady heard a car horn honk and taking one last look at the figure in the mirror, touched a finger to the brim of his hat and with a sharp salute said, "It's show time!"

As he walked down the hallway which led from his ground floor apartment to the street, he thought about the other things he'd learned about Joshua White.

White was a twelve-year veteran who had already won two Commendations for Valor, one Civil Servant Award, and Civic Leader of the Year Award. The older veterans didn't say much about White, good or bad; they left the younger ones to their own opinions.

At his "indoctrination" which took place in a local police bar, Grady had received some wise advice as well as some other more ribald comments. Someone had yelled to Grady, "Hey, O'Leary, you gonna have to ask Jesus if you can blow your nose now?" Another said, "Yeah, every time he gets a call, they'll drop to their knees to pray and we'll have to handle their calls for them." Joshua had come late. He drank one Coke, said his congratulations, and then left. He was the topic of conversation for quite a while after, until it drifted to women and sports.

As Grady approached the squad car he thought, *Well, I'll see for myself what this man is made of.*

White got out the squad car and came around to shake Grady's hand and welcome him to his first patrol. He told Grady to get in the driver's seat as he got back in the car on the passenger side. Most officers considered driving a matter of seniority. They're in control when they drive, so they usually made it very clear to new people that the driver's seat belonged to the veteran. Grady was taken aback by this gesture of acceptance. White was already treating him as an equal. This made Grady feel more at ease, but also a little guilty because of the bad-mouthing he'd participated in about this man.

Grady got behind the wheel and the feeling of power overtook him. He was now in control of a large sedan that had been specially made to travel up to 180 m.p.h. It was a shining black and white unit with the standard police lights on top and loud siren.

Grady was a bit nervous though, and asked, "Are you sure you want me to drive?"

Joshua smiled and said, "You do have a license, don't you?"

Grady nodded and looked back as he pulled into the traffic flow.

"Where do you want me to go?"

"We have the residential area today; I'll show you where to turn."

With a smile, for he was aware of the comments made about him, Joshua added, "By the way, Grady, where do you go to church?"

Grady's expression was priceless, an "Oh boy, here we go" look.

Without waiting for an answer, Joshua laughed and went on, "Well, I see you've already heard all the rumors about me. I'll make it easy for you, Grady. I'll tell you what I believe and then you won't have to guess.

"I'm a follower of Jesus Christ above all else and I bring my Christian values into everything I do. I want everyone to hear about the freedom that Jesus brings to their life both here in this world and in the world to come. I'm not ashamed to talk about Jesus to anyone, including the people I arrest. There's no task more important than helping people receive Jesus into their hearts so they can start to live for Him.

"My methods haven't set well with certain people and that's how the rumors were born. I'm the butt of many a joke; it goes with the territory. I never hound people, however, for Jesus invites people to join Him. He never twists their arms, nor will I.

"That said, where do you go to church, Grady?"

Grady said proudly, "I'm a Catholic, sir, and I go to church on Easter and Christmas. I haven't seen the point in going anymore than that."

Joshua smiled. "What's this sir stuff? Call me Joshua. Well, good, I'll give you an invitation then. We're having a revival this week and it starts tonight. How about I pick you up at 6:30 and you can see firsthand where I get my faith from. Then you can decide for yourself if I'm nuts or not. If you don't enjoy it, I'll not ask you again. What do you say?"

Grady looked over at Joshua, feeling a little uncomfortable. "I don't know if church is what I had in mind for fun after my first day in the field."

Grady's face was hot. He turned his attention back to the road and found that the car in front of him had suddenly decided to slam on his brakes and the back end of the car was coming up at an alarming rate. He slammed on the brakes, squealing his tires in the process. This action threw both officers hard against their safety harnesses and then back into their seats as they stopped. Grady's heart was racing and headlines jumped into his head: "Rookie Officer Wrecks Squad Car in First Five Minutes of His First Shift."

Joshua read the expression on Grady's face and started to laugh as he said, "I can already see that there will never be a dull moment around you, Grady. Well, don't worry, it's the one you don't see that'll get you."

Grady was beginning to like this man despite all the rumors he'd heard. White was okay. He didn't seem to take anything too seriously, at least not yet. Grady didn't want to hurt White's feelings and at the same time he wanted to get him off of his back about religion, so he decided to go with him to the first night of the revival meeting. He would go once and then he could say he'd given it a fair chance.

Without taking his eyes off the road since the traffic had started up again, Grady said, "I'll tell you what, I'll go with you tonight, but if it doesn't do anything for me, you have to promise not to bug me about going anymore. Is it a deal?"

Joshua smiled as he said, "That'll be great, Grady! I'll pick you up at 6:30. I think you'll have a great time."

Grady felt a little more comfortable with that decision out of the way.

They were now clearing the downtown area and entering the suburbs. They were covering the eastern subdivisions today which consisted of about twenty different neighborhoods. Grady noticed that most of the neighborhoods were made up of every thing from split-level homes to small three-bedroom, ranch-style homes. Most had a two-car attached garage and neat little privacy fences around their yards.

As they turned onto Maple Street, the early morning sun was vaporizing the dew from the grass and causing long shadows to move across the yards. They could see mothers standing at their fences talking about their plans for the day as their pre-school children played. Grady could hear the birds in the maple trees lining the street singing through his open window. All in all, it was a very peaceful picture.

Grady was about to make that observation when he saw Joshua tense slightly. He turned to look in the direction of Joshua's gaze. About a block ahead of them they saw a moving van backed up to a house, with movers carrying furniture down the ramp at the back of the truck. There was a black family trying to carry some of the smaller boxes they had loaded into their van. Parked in the middle of the street was a blue sedan with four youths sitting on the hood, yelling obscenities at the family. As they pulled closer, one of the youths threw something, striking the black man and knocking him down.

Joshua called on the radio, "Central, C-4. We'll be out at a disturbance at 312 E. Maple Street. There are four white males who are throwing things at a black male."

"10-4. Do you need backup, C-4?"

"Negative, Central."

"10-4, Central out."

Joshua got out of the squad car and walked up to the young men, with Grady right behind him. The boys looked at the officers and the one who had thrown what turned out to be a brick, asked, "What brings you out this way, Officer White?"

He ignored the young man and approached the injured black man who was just picking himself up. He had a gash in his forehead which would need stitches. Joshua hit the button on his pack radio at his hip,

"Central, C-4."

"Go ahead C-4."

"Central, we'll need an ambulance out here for a head injury."

"10-4, Josh."

The black man protested, "I don't need an ambulance, Officer. Just do your job and arrest these hoods."

Joshua smiled and said, "Yes, Pastor, I am doing my job. You see, we'll need the medical record of your injury in court when this incident goes to trial, and you must go by ambulance for liability purposes. Don't worry, though, your insurance covers it."

The black pastor was about to say more but Joshua pressed his own handkerchief against the cut and put the pastor's hand on it.

"Just hold this tight against the wound until they get here."

Joshua walked up to the young man who had thrown the brick and said, "Sir, you're under arrest for battery."

The youth said, "What for? They're the ones who are moving into an all-white neighborhood. We don't need their kind around here!"

The boy was big and muscular, and like the other three, this one was smoking a marijuana cigarette. Grady never did understand why the government had legalized it. Violent crime had gone up, while efficiency at work had gone down. In their "high" state, it was certain that none of these four were going to be very cooperative.

Joshua repeated, "You're under arrest. Please turn around and put your hands behind your back."

The youth smiled and said, "Yeah, right!" and pulled a knife and slashed out at Joshua.

Before Grady could even react, Joshua had grabbed the boy's knife hand, twisted it behind his back and with a sweeping motion of his foot, knocked him on his face. As he was handcuffing him, a second boy brought out a baseball bat and advanced on Joshua. Grady pulled his .357 Magnum, pointed it at the youth, and yelled, "Freeze or I'll shoot!"

The youth ignored his warning and as Grady was applying pressure to the trigger and the hammer was coming back, he heard Joshua yell, "Don't shoot, Grady!"

Grady, against his training, eased up on the trigger and watched as the bat came down toward Joshua. Suddenly, Joshua was not where he had been and the bat crashed down on the street. Joshua, who had rolled to the side, now, from his back, kicked the youth in the groin. Reaching up, he grabbed the boy by the shirt, placed a foot in his stomach, and flipped him over his own body and onto his back. The youth groaned in pain.

Meanwhile, a third boy had pulled a gun which had been concealed in his pocket and was about to shoot Joshua in the back, but Grady fired his own revolver twice, hitting the eighteen-year-old boy in the chest with both shots. Grady then turned his revolver on the fourth youth, who put his hands up in surrender.

Joshua rushed to the downed youth, tore open his shirt and saw that he was beyond help. He yelled to the black man, "Pastor Smith, please come here and pray for this young man."

The black man just stood there, shaking.

Joshua saw that shock was setting in and turned to Grady. "Grady, handcuff the other two and call this in."

Grady complied. As he called in, his voice was very shaky.

"Central, C-69."

"Go ahead, 69."

"Shots fired, suspect down, officer's secure."

"10-4, 69. A supervisor is on the way."

As Grady called the report in, he watched Joshua place his hands on the young man's chest and pray, "Jesus, if it is Your will, heal this young man. If not then please help him to accept You before he dies so he can escape eternal damnation."

The dying youth said in a whisper, "I spit on your God."

Joshua replied, "Jesus forgive him for he doesn't understand the truth. Help him to see before it is too late."

Sirens could be heard in the distance, approaching fast. Joshua got up, walked to the squad car and opened the trunk. He pulled out a blanket and covered the youth to keep his body warm. The ambulance screeched to a stop, and the crew jumped out and ran to the boy that Joshua indicated needed the most help. One of the crew also went over to help the injured black man.

Joshua walked over to Grady and removed the revolver from his shaking hands. He directed Grady to the squad car and sat him down on the passenger side, leaning over the door to talk to him.

As if in a trance Grady said, "They told me that most officers never have to use their guns, in their whole career. Here, it is my first day on the job and I've already shot someone."

Joshua laid a comforting hand on his shoulder. "You did the right thing. He gave you no choice, and you saved my life. Don't be too hard on yourself."

He left Grady there for a moment and walked over to the fourth youth, who was still standing with his arms in the air seemingly oblivious to the wet spot that was spreading down his leg. Grady had forgotten, in his own shock, to handcuff this youth or the one who was still moaning on the ground. Joshua corrected this now and sat the two young men next to the one that he had handcuffed earlier—the one who had pulled the knife.

After having a temporary bandage placed on his forehead, the minister had gone over to the young man who had been shot and had started praying for him. Joshua helped the ambulance crew pick up the litter and place the man in the ambulance. As the minister got into the ambulance, Joshua said, "Rev. Smith, please do what you can to lead this young man to salvation."

Rev. Smith looked down and asked, "How do you know my name, Officer?"

"Well, Pastor, the day the elders of the church hired you, I was gone. I'm one of the elders, and I read your file and voted in favor of you. Since this house is our pastor's house, I assumed that you were Rev. Smith. By the way, you see that house next door?"

Pastor Smith nodded.

"That's my house. We're neighbors."

Joshua could see the look of surprise on the pastor's face. Before the pastor could say more, however, the ambulance driver hit the side of the ambulance to indicate that it was time to go, and Joshua closed the back door and watched as the ambulance pulled away.

At the same moment, several police cars came screaming into the scene. Some stopped on either side of the scene to stop all traffic. Chief Wilson arrived and took control of the scene. Joshua turned Grady's gun over to the crime scene officer, who also took the suspect's gun, knife, and ball bat. Statements were taken from the pastor's family. A statement would be taken from the pastor later at the hospital, along with the wounded man, if he lived.

Grady would be given a three-day, paid suspension to take the mandatory psychiatric counseling, to help him cope with the stress of the incident.

Chief Wilson asked Joshua to drive Grady home and stay with him until his shift was over. As Joshua drove them away from the scene, Grady got tears in his eyes and felt he was about to cry like a baby.

Joshua said, "Go ahead, Grady, cry. It will make you feel better."

Grady cried deep, shaking sobs, all the way home.

Joshua smiled, knowing that the healing process had already begun.

Grady came back to the present when he cut himself shaving. He slapped a dry tissue on the cut and watched as it soaked up the blood and stuck to his face. He hadn't thought of that incident for quite a while now. It was strange how little things could trigger such memories. The feeling of sadness came flooding back as he remembered that the boy had died of his wounds. Grady also recalled the hours of questions asked during the investigation into whether or not he acted properly. He relived the relief he had felt when Joshua told him that it was judged a righteous shoot. It had taken Grady a few weeks to get over the shooting, but, with Joshua's help, he did get over it. Since that shooting incident, Grady had not had to fire his weapon, except on the range for practice, and for that he was grateful.

He spoke out-loud to himself, "One good thing came out of that incident, Lord; that revival that I went to, every night that week, brought me to You and gave me a new sense of importance and acceptance."

He had gone to Mass every Sunday since and had become a new source of the Spirit to the Catholic church. Grady also went to Rev. Smith's church on Wednesday and Sunday nights, and hadn't missed a revival since his first one.

He finished dressing and went into the kitchen to make a cup of instant coffee. As he waited for the water to boil, Grady switched the television set on and found the news channel. It was only 3 o'clock; he had about a half hour before he had to leave to meet Chief Wilson.

He had turned his back on the TV set to spoon the coffee into his cup when he heard a deep male voice say, "This is a special news bulletin, please stand by."

Grady turned to watch as he added sugar to the black powder and stirred in the boiling water.

"Good afternoon, I'm Marla Brinkle, coming to you live from the State Capitol. Behind me are protesters who object to the city of Covenant's continual rejection of state policy."

Grady whistled softly at the reporter's image on the screen. She had beautiful, long flowing blonde hair, a traffic-stopping smile and—*Man, those eyes are the deepest green I've ever seen*, thought Grady, as he pulled out a stool and sat at his food bar to watch the report.

The pretty young reporter walked over to a protester and asked, "Sir, what is it that you're trying to accomplish here today?"

The burly man spoke with a deep voice pushed through angry features, "We want the city of Covenant to stop persecuting our brothers and sisters of the Witches Guild. The State has declared witchcraft a legal religion in its own right, and yet Covenant still insists on persecuting the covens that operate out of Covenant. We say that it's about time that they come into the twentieth century with the rest of us. Governor Bradley has assured me that he will see to it that Covenant complies with the law, one way or another."

"Thank you, sir!"

The young reporter moved to an elderly lady whose face wore a particularly sour expression. Ms. Brinkle asked her, "And you, why are you here today?"

"Well, I've been working for years to get an abortion clinic into Covenant, but they won't allow it. They closed down the first one we opened. Women have a right, by law, to terminate a pregnancy right up until the time of birth. They're denying the women of Covenant the freedom they deserve and have coming by law. Governor Bradley has assured my group that he'll make Covenant comply with this law as well. He'll personally authorize the building of a fine clinic in which women can safely rid themselves of this unwanted tissue. After all, we have clinics in which cancer cells can be safely removed, or tumors, or bad teeth, so why not unwanted pregnancies."

Again, the reporter thanked the speaker and moved to another person in the crowd; a man who was wearing a suit and carrying a briefcase.

"And sir, why are you here today?"

"Well, ma'am, I've heard that in Covenant they still insist on praying in schools, and I mean public schools!"

The entire crowd let out a gasp and looked shocked by the news.

The man continued, "Not only that, but those people are still refusing to remove those obnoxious tablets from their public square and the plaques from the walls of their schools on which are written the outdated, poisonous Ten Commandments."

Ms. Brinkle asked, "What do you mean by poisonous?"

"I mean that they teach those so-called laws in their schools, damage the minds of innocent children with guilt trips and inferiority complexes. It must stop. There are children in Covenant who don't believe in God, or in these mind-bending rules, and they have a right to be protected by the state. Governor Bradley has promised to right this injustice."

"How many children are there in Covenant who are at risk from this onslaught of forced religion in public?"

The man answered, "The numbers aren't important. If even one child doesn't want to be force-fed this propaganda, then they should have the right not to have it displayed or heard in public."

The crowd exploded into a loud applause.

Two couples approached Ms. Brinkle. The two men were holding hands and the women had their arms around each other. Ms. Brinkle asked the two couples what they were protesting and one of the women stepped forward.

"All we want is for gays to have the freedom to work, marry, and raise our adopted children in Covenant, just like anywhere else in this country. Those high and mighty Covenant people say that being gay is a sin and that we must renounce who we are before we can follow Jesus. What nonsense! We're good Christians and only want to raise our families in peace, and in Christian love. Governor Bradley has assured us that we have a right to live any way we choose and that Covenant will no longer be able to discriminate against us."

The crowd applauded again.

Ms. Brinkle turned toward the camera and said, "You've heard for yourself the many concerns these citizens have for their rights and their belief that those rights are being blatantly violated by the Covenant people. This brings a question to the mind of this reporter. What will these Covenant militants do when we remove the word "God" from our money as we did from the Pledge of Allegiance? Will they write "In God We Trust" on every bill they spend in the future?"

Marla smiled at her joke and said, "This is Marla Brinkle reporting live from the Capitol building."

Grady turned off the set and sat down, stunned by what he had just heard. He stared into the black liquid swirling in his cup.

Fear gripped Grady's stomach. Had he awakened into some alternate universe where all reason was slowly leaking from the earth? He thought about the attempt on Joshua's life and now, the attempt by the state government to sanction sinful, inhumane, and blatantly antichrist behavior. Grady spoke aloud to himself again, "I hope the chief can shed some light on this at our meeting."

He drank his coffee in a couple of deep gulps, set the cup in the sink, and walked out of the apartment.

Warren had drawn his sword as soon as the demon entered the apartment. The foul imp had come in fast, attaching itself to Grady's neck before Warren could react. The demon began to pump fear and dread into Grady's soul.

Warren crossed the room in a flash and with one powerful swing of his sword, he cut the accursed creature in half. After the red smoke cleared, Warren saw that the black, infectious poison of fear and doubt, which the demon had just injected into Grady's soul, was spreading fast. Warren prayed, and then placed his free hand on Grady's neck and said, "Do not fear, my friend, but be filled with the peace of Jesus Christ."

Even as Warren was leading Grady down the long hallway which leads to his apartment's parking area, he saw the black fog roll back, leaving Grady's soul white and pure and peaceful once again.

Chapter 10

The Heavenly Life

As Jesus led Joshua toward the Holy City, He pointed out the assorted animals and flowers that grew and lived together among the trees of the forest. There were all manner of mammals, reptiles, birds, and insects; all living in harmony with each other and their Creator. They passed a wolf sleeping contentedly. Rolled up and sleeping under the wolf's chin was a small lamb. Joshua was reminded of the description of the peace in heaven by the prophet Isaiah. It brought tears to his eyes as he thrilled at the literal truth of the Word of God.

Joshua was readily accepted by the normally wild animals. A cougar came right up to him and nudged him with his nose. He rubbed the big cat under the chin and petted his head before they moved on. He did the same with the bear, the tiger, and the ape who paused to inspect the newcomer as Jesus and Joshua passed their way. They laughed at the comical antics of the ape family as they played with some bear cubs.

Joshua looked up when he heard the sudden flapping of millions of wings as the birds left the trees and took flight forming a rainbow of colors in the sky above them. These birds sang the most joyous songs that Joshua had ever heard.

Mice were hitching rides with the owls, lions were caring for the cattle—it was a so perfectly harmonious.

The fragrance of the plants and flowers was indescribable; they pleased every sense at once. None of the plants were toxic to the touch and could be eaten of freely without harmful consequence.

Joshua was already in awe of this place, but what he saw next took his breath away. They were ascending the hill which led to the front gate of the Holy City. It had been beautiful from a distance, but, up close, he could feel the peace and love radiating from the walls that surrounded the city. The stone seemed to change color as they approached.

As they walked, Jesus had been teaching Joshua all the things that he would need to know when he returned to earth. As Jesus spoke, Joshua took time to commit to memory every feature of his Savior's face.

Jesus was not as tall as Joshua but he had a strong bearing and muscular body. His dark features were those of an outdoorsman—rugged and weathered. His dark brown hair was shorter than Joshua would have pictured it and was windblown and unruly yet shone with a supernatural light. The scars on the Lord's forehead were still visible where His crown of thorns had pierced to the bone. The scars on His hands and feet were testimonies to His love and longsuffering.

The thought of Jesus suffering on the Cross brought more tears to Joshua's eyes. Yet he was filled with joy knowing that Jesus loved him so much that He would have died just to save Joshua alone.

Jesus stopped and smiled up at Joshua. "You know, no one is supposed to be sad in heaven, so why do you weep, Joshua?"

Joshua shuddered as if he was just waking up and stammered, "Oh! I'm not sad, Lord. On the contrary, I was thinking of the sacrifice You made for me on the Cross. I am so thankful for it. I feel such peace and joy that I can't hold back my tears. If I feel any sadness, it is only at the fact that not all people believe in You yet. I wish You had remained on the earth and taught the human race first hand about the kingdom of God."

Jesus smiled at Joshua, and Joshua thought he might get lost in that smile; it was filled with such love.

"Joshua, My Father and I agreed that the human race needed a chance to choose love over hate and that We would have to show them by example. So I became flesh and dwelt among the human race for a time. People could actually touch God by touching Me. They could see and feel love for perhaps the first time. I became the new covenant between God and the human race. But a sacrifice had to be satisfied and it was ordained that I die on the Cross for all. Therefore, I suffered and died in the place of each sinner who had been condemned to death by their own sinful nature.

"I rose from the grave on the third day and conquered death forever. I taught the apostles for many days to make sure that they understood what task I had given them to do. Then, having completed my mission on earth, I rose to be with My Father in heaven again.

"But I sent the Holy Spirit to guide My people and keep them from the wrong path. I also assigned an angel to each true follower of the Way.

"Now, I am training a new prophet to tell my people to return to that Way and to live in peace and fellowship with one another."

Joshua realized that Jesus had directed that last statement at him, that he was the new prophet. Before he could object, Jesus continued, "Joshua, even with all of the events of My life spelled out in My Word, the

Bible, it hasn't been enough to melt the cold, calculating hearts, who even as we speak, are leading many astray with logic and false reasonings. There are learned men who say that My Word is nothing but a collection of stories which soothe the human spirit, but little more.

"These same people would have my followers believe that nothing that is told in the Bible is an accurate accounting of My life, that I didn't even perform any miracles. It is so hard for the reasoning mind of humans to make way for the faithful heart. These people are not seeing through the eyes of faith, but rather are believing the lie of Satan that they understand the world better than the God who created it.

"Until recently, the United States was a bright spot of faith and hope. These were a people of faith, hope, and integrity. They believed in My Father and honored His name in every thing they did. They had faith in My sacrifice and believed in Me as their Lord and Savior.

"Now their hearts grow cold and distant. As We knew they would, they have embraced this new false teaching and have taken the honor from both My Father's name and from My name. They no longer allow the children to come to Me in prayer. Their chosen leaders are corrupt. In many churches, doubt of Our mighty power is taught by the learned leaders.

"Once, We blessed this country for its faithfulness. Now, We have withheld Our blessing as its people have chosen corruption and destroy themselves with their greed, their pride, and their own self-serving wisdom. They are a proud and boastful people. They have said that they no longer need a God, yet have embraced the lies of Satan and worship the many gods that he gives to them. "They outlawed God in school, in the work place, in every area of public life, and in so doing have condemned themselves to suffer the cancer that eats away at the core, the strength of any country—the family. In destroying the family, they destroy the country, and, ultimately, themselves.

"They have turned abominations—homosexuality, witchcraft, devil worship, and astrology—into mere alternate lifestyles, thereby condemning themselves to hell and destruction. "They have become murderers of the innocent, sacrificing precious lives to the god of their convenience and comfort.

"I tell you, Joshua, that Sodom and Gomorrah's fate was less harsh than the one that will befall these people, if they do not repent and turn from their wickedness, and worship the only true God.

"This is the task which is being given to you, Joshua. You will go back and tell them the truth. Tell them what you have seen and heard here. They must believe you—or they will die."

Suddenly, Jesus stopped talking and pointed to the huge gate which stood before them. Joshua had been so engrossed in their conversation that he hadn't made note of their progress up the path. The excitement of the moment welled up inside him.

The doors of the gate thundered as they began to move. They opened wide, allowing the brilliance of God to come flowing out upon Joshua. He fell to his knees in awe at the sight of God's city of a million lights. When he finally raised his head and held up a hand against the brightness, a beautiful panorama unfolded before his eyes. Beings as bright as the stars walked the streets of gold.

The buildings were built of every precious metal and stone imaginable. As Joshua stepped through the gate, the huge doors began to shut behind him. Jesus led him to a large mansion which rested on the top of a hill. There were steps of gold leading to the ivory door.

As he began to ascend the stairs, he realized that Jesus had vanished and that he was alone again.

Suddenly the ivory door opened up and his mother stepped out. She looked years younger than he did right now.

They embraced, and then Joshua saw his father and embraced him as well.

His mother said, "Son, we've been waiting for this day for a very long time. Come, our time is short and we have much to share with you."

They pulled him into the mansion and the large door closed without a sound.

As Jesus approached the throne of His Father, His body began to emit light; first from the wounds on His forehead, and then from the wounds in His hands and feet, and finally from His wounded side. Within just a few feet of the throne, His entire body disappeared into the Father. The Father and Son are One.

"Father, all is prepared as We planned. Joshua White is a faithful servant and a brave and courageous warrior. He will lead many back to the Way. This will lead to war, just as We foresaw."

God's love for the Son was evident in Their exchange as the Father spoke. "Yes, Son, it is so. The time of Your return grows near, but We will give the people a chance to repent and return to Us before the end."

"Holy Spirit, Your task is great. This battle will be the first of many in this final war." The three Persons of the one true God agreed to give, yet again, of Their love to the very people who denied Their existence.

Chapter 11

Demonic Bombs— Angelic Shields

The anger of Worl and his ever present guards, Left and Right, was growing thicker with every passing moment. They had witnessed Aaron's glorious battle and then endured his cowardly assassination by the twins. It was all Worl could do to stop his guards from hunting down and ripping out the throats of the twins. He had managed to control them, and himself, but it was a close thing.

Right leaned out of the cloud in which they were hiding and was about to protest this inactivity, when Worl pulled him back into the cloud, signing for him to remain silent. Just at that moment, the sentry, now turned messenger, which Crygen had dispatched at Tumult's order, flashed by the angels' hiding place at a great rate of speed. He landed on the roof of Cono's command center, arrogantly pushing past the guards and entering the building.

The demonic messenger allowed the guard to show him into Cono's spacious chamber. He approached Cono, who pretended that he didn't notice the fledgling's arrival.

The messenger bowed low in the expected sign of a submissive servant, but the way he did it showed only contempt.

He raised himself up and arrogantly declared, "My master, Tumult, sends his greetings to Cono, once commander of this region. By order of Lucifer himself, Tumult is to take immediate command of this region. He orders you to meet him at his campsite by dusk to transfer command. Tumult further orders that his host, Bradley, will conduct the human sacrifice tonight, instead of your host. Will you comply?"

This last was issued as a challenge.

Cono had just about enough of this whelp. He'd grown more furious with every word that issued from the demon's mouth. With unbelievable control, Cono walked over and stood in front of the messenger.

In a deceptively quiet voice, Cono said, "I, of course, live to serve my master Lucifer, and I will comply with his plans in the fullest."

With a smug look on his face, the messenger turned to leave. Before he could make his exit, Cono called out to him. When he turned, he heard, rather than saw the dagger as it "swished" through the air. Fire exploded in his head as the dagger pinned the demon's large ear to the chamber wall.

Cono calmly walked up to the struggling demon, placed his left hand on the hilt of the dagger and spoke directly into his face. This time he didn't hide his anger or contempt from the simpering spirit. He spit out each word.

"Tell your boss, Tumult, that according to protocol, he must come to me and transfer command in an environment of my choice. Tell him that even though he has been very rude by sending me his obviously most incompetent slave, I will still throw a magnificent dinner in his honor tonight, at Connelly's mansion.

The transfer of command will take place in the full assembly of demons."

Cono held the dagger with his left hand and with his right; he pulled the demon toward him. The demon screamed in pain as the dagger sliced through his ear. Cono then shoved the demon to the ground.

"Now, get out before I decide to send you back to hell myself!"

Holding his bleeding ear with his right hand, the demon pointed at Cono and said, "You'll be sorry for this, you . . . you . . . has been."

Cono, who had been walking back toward his chair, stopped, drawing his sword as he turned. The red glare of the steel gave the chamber an eerie glow, in which the demon's shadow danced. Cono advanced on the demon, who decided to take the wiser course, and scrambled from Cono's presence.

Cono put his sword back in its sheath and turned to face Lt. Poe as he stepped out of the shadows.

"Can Tumult really just waltz in here and take over all of the territory that we've worked so hard to build up?"

Cono nodded thoughtfully, "Yes, I'm afraid he can, for now, anyway. However, I'll be watching his every move, and the first slip he makes, I'll be there to kill him."

Poe left Cono to his musing to prepare for the evening's festivities.

The messenger, though not pleased with having his ear sliced open, was very pleased with Cono's response. Tumult had said that Cono would blow a fuse and he sure had. He had actually refused a direct order from Tumult, and the penalty for that could be death.

The demon was smiling at the prospect of torturing Cono himself, and so he failed to see the movement just above him. Out of the corner of his eye he saw a flash, but before he could collect himself enough to realize the danger he was in, it was too late. Three strong pairs of hands ensnared him, and with his screams silenced by one angelic hand over his mouth, the other hands silently dragged the terror-stricken demon into the cloud above Cono's headquarters.

* * *

Grady stepped out onto the sidewalk and looked around. It was still a beautiful day outside and he noticed the neighbors washing their car while their children rode bikes in the parking lot. As he walked toward his own car, he saw Mandy, the police dispatcher, crossing from his side of the street to the other side. He knew her shift was coming up so he yelled, "Hey, Mandy, I'm going to the office; want a lift?"

Startled, Mandy turned, quickly hiding her look of fear. With a slight tremor in her voice she said, "No thanks, Grady, I just want to stretch my legs before work."

With that, she turned and walked briskly away.

Grady watched her go, then shrugged his shoulders and walked to his car. He put his key in the lock and the two metal contacts touched each other causing the entire squad car to explode in Grady's face.

Chief Wilson entered his office with his usual cup of coffee in his hand. He sat at his desk and took a sip of the hot brew, looking out into the officer's squad room through the glass walls of his office. The glass office walls gave him the feeling of working in a fish bowl, but it seemed to motivate the officers to get their work done. Right now, he could see officers looking up information on their computers, talking on the phone, or following up on the latest leads of one crime or another.

"Well, enough stalling," Wilson whispered to himself. He was thinking of that strange file that Joshua had given him. He had, at first, thought the information that it contained was fiction, but now, with Joshua in the hospital from a possible hit, he wasn't sure what he thought.

He put his cup down and dug the key to his desk out of his pocket. He put the key in the lock of the drawer which held the file in question. When he turned the key, Wilson heard a metallic click and an electric crackling noise. He looked stunned; he knew from his years of working around explosives just what the sound meant.

Wilson prayed, "Jesus, help . . ." as his desk and office exploded into a nightmare of flames and shattering glass. Every window on the first floor was shattered as people threw themselves to the floor and covered their heads.

* * *

Assistant Chief Anderson pulled up to the local motel's cafe, turned off his squad car and got out. He saw the semi-truck parked in the lot, but he turned and walked into the cafe as he'd been instructed to do. As he entered, he took the picture out of his shirt pocket for one last look. On the back of the picture was one word: Butch.

Anderson walked over to the man whose face he had just seen in the picture and sat down across from him. He said, "Butch?"

The man nodded.

Anderson continued, "I'm interested in a package."

Butch said, "What kind of a package?"

Anderson smiled and said, "The kind that wars are made of."

Without a word, Butch got up and threw a twenty onto the table and left the cafe with Anderson in tow. He climbed into the cab of the semi and pointed Anderson to the sleeper. Anderson climbed in and sat on the bed. Butch leaned back and said, "Lie down on the bed, please."

When Anderson was flat on his back, Butch pushed a button that caused the bed to tilt sideways, rolling a surprised Anderson through a trap door, depositing him unceremoniously on the floor of the truck's trailer which housed the secret mobile office of Governor Bradley.

* * *

As Warren led Grady out onto the parking lot of his apartment building, he received a message from Michael the Archangel. Quite often, Satan overstepped his authority and caused one or more of his human hosts to take the life of a saint of God. When he did this, the angels were, at times, given permission to intervene. This is called, "Maximum Intervention".

This was the content of Warren's last message and it couldn't have come at a more opportune time. This meant that Warren was authorized to intervene in the physical world, if need be, to protect Grady's life.

As Grady approached his car, Warren knew that an evil presence had just tampered with it. He'd watched Grady's conversation with Mandy and had seen the ugly demon, Deceit, clinging to her neck as though he was afraid that Warren might try to steal his prize.

When Grady turned the key in the lock, Warren heard the click which would activate the detonator.

A millisecond before the explosion, Warren picked Grady up and threw him toward the apartment building, calculating his throw so that Grady would land just short of the building.

The demon that was clinging to Mandy watched in open-mouthed shock at seeing an angel physically intervene in an attempt to thwart his plans. He fled to report to Cono, leaving behind a confused and fearful Mandy.

As the fire raced toward him, Grady felt an unseen pair of hands grab him and send him flying backwards toward his apartment building. His car was quickly and completely engulfed by the hungry flames, which reached out for Grady with its deadly embrace. Grady landed at the foot of the apartment building wall and fell flat on his back. The full effect of the blast was spent on the brick wall just inches above and behind his head.

Grady didn't see Warren's wings as they covered his body, protecting the human flesh from the scorching heat of the flames as he had once done long ago for three faithful boys in a fiery oven. Only a small amount of harmless dust, brick chips, and ashes was allowed to shower down upon Warren's charge.

Mandy was in a panic. Unbeknownst to her, she had just been deserted by her spirit guide. The bomb was just supposed to scare Grady, not kill him. She didn't know what went wrong, but she knew that she had better run over and see if she could help Grady. She had to keep up her act a little longer.

* * *

Beriack had been assigned to Chief Wilson from the very first day Wilson was saved. He'd spent many a day in this office, watching his charge make one decision or another, and even giving him an insight or two. Beriack knew his routine and he knew when Wilson was upset or worried. Today he was both.

The order from Michael had put him on his guard even more than usual. Orders like that just weren't handed down unless a situation had turned severe. Beriack became alert as Wilson put the key in the desk drawer lock and the angel noticed the telltale slime left behind by a demon's tampering. Beriack made his move as he heard the click of the detonator.

Chief Wilson saw a gleaming, translucent man standing on his desk. No—not a man—an angel! He'd heard of angels, but like most people, he hadn't given them much serious thought. When he saw this one, he knew he was dead, especially when the angel jumped down, grabbed him by the front of the shirt and slammed him against the wall.

Just before the angel appeared, Wilson had started to pray, but he was stunned into silence, first by the appearance of the angel and then by the explosion itself.

As Wilson's back hit the wall his breath was knocked out of him, saving him from getting a lung full of fire from the explosion. He saw the angel extend his wings to the side and then felt them being wrapped around him. He could hear the roar of the flames and the pinging sound of the debris that was hurled everywhere.

Without the awareness that he had moved, Wilson found himself standing in the middle of his office looking at its total destruction. Even though the four walls around him were scorched and dug out from the debris, he was unharmed.

Whoever set the charge had not intended for him to live. He looked back at the wall behind his desk and saw his silhouette cut into the wall. As he was trying to remember what had just occurred, officers from the squad room picked themselves up and gathered at the broken windows of Wilson's office.

By rights, the entire building should have been in flames, however, there were just a few small fires here and there. *This is not the way it works*, thought Wilson. By now, there were over thirty employees staring at him. They all looked as though they were shell-shocked.

One of his men came forward and held up a piece of broken mirror in which Wilson could see his reflection. This morning he'd had jet-black hair but now his hair was as white as snow, giving him the appearance of being bald because of his butch-style cut. Wilson also noted that his face was sooty and his shirt was torn, but he was alive.

He gently pushed the mirror away and looked toward the squad room.

"I don't know exactly how it worked, but I was just saved from sure death by an angel of the Lord Jesus Christ. If any one would like to pray with me, we'll thank Jesus for His protecting power and the grace with which He has saved us all from Satan."

Wilson knelt down on his ash-covered floor.

"Thank You, Lord Jesus, for saving first my soul and now my life. I will accept this gift from You and I pledge to You this very day that I will do whatever You make clear to me that You wish for me to do..."

As Wilson prayed, more and more of the officers and other employees began to kneel and pray with him. Some hadn't prayed since they were children. Some had never prayed at all.

Before his prayer was through, every officer, employee, and suspect awaiting booking were on their knees.

* * *

Governor Bradley looked up as Anderson made his humiliating entrance into the office. Anderson picked himself up and brushed the dust off his otherwise meticulous uniform.

The Governor asked, "Is it accomplished yet?"

Anderson tried to hide the anger and humiliation he felt at the accusatory tone the Governor was using. He answered with an equally icy tone. "I should be hearing any time now." He indicated the pack radio on his belt.

Governor Bradley sat back in his chair. "I asked you and Connelly to do a couple of minor assassinations for me, and all I have so far is one slightly wounded cop."

Anderson lost his temper. "Look, sir! You sent us a sniper who couldn't hit this truck on a clear day. His back-up didn't show up so we had to use two of our own people who weren't trained for this sort of work. We aren't taking all the blame for this screw-up. At least we made arrangements that will insure that Joshua won't leave the hospital alive. He'll be dead by tomorrow." Bradley's guards had automatically raised their assault rifles when Anderson lost his temper. The Governor nodded to the one closest to Anderson and the guard brought the butt of his rifle up hard against Anderson's chin. The Governor got up and stood over the bleeding assistant police chief.

"First thing is, Mr. Anderson; never, ever raise your voice to me again. Second . . ."

He was interrupted by the squawk of Anderson's radio.

"C-2, Central, come in C-2."

Anderson looked up at the Governor, who nodded.

"Go ahead Central for C-2.

"C-2, it's terrible, there's been an explosion at headquarters and another at Grady's apartment building. We need you to go over to Grady's and check it out."

Anderson tried not to sound too anxious, "Did anyone get hurt, Central?"

"Negative. It was a miracle, sir! No one was seriously hurt. I'll tell ya', a lot of us will be going to church after this one!"

"That's . . . !" Anderson was going to say that's impossible, but instead he said, "That's great Central, glad to hear it."

"Oh, and C-2, the chief would like to see you in his office within the hour."

"Tell, the chief that I'll go to Grady's and then come straight over. C-2 out."

Chief Wilson stood by the radio during this exchange. He didn't miss Anderson's tone of surprise in his voice when he found out that no one was hurt. There was doubt forming in Wilson's mind about Anderson's loyalty.

The Governor glared down at Anderson, who was still on the floor.

"What kind of operation are you running here, anyway? We sent you tons of the best plastic explosives available and no one was even hurt? I can't afford any more mistakes.

"You tell Connelly that I've already set the war in motion. I declared it with that demonstration in front of the Capitol. Joshua White was supposed to be dead when it started and Wilson and Grady were supposed to be dead by now too. Instead, I find that everybody is still alive!

"As of now, I'm taking over the control of this entire operation. I'll be at the Coven meeting tonight and I'll do the human sacrifice myself. At least that way I'll be sure of at least one death in this area. If I didn't need you two idiots, I'd kill you both myself . . . and I may yet."

Anderson blurted out, "Look, sir, I used enough plastic to kill a hundred men. I don't understand what happened!"

Bradley cut him off with a kick to his already bloodied chin.

"I don't want to hear any more of your excuses! Go and tell Connelly that I'll be there for the dinner tonight. Got it!"

Anderson nodded. Wiping blood from his mouth, he slowly crawled back through the trap door and out of the Governor's office. Tears streamed down Anderson's cheeks as fear and rage collided deep in his soul.

* * *

Mandy helped Grady extract himself from the bushes. Grady exclaimed, "Praise God!" He flexed his muscles, hopped up and down, and then exclaimed again, "Praise God, I don't think anything is even broken."

Mandy looked down and whispered, "Yeah, praise God."

He noticed that Mandy looked more shaken than even he felt.

"Well, Mandy, since I'm suddenly left without transportation, why don't you walk me to the station?"

Mandy gave him a weak smile.

"Shouldn't you call in first?"

Grady hit his forehead with the palm of his hand as he realized that he wasn't following police procedure. He hadn't even thought of the fire. He picked up the mike at his shoulder and said, "Central from C-69."

"Go ahead, 69."

"Uh, Central, someone just blew up my squad car. I somehow wasn't hurt but I need the fire department and a wrecker at my home parking lot. Mandy and I will be walking to the station."

"10-4, Grady. Are you sure you don't need an ambulance?"

"I'm positive, Central. You better send the crime scene boys out here also to see if they can find out who may have done this."

"10-4."

As the dispatcher signed off, Grady thought that he heard an explosion on Central's end, but he figured he was probably still hearing the roaring in his ears from the car bomb. He shrugged, put a brotherly arm around Mandy's shoulders and they began their walk to the police station. Grady didn't notice the fear and confusion that crossed Mandy's face as she tried desperately to figure out just what had gone wrong.

* * *

Worl faced the messenger that Left and Right held securely between them, their powerful hands digging painfully into his arms. As he struggled, Worl took note of just how ugly this little creature was, with his fierce red eyes and a foul tongue that matched his foul breath. They had transported him a safe distance away from Cono's office so that no other demons could hear his ranting and cursing.

When Worl had heard enough, he drew his sword and placed the point of it gently against the throat of the demon. The vile creature flinched and shut his mouth, but still glared his hatred at Worl.

Worl ignored the demon's indignation and calmly began his interrogation, "Now, you and I both know that with one little push of this sword, I can send you back to your master, Lucifer. We also both know what that would mean for you, don't we?"

The demon stupidly nodded his head, causing the sharp point of Worl's sword to nick his greasy chin. He shrieked in exaggerated pain.

Worl continued, "Or, with just a little information, I could let you go back to Tumult and you could forget that this meeting ever took place. Now, it matters very little to me which way you choose, but from what I've heard of your master's torture chambers, I don't think you want to go there. Now, do you want to help me or do I push?"

Worl added a little more pressure causing the tip of his sword to pierce the demon's throat a little deeper.

The demon squealed, "I'll talk! But you must hurry, I'm due back any minute, and Tumult will know that something is wrong."

Worl left the sword in place and said, "Good! Now all I want to know is where and when the sacrifices are to take place and who will be there."

The demon spilled his guts, telling Worl all about Tumult's plans to overrun Covenant, his attempts to take Joshua out, and also his attempts on other lives as well. He told Worl about the sacrifice at the warehouse that evening and that Tumult would be there himself to conduct it through his host, Governor Bradley. He rambled on and gave Worl information that he hadn't even thought to ask for.

Worl let him ramble. When he could tell that the demon had given him all the information he needed, he reminded the spineless little demon of his fate if he talked.

He had his men release the demon, who wasted no time in beating a swift retreat back toward Tumult's building army.

Worl and his faithful guards, having completed this stage of Jesus' plan, now moved on to the hospital to complete the next stage.

* * *

As Grady and Mandy approached the police station, they were astonished at the spectacle they encountered. There were fire trucks with ladders extended up to the third floor, hoses stretched out in every direction. It looked to them as if a mad octopus had attacked headquarters, and the firefighters were trying to ward it off.

The firefighters were actually looking for fires which may have started in the walls before the power could be cut to the building. More than once, a building had burned down from hidden smoldering fires that went undetected until it was too late. The police officers were pitching in and clearing debris from the area to make room for firefighting equipment.

Grady and Mandy crunched across the broken glass which covered the first floor entrance. Grady left Mandy at the radio room and went on to Chief Wilson's office—or at least what was left of his office.

What he saw gave him mixed feelings. He was appalled at the destruction, but his heart soared when he saw Chief Wilson standing in the middle of his office, staring at what was left of his coffee mug. Grady couldn't contain his laughter—the sight of Chief Wilson standing in the middle of a shambles of an office, holding half a coffee mug, wearing a charred uniform (that matched Grady's own charred uniform), with his face covered with soot, and sporting the whitest hair that Grady had ever seen—it was just too much!

At the sound of Grady's laughter, Wilson looked up from the mental funeral he was having for the mug his wife had given him on his twenty-fifth anniversary as a police officer. He saw him standing in the hall. Wilson took note of Grady's torn and charred uniform and without asking knew that he had just had a similar experience to his own.

Wilson faked a scowl and yelled, "Mister, you are out of uniform, I wouldn't push my luck if I were you."

Grady tried, unsuccessfully, to keep a straight face.

"I only have one question, Chief. Did the explosion scare the color out of your hair or did it blast the hair dye off of it?"

Wilson good-naturedly threw the remainder of the cup at Grady, who easily dodged it.

Grady entered the chief's office through one of the broken windows. Wilson picked up a wooden chair and pointed to it. "Sit down."

Wilson balanced himself on what remained of another wooden chair.

After Grady filled him in on the car explosion, the chief asked, "Grady, during your experience, did you see anything . . . uh, how should I say it? Anything . . . supernatural?"

After what they had both been through, Grady took this question very seriously. He thought for a minute and then said, "No, I can't say that I saw anything, but I did feel a force pick me up and throw me a great distance. At first I thought it was the force of the blast itself. But now I think it had to be something else, though I don't know what. Why? Did you see something, Chief?"

"Yes, I did. It's incredible, I know, but I saw an angel standing on my desk! I watched him as he picked me up, threw me against the wall, knocking the breath out of me, and then he wrapped his wings all around me and shielded me from the blast. The way my bones feel right now, though, I wish he had just defused the bomb."

Grady and Wilson looked at each other in disbelief, as though neither of them could believe he had said that.

"I can't believe I'm complaining about how an angel saved my life!" Wilson said sheepishly. "I won't question their methods again. Why don't we stop and give thanks to God, Grady, for allowing us to live through this experience."

The two men knelt down in the ashes of what should have been Wilson's funeral pyre and prayed for the wisdom to use this gift of life to defeat the enemy at his own game.

The two men then got up and, at Wilson's suggestion, went across the street to Maggie's cafe to get a bite to eat. They sat in a corner booth, ignoring the stares of the other customers, due to their appearance. Maggie came over with two cups of steaming coffee and two pieces of apple pie, and said, "You boys look like you could use this. What happened over there, Chief?"

"Thanks Maggie. We'll both have the special of the day. I'm sorry, but I don't know exactly what did happen, but when I find out, I'll let you know."

Maggie turned to get their order after giving Wilson a quizzical look. Wilson spoke just loud enough for Maggie to hear. "She's a good woman, but she's just a little too nosy for her own good." He slapped Grady on the shoulder and smiled.

Maggie pitched over her shoulder, "Don't make the cook mad, Chief, especially right before I'm gonna serve your food."

With Maggie gone, the two men filled each other in on their experiences again and got serious about trying to figure out just what it was they had stepped into. Both Grady and Wilson had seen Marla Brinkle's bizarre news broadcast. Wilson went on to fill Grady in on everything that had been discovered about Joshua's would-be assassins. Then he explained the far-fetched story that Joshua had shared with him just a couple of days before.

Grady whispered, "Ah, come on, Chief! The governor, a warlock! That's a bit much to believe, even from Joshua."

"I felt the same way when Josh told me. If it had been anyone else I would have ripped the report up and put him on midnights for a year, but this is Joshua we're talking about. So, while I had my doubts, I kept the file and thought about it. What you don't know, Grady, is that Josh has been working on this case for about three months now. On his own, he dug around and found a motive for Governor Bradley wanting to shut Covenant down.

"Our illustrious governor is the power and the money behind Senator Brice's bill. The Brice Bill is calling for the removal of Jesus' name from all public places. It states that it would be unlawful to mention Jesus to anyone in public verbally or in written form. This is being done under the guise of protecting people from Christians who want to force their religion on everyone. Christianity is described as a cold, uncaring, and bigoted religion that would have to be confined to a follower's home. There would be no outward signs allowed that would show that a person was a Christian."

Grady shook his head, "I can't believe that a bill like that would ever get through."

Wilson held up his hand, "No, wait, it gets better. The bill also calls for a government-sponsored mandate which would give full constitutional rights to the practice of witchcraft, soothsaying, psychic revelations, and any other mystical religion that teaches the power of the universal force. This would include Satan worshipers.

"Governor Bradley has been quietly pushing this bill through the process with bribes and threats, and had just gotten the ear of the President herself. Joshua notified him that he was going to blow this wide open in the press and see if the people really knew of what this bill consisted. Joshua had already started a local opposition group and was beginning to hear from other parts of the country by the time he reported to me.

"Now he's in the hospital, close to death, from an attempt on his life. That's too coincidental for me."

Grady was nodding his agreement as Maggie brought their food and put it in front of them. Maggie didn't say a word, but politely left them to their talk.

"Chief, did Joshua come up with any hard evidence?"

Wilson lowered his voice. "He did more than that. He states in his report that Theodore Connelly is a warlock in charge of the local coven and that Governor Bradley is the top warlock state-wide."

Grady rubbed his aching temples and let out a low whistle.

Wilson continued, his voice still a whisper. "Grady, we're surrounded by witches and there is no way of knowing who is or is not one. Even our police department is not exempt from witches.

"I'd say that they've declared war on our little town of Covenant. We're the testing ground for their theories. If they can shut us down, they can take the country.

"Grady, I believe there is still hope. Based on our own experiences, there is obviously some heavenly intervention going on here. But we also have to do our part. Now, if you're up to a little espionage..."

Grady nodded and for well over an hour Wilson shared his plans with him.

A smile began to form on Grady's face.

Chapter 12

The Temple

Deceit, the demon who had clung so selfishly to Mandy only to desert her in the face of the enemy, was led into Cono's office by Lt. Poe.

Lt. Poe addressed Cono, "Sir! This fool has something so important to tell you that he disobeyed your direct orders by leaving his assigned host."

Deceit was suddenly filled with terror at the revelation that he had disobeyed Cono. He had been so shocked and afraid of the angelic intervention, that he hadn't thought of the consequences of leaving his post. He began to shake violently.

Cono snarled, "Speak, you fool!"

"We tried to kill Grady today, but we couldn't," Deceit whimpered.

Cono glared at him. "What do you mean you couldn't?"

The demon was shaking so hard he could barely speak. In a voice just above a whisper, he continued, "Right before the bomb went off in Grady's car, Grady's guardian, the one named Warrior, no, I think his name is Walter, or maybe . . . "

Cono couldn't take it anymore; he kicked Deceit right in the mouth, dislodging several of his yellow teeth and knocking him flat on his back. Cono drew his sword and slime oozed from his mouth, and dropped onto Deceit's face. He bent over him and threatened, "Get to the point, you blithering idiot, or die!"

Deceit tried to wipe away the blood which was running freely from his mouth. Very timidly, he continued, "The angel picked Grady up and physically threw him away from the blast . . . . " Cono screamed and started swinging his sword in a dangerous arc. Lt. Poe had to duck twice to prevent his own decapitation. Cono ranted, "That's against all the articles of war! We can only suggest mental images, not get physically involved! What kind of treachery is this?" Cono screamed again and brought his sword down with all his might.

Now, it was Deceit's scream that was heard as Cono's sword severed his right ear from his head. Deceit jumped up from the floor and began to hop around, clutching his bleeding head with one hand and sifting through the dirt for his severed ear with the other.

Cono yelled, "Get out before I decide to kill you where you stand!"

Deceit flew out of the compound just as fast as he could. As he soared into the sky, a red sword flashed and Deceit's head fell from his shoulders. Poe had left word with the sentry that Deceit was not to leave alive, and he had carried out his orders with experienced ease. The sentry smiled as he watched Deceit explode in a puff of red smoke.

Cono felt better now. He told Lt. Poe, "Let's not tell Tumult about this development just yet. It may come in handy for us to know something that he doesn't know.

"Poe! This is unprecedented in recent history. I still can't believe that those angels would intervene in the physical world. They're supposed to obey the rules. This could be a much fiercer war than we anticipated."

Poe nodded and asked, "What about the woman, Mandy? Do I assign someone else to take care of her?"

Cono thought for a moment, then replied, "No, just leave her for awhile. We're done using her for now. She's harmless to us and useless to them."

With that settled, the two demons turned their attention back to the preparations for the evening's service.

* * *

Mandy relieved Paul of his post at the radio, flopping into the vacated chair. She was pale and obviously shaken. It concerned Paul enough to comment, "Mandy, maybe you should take off sick today, you don't look so hot."

She shook her head and gave him a look that made it clear that he should mind his own business. With Paul gone Mandy was left deep in her own thoughts. How could things have gotten so out of hand? She was shaking so badly that she wished she had taken Paul's advice to go home sick. She needed to get away from here and think.

The hatred she felt for Asst. Chief Anderson flared as he came through the door. He stopped and stared at Mandy and then hissed, "I'll deal with you later."

As he walked away, Mandy's stomach knotted up as she thought of all the things that message could mean. She began to think about the first time she had been approached by Anderson.

Mandy had been lonely and in need of company. Anderson had told her of this "club" for lonely people, in which she could learn calming techniques and ways to expand her consciousness.

For a while, it was just wonderful. From day one, people greeted her with a hug and a friendly kiss on the cheek. They were pleasant and kind, and she grew to trust them.

They taught Mandy to listen to soft, relaxing music, while staring at a lighted candle. If she tried real hard she would be able to see a foggy, cloudy-type being just above the candle. As Mandy mastered this technique, she was taught how to change the color of the being in the flame.

Then she met her spirit guide for the first time.

He was a kind and generous spirit who would come whenever she called and would give her good, sound advice. She grew to trust him also.

Next, Anderson personally taught her how to astral-project her spirit from her body anywhere and contact anyone she wished.

While in the astral-projected state, Mandy would meet face to face with Ambro, her spirit guide. He was a former Egyptian ruler and was strikingly handsome and very wise in all matters. He was also very affectionate. Mandy soon fell in love with him.

Ambro taught Mandy all the secrets of the universe. He ended his teaching by leading her down the path of free love. He convinced her that she would obtain wisdom and knowledge beyond belief through the powers of human sexuality. When Mandy hesitated, he argued that he loved Mandy very much, but the only way that they would ever know the bliss of sexual union would be for him to possess a man who would then have relations with Mandy.

Mandy resisted this argument at first, but it seemed that Ambro was so saddened by her refusal that she soon agreed. She was very self-conscious the first time Anderson seduced her, but she reminded herself that it was Ambro and not Anderson at all. After Anderson, there were many other men, all hand-picked by Ambro. They were all very gentle and kind.

After about three months of this instruction, Ambro urged Mandy to join the temple. In doing so, she would obtain the true knowledge of an advanced mystic. She agreed—she wanted to please these people who had been so kind to her. She studied the laws and rituals of the order. Then she took the blood oath of lifetime obedience. She was now well on her way to learning the secrets of witchcraft, demonism, and Satanism.

Mandy was assured that the temple gleaned only the good attributes and practices from each of these religions and incorporated those principles into the religion practiced in the temple. She was an excellent student, hungry for knowledge, for love, and acceptance.

At the swearing in, Mandy and the other candidates, or postulants, promised to obey the leaders of the order without question. The penalty for refusal to carry out an assigned task was death. The postulants made the promise, but thought it was surely just a leftover, figurative part of the oath.

They were wrong.

After the oath was sworn, each postulant had to submit to a test. Mandy's test required her to rape a ten-year-old boy, who was tied down and helpless. He was crying and embarrassed at his nakedness. Before Mandy could refuse, Anderson showed her the corpse of a woman who had refused her first order.

Suddenly the realization that she was now nothing more than a slave in the hands of evil people hit Mandy like a truck. She lost her hope, her innocence, and her soul that night.

After committing the evil and malicious deed required of her, Mandy was viciously raped again and again. Mandy's spirit guide, Ambro, appeared to her that night in his true form—as a horrifyingly grotesque demon. She screamed and went into shock and never fully erased that face from her mind.

The next night, the elders tied Mandy to the sacrificial altar and, on her bared stomach, slaughtered a small infant. She wept bitterly, begging for the child's life, and ultimately for her own. She realized now that she had no chance to get free from these people.

At times, Anderson would beat Mandy for no apparent reason, and then, at other times, he would pamper and pet her as though she were a queen. Anderson would come and dress her up in an expensive gown and take her to an elegant ballroom for dinner and dancing. During these times she would mentally withdraw and fantasize about being a princess at a gala ball.

Later, however, after they had snorted cocaine together, Anderson would take her to his home and rape her. Afterward, he would look down at her with disgust and say, "Get out of my sight, you pig!"

Mandy began to starve herself into painful thinness so that she could please him. It made little difference.

When she got pregnant, they made her carry it to full term. She was forced to deliver the baby on the altar of sacrifice. The doctor held the baby up for all the admiring coven to see and then he laid it on Mandy's belly, cut its throat and let it bleed to death over her stomach. They ordered her not to mourn—it was an honor to bear a sacrifice to Satan.

Her hatred began to grow. As punishment for questioning the beliefs of the temple, they had the temple doctor "fix" Mandy so that she could never bear children again. She swore to herself that given the chance she would bring the temple down.

Mandy got her chance months later when the police doctor, through routine blood checks, found that Mandy had contracted AIDS. The doctor couldn't tell anyone and Mandy would not.

She went to her temple duties with a new vigor and enthusiasm that was greeted by all with praise. She had finally embraced their beliefs. Mandy "worked" her way through both the men and women leaders of the coven, infecting as many of the hierarchy with the virus as she was able.

Mandy had been with Anderson the night before Joshua was ambushed. Afterward, Anderson explained to her that Joshua, Grady, and the chief were snooping around in temple business and that they had to be warned. She was to send Joshua on a fake call and set him up for a warning shot. He would then receive a note telling him to back off. Grady and Chief Wilson would be warned by some carefully planted smoke bombs--bombs she was to plant.

Anderson showed her how to hook up the bombs, and she had done the chief's office last night and Grady's vehicle on the way to work.

When Mandy saw Joshua's condition and the destructive power of the bomb blasts, she knew Anderson had lied to her--again.

Mandy was roused from her thoughts when the desk phone rang. After taking the call, she decided to take Paul's advice. She called her supervisor and got the night off. She decided, once and for all, she was going to confront Anderson.

Anderson reported to Chief Wilson as ordered. What a waste of time that had been! Wilson had rambled on about scheduling and repair plans, and Anderson spent the time looking at his watch and fidgeting. It was time for him to get off duty, and he left as soon as he could.

As he drove home, Anderson dismissed his concerns about Wilson. *What a fool! The simpleton didn't suspect a thing.*

Anderson knew how to cover himself. He had used Mandy for the job of blowing up those two nosy clods; if anything went wrong, it would be Mandy who went to jail. She hadn't gotten caught, but she sure had bungled the job.

Anderson grinned as he thought of the punishment he would inflict on her just as soon as these sacrifices were out of the way. Until then he would let her do her duty to the temple.

When he arrived home, he took off his uniform and flung it on the bed like a soiled rag. He checked the tuxedo he would be wearing to dinner that evening—it was vital that he looked his best. For now, however, he pulled on jeans and a blue pullover shirt and sneakers.

He left his house and drove to Connelly's warehouse. He unlocked the door and entered the section of the building which housed the temple.

He was excited about tonight. He'd worked hard to reach the enviable post of a level 2 warlock, or Warlock II, one of the higher ranks of the temple. It meant that he knew his Satanic bible very well and that he was an accomplished sorcerer.

Anderson's spirit guide told him that he would be promoted to Priest of Mandes III as a result of his participation in the service tonight. This was an honor bestowed personally by the powers of darkness and he had finally been chosen. The honor would allow him to take the unoccupied seat on the council of nine, replacing the temple doctor, who had committed suicide. As a member of the elite council, he would allow the powers of darkness to enter his body and they would teach him knowledge and power beyond his imagination.

Anderson had watched Connelly take this same step and it sure had helped him get rich and powerful. Connelly was now a Magister IV with the exalted

The Temple

designation of Master of the temple. His magical powers had grown immensely over the last couple of years. Anderson fully intended to follow in every one of Connelly's footsteps. Connelly had been promised by his own spirit guide that he would move up to Magus V tonight, the highest degree conferred within the authority of the church of Satan. Anderson was dripping with envy.

Governor Bradley was a jerk as far as Anderson was concerned, but he was a powerful jerk. He was already a Magus V. His powers were enormous and it was rumored that he once killed a man by merely thinking it. Bradley could travel long distances by moving from one astral plain to another--a very handy tool when you needed an alibi to cover your tracks. Bradley had used it for that purpose many times.

Bradley had bragged once that he had no less than twelve demons living in his body. At this ceremony, Bradley would receive his thirteenth spirit, a spirit named Tumult, who would bring Bradley to the pinnacle of his career by promoting him to Ipsissimus. This title would give Bradley complete ruling authority over the powers of darkness. Bradley's power over the physical world would be complete—he would be invincible.

Anderson walked through the warehouse and stood before a solid brick wall. He pulled on one of the bricks and a small access panel was exposed. He punched in the code, known only to himself, Connelly, and Mandy. Mandy had been given the secret code so that she could carry out the menial tasks that he and Connelly didn't want to do.

As Anderson punched in the final digit in the code and the engage button, the hidden door slid aside and he stepped into the temple. The temple was large enough to accommodate over one thousand people.

This evening it would entertain only five hundred of the most powerful, elite members of the coven. Out of these five hundred, only two hundred had been invited to Connelly's banquet.

Anderson flipped on the lights and the temple was flooded with harsh light. During the ceremony it would be lit only by torches lining the top portion of all four walls. That was one of the many menial chores that he had assigned to Mandy—keeping those torches full of fuel and ready at all times.

He stopped in the middle of the temple floor and looked around with admiration and a sense of power and well being. Anderson was very full of himself.

Everything was in place. A banner hung in the place of honor directly above the altar of sacrifice. The banner was large—ten feet long by five feet wide—yet the bottom of the banner was still ten feet from the floor of the temple. Printed on the banner in large violet letters were the words: WALPURGIS NIGHT, which is the holy feast of May's Eve, one of the greatest Sabbath's of the year. Below this name was a large sign of "Baphomet"—a goat's head inside an inverted pentagram, within two circles.

They would celebrate that feast tonight and it was made even more significant by the powerful full moon that would be hanging in the night sky, as well as the human sacrifice that would be offered.

Anderson quickly checked each wall banner that depicted a lesser demon whose task was to protect the temple from the outside world. On the north wall was Astaroth, on the south, Baal, the east held Asmodeus, and the west, Belial. They were a ghastly crew and Anderson loved them.

He walked across the floor that was covered with soft mats, which protected their naked bodies from the concrete during the service. On his right was the bathroom--he'd have Mandy make sure it was clean--another menial and degrading task.

In the center of the temple was a concrete platform which stood five feet above the rest of the floor. The platform was circular with a diameter of thirteen feet. Anderson walked up the steps and looked at the "Seal of Solomon" which was centered on the platform and etched about four inches into the concrete. Nine feet in diameter, the hexagram had two inverted triangles, one facing one direction, the other facing the opposite direction. In the center of this sign was placed a marble altar which had once celebrated the Holy Sacrament of the Eucharist. Connelly had imported it from England, along with the sacred stones and pillars from a deserted Catholic church.

Anderson checked the censer, candles, chalice, and surgical instruments to make sure that all was ready for tonight. He lovingly traced the Pentagram that was etched into the center of the altar with his finger and thought about the power that Bradley would receive when the Pentagram filled with human blood. Bradley had once bragged that he would even surpass the false prophet, Jesus, in power some day. Well, that day was here. Anderson longed for the day when he too would reach such heights.

He placed a large candle at each corner of the altar and placed the book of shadows in the center of the Pentagram. On the book, he solemnly placed the ornate and razor-sharp knife which was to be used for the sacrifice.

There was a life-size Crucifix sitting on a stand, which Anderson now took and turned upside down, the sign of the defeated Christ. For his final sacrilege, at least for now, Anderson took the consecrated host, which had been stolen from the local Catholic church, and spread them out on the floor. They would trample on the host with their bare feet and urinate on them, in order to purify the temple.

He checked the boat of the censer; it was full of marijuana laced with PCP, a strong hallucinatory drug.

He checked the large two-way mirror at the back of the temple, directly above the entrance door. Behind that mirror was a secret room which housed a video camera and recording equipment. It was to this room that Anderson now headed.

As Anderson left the temple, he turned off the lights and then closed and secured the door, which assumed the appearance of a brick wall again. Next to the door was a metal ladder fastened directly to the brick wall. He climbed up this ladder to a small metal door, also set flush into the wall with a secret access panel. He punched in the access code and when the lock clicked open, pushed the door inward and climbed into the secret room.

Opposite the entrance was the back side of the two-way mirror out of which Anderson could see the darkened temple. In front of the window a video camera fitted with a wide-angle lens stood securely on a tripod.

No one but he and Connelly had access to this room, most were not even aware it existed. Connelly had taught him time and again that it never hurt to have insurance, just in case one of the followers decided to quit the order and turn informant. The rat would then be shown one of many tape recordings that showed them participating in a human sacrifice. They usually changed their minds about quitting--if not, they were terminated at the next gathering.

Anderson turned the camera on, along with the recording device and then narrated, "What you see before you is the temple, which is now the sight of the May Eve's Sacrifice of a holy virgin and the birth of the infant sacrifice. The celebrant is Governor Bradley, leader of our state-wide coven."

Anderson set the equipment on standby and then dropped the remote control device in his pocket. Later when the celebration began he would simply press the button and they would have instant leverage over Governor Bradley. Anderson opened the door and exited feet first.

When Mandy got to the warehouse, she used her key to gain access and then walked toward the temple. She was sure that Anderson would still be there, and as she rounded the corner she saw his back-end exiting the door to the secret room. She could see the video recorder over his shoulder and suddenly realized that they had video-taped everything that she and the others had done in the temple. She shuddered at the thought of those tapes falling into the wrong hands. A plan began to form in Mandy's mind.

She yelled out, "Hey! What are you doing up there; fixing something?"

To her delight she watched as Anderson jumped and nearly lost his footing and fell from the ladder. He hurriedly closed the door to the secret room, but, in his haste, didn't notice that it hadn't latched all the way.

"Oh, there you are, Mandy. I wanted to talk to you for a minute."

He climbed down the ladder and faced Mandy with a broad smile on his face. In a brotherly tone, he said, "Look, Mandy, I know that we lied to you about Joshua and the others but, honestly, we were afraid that you'd get too nervous if you knew the truth." Calmly, hiding her delight in her new plan, Mandy replied, "Oh, that's all right. I'd rather not know the details, anyway. I just stopped by to see if anything else has to be done to prepare for tonight."

Anderson put his arm around her waist and led her out of the warehouse. Once outside he said, "Now, remember, we want you here at ten o'clock tonight to open the temple and welcome the least important quests. The rest will arrive later from the Connelly Mansion."

Mandy nodded. "I'll be here. I'm looking forward to seeing the temple grow."

They each went their separate ways, immersed in their own dreams of power and revenge.

Grady had followed Anderson from the police station as the chief had instructed him. He was shocked and saddened to see Mandy arrive at the warehouse, use a key, and go in.

First Anderson, now Mandy. Who else in the department was involved in this conspiracy?

Grady heard the time of the meeting and vowed to be an uninvited guest at the festivities. He left to report back to the chief.

Chapter 13

The Angels Flee

Chief Wilson left the station immediately after Mandy. He'd sent Grady to tail Anderson and now he was headed for the hospital to see how Joshua was doing and to check on the preparations for the prayer meeting.

When he arrived at the hospital, Wilson noted that the platform had already been built on which the ministers would stand and preach. As he got out of his car, a smiling Rev. Smith came up to greet him.

"Chief, the response has been enormous! There are volunteers here from all the different churches in the area. The Boy Scouts and Girl Scouts are going to set up concession stands to feed the thousands that we're anticipating. Even the portable potty people have agreed to provide free service for us. I mean, God is really coming through with all of our needs."

The chief agreed, "Yes, and He's also provided us with some leads, which I can't tell you about—not just yet anyway. However, I do want you to pray for a successful conclusion to our investigation."

As they walked toward the hospital, Wilson heard Marla Brinkle, the TV news reporter, ask one of the workers, "Why all of this fuss over one wounded cop? I mean he certainly wasn't anyone special."

The worker spotted the chief and pointed to him saying, "There's the man you need to ask," and then turned back to his work.

Wilson wasn't sure that he liked this beautiful young woman, but he knew that he didn't like the sound of her question. He waited while she made her way over to him.

"Good afternoon, Ms. Brinkle, how are you today?"

Marla flashed him a brilliant smile and answered, "I'm fine, Chief Wilson. Could I ask you a few questions?"

Not in the least swayed by her charm, Wilson replied, "I'm afraid I've already heard your question, and even though I don't like the way you put it, I'll tell you why all this fuss over one cop. Joshua White has done more for this city than any ten people have. He's a fine officer and an even finer man. I also . . ."

Marla cut him off, "That's all very nice, Chief Wilson, but did you know that Governor Bradley is seeking a warrant for his arrest?"

Wilson's face got dangerously red. "Why would he do that?"

Marla was smug in her reply, "Governor Bradley stated that Officer White has incited riots and encouraged people to break the law. He's responsible for the city council voting to return prayer in the schools and keeping the Ten Commandments and religious articles accessible there. And was it not Officer White who fought to keep the abortion clinic out of Covenant, causing many nurses and doctors to lose their jobs and the city to lose much needed tax revenue?"

Wilson proudly stated, "Yes, Joshua certainly led us in the right direction in all of those matters. He . . ."

Marla cut him off again. "Furthermore, Chief, because of his misguided efforts and your unfortunate acceptance, marshal law has been declared by Governor Bradley, and will take effect in the morning."

She opened a letter and read enthusiastically, "The order states that Christians will not be allowed to gather in groups larger than ten people. Wouldn't this hamper your prayer meeting here?"

Flustered, Wilson said, "Yes it would, but..."

Warming to the subject, Marla went on, "Chief, isn't it true that Officer White is the leader of a militant group of Christians, who are fighting the governor's efforts on the Brice Bill?"

"Yes, I mean, no, he..."

"And isn't it equally true that Officer White repeatedly made misleading statements about the bill in order to sway people against it, and that he said that he wouldn't comply with it even if it was the law?"

Angrily, Wilson answered, "Yes, he is against the Brice Bill and he, along with most of the people in Covenant, will resist its passage and enforcement."

Marla Brinkle turned her back on the police chief and faced the camera, "There you have it, ladies and gentlemen. Not only does Officer Joshua White willingly break the law and get away with it, but the people in this area encourage his activity. Even the chief of police is sympathetic to his cause. Is it any wonder that the governor of this fine state has had to order the National Guard to the area to keep the peace? He has also asked me to make this statement for him, and I quote, 'The Christians of Covenant are dangerous people. They are misguided zealots who will stop at nothing to hinder world peace, which is within our grasp. They cling to their outdated, exclusionary, and bigoted God, who discriminates against gays, witches, demonists, and Satanists. As your governor, it is my duty to make sure that this minority religion finally bows to the New World Order, which is this planet's only hope. I will force them to obey the law or they will pay the consequences.'

"Governor Bradley made this statement just before he departed from the Capitol. Rumor has it that the governor has chosen to accompany his troops here in person.

"This action stems from the demonstration earlier today at the capitol, when some so-called peaceful Christians bombed several buildings, causing over one hundred casualties. We may finally see justice fall upon these people, so please tune in for updated reports.

"This is Marla Brinkle, reporting live from Covenant, a city that may well have blood on its hands come tomorrow."

Chief Wilson grabbed Marla's arm. "How can you present that report as the truth?"

Marla laughed, "Come on, Chief! The news isn't about truth anymore, it's about ratings. It's about scooping the other networks, and in order to do that, you have to be able and willing to stick your neck out and predict the outcome of certain events."

"You mean you have to be willing to manipulate, bend, and fabricate it, if need be, all in the name of ratings. What happened to reporting the truth in order to protect people from manipulators like Bradley who seek only their own gain?"

Marla didn't bother to answer. "Good day, Chief!" She grabbed her cameraman and left.

Wilson watched her go, wondering if he was indeed still in the United States of America. As he recalled, the country had been founded by good Christian men and women and its laws were based on sound Christian morals. After the last couple of days and this interview, he wasn't sure anymore just exactly who was running the government these days.

He said a prayer for the leaders of the country and the leaders of the news industry, as he entered the hospital. The lobby was filled with concerned citizens, ministers and council members. They all clamored around him, looking for an answer to these new threats.

The chief had none.

Beriack touched Chief Wilson's shoulder and whispered in his ear.

Suddenly an idea popped into Wilson's head. He liked the idea. It was simple, and obeyed the letter of the law, if not the spirit of it.

He turned to the anxious crowd. "I just got an idea that will help us tomorrow. This is what we'll do . . ."

* * *

Worl and his men arrived at the hospital just in time to see Aaron return to duty. He looked stronger than ever.

Worl and Aaron exchanged salutes then embraced in greeting. Worl whispered in Aaron's ear, "Do you understand your new orders, Aaron?"

Aaron stood back and looked into Worl's eyes. Aaron was no match for Worl's intensity and he finally lowered his eyes and nodded acceptance of his task.

Satisfied, Worl slapped him on the back and presented him to the other angels gathered there.

Worl said, "Except for those angels that are assigned to a specific Christian, all other angels are to pull out, immediately. We are to withdraw to the north and are not to return to Covenant unless summoned by our Lord. Tonight is a dark and evil night; keep the saints off the streets.

"The Christians should make a large showing tomorrow at the hospital for the prayer service.

"The angels that remain to guard the hospital are not to make contact with the enemy, unless absolutely necessary.

"Remember, Jesus is Lord! Now let's get to our assigned duties. Everyone's dismissed except Aaron, Warren, Beriack, and Oath."

After repeating "Jesus is Lord" the other angels left.

Worl continued, "Here's what I want you to do, very early tomorrow morning..."

* * *

Grady met with the chief and filled him in on what he had learned while tailing Anderson.

Wilson said, "As shocking as it is, Grady, we can't do anything to them until they break the law. We can, however, keep them under close observation. I want you to stay at that temple all night if necessary. Take down license numbers, identify citizens and fellow police officers, and anyone else that shows up there.

"Joshua found out that the temple is a merging of witchcraft, demonism, and Satanism—a very dangerous combination. Grady, stay as long as you can after their meeting to see what they do with the trash. We may find some clues in there as to what they do in that temple of theirs. We need something concrete to use to get a search warrant."

Grady made a few notes, then said, "I'll go home and get some sleep and be in place by 8:30."

"Just be careful out there, Grady. I don't want another wounded officer on my hands."

Grady said, "Don't go and get mushy on me, Chief."

They clasped hands, then departed, each intent on serving the Lord in his own way.

* * *

The Angels Flee

Aaron watched as ten thousand angels headed north, leaving Covenant virtually unprotected. They had all fought so hard to defeat the demons in the battle over the hospital and now they were turning the town over to them! The Lord hadn't told Aaron why this must be, just that it must be. Aaron trusted the Lord—He who knew all that was and is and is to come—and he would obey Him. He would always obey.

Tumult's soldiers jeered and shouted obscenities at Worl's men as they went by. They taunted the angels, "Run, cowards, and don't bother to show your yellow faces here again. After tonight, this will be our town."

For all of their brave shouting, however, Tumult's men still waited until all of the angels were gone before they moved into their new home.

Chapter 14

Unthinkable Acts

Theodore Connelly owned the largest trucking and transport firm in Covenant and was the city's largest employer. His fortune, however, was made selling drugs.

He had lobbied hard to get marijuana legalized and now that it was, his sales had more than doubled. Other drug sales had also increased dramatically.

Connelly was a very happy man.

He was worth several million dollars and his biggest thrill in life was entertaining his friends and showing off his wealth.

Tonight would be such an occasion. He had invited two hundred of the most prominent members of the coven to dine with him and celebrate May's Eve. It would be a glorious feast. He had flown in the best chef from Paris, France, that money could buy, including his entire culinary staff. They would prepare and serve the meal at the feast.

Connelly couldn't pronounce what they were going to eat, but he knew it would be impressive, and that's what he was after.

Formal attire was expected, of course.

He finished tying his bow tie and then looked at himself in the full length mirror hanging on his bedroom wall. He was wearing a deep violet tuxedo—violet being the most powerful color to wear on a Monday, especially on May's Eve. He was inordinately proud of his five-foot-five inch, rounded frame and balding head and he always dressed a trifle flamboyantly. After one more admiring look in the mirror, Connelly headed down to greet his guests.

Normally, a dinner of this magnitude and magnificence would be followed by a dance with a full orchestra. Tonight, however, the dinner would be followed by a human sacrifice and several promotions in the Order.

Dr. Chad White drove through the gate of Connelly's estate and stopped at the guard house to show his invitation. He then continued up the long concrete driveway which led to Connelly's Mansion. Ellen had refused to come with him. This really irritated him but he didn't push it; after all, there would be plenty of unattached women here tonight.

As he rounded the final curve in the driveway, the full majesty of Connelly's estate hit him. The English estate house had been moved brick by brick from England and then rebuilt on this spot. The house was surrounded by beautifully landscaped grounds which sported complete horse stables as well as kennels in which he raised foxes and fox hounds. At least once a year Connelly held a fox hunt on these massive acres of land.

Near the house, Connelly had built an indoor pool, hot tub, tennis court, and handball court. The lane which led the half mile to the rolling eighteen-hole golf course could be seen in the distance. He used these toys to entertain his connections in the government, judges, states attorneys, as well as sheriffs.

Dr. White's attention returned to the house. It was lighted by bright floodlights and guarded by several two-man teams, each accompanied by a guard dog on a chain. Each person on the team had an automatic rifle slung over his shoulder.

The three-story house was built of stone. It had twenty bedrooms, each with its own bathroom, a large den, a library, a huge kitchen, and a ballroom that would hold up to four hundred people.

The finest room was the dining hall in which Connelly had placed the largest, one piece, horseshoe-shaped dining table in the world. It was made of mahogany and polished to a mirror finish. It could seat exactly two hundred people and cost three million dollars to carve.

White left his car at the front door where a neatly dressed valet parked it for him, and entered a world that even he could only dream of. In the entrance way was a large spiral staircase which led to the upstairs rooms and boasted of a mahogany banister, which was inlaid with mother of pearl. From the ceiling, two stories above, a large chandelier, made of genuine crystal, hung elegantly.

While White stood gaping at the house and at the important guests who were arriving in a steady stream, Connelly had approached him unnoticed.

"Welcome, doctor! Welcome both to my house and to the temple. I think you'll be pleasantly surprised at the life we have planned for you. Get yourself a drink and mingle. Everyone is dying to meet you ."

With that he walked away, greeting other guests and tending to other details.

At eight o' clock sharp the guests were seated for the meal. Dr. White was surprised to find that he was seated with Connelly and Governor Bradley in the place of honor. Connelly was still standing behind his chair, and Governor Bradley had not arrived yet.

Connelly was glad the Governor hadn't arrived on time—now he could lock him out and he would have to knock to get in. He nodded to Anderson, who closed and locked the large double doors. The last door slammed into place and echoed throughout the chamber. Connelly watched as the guests looked at each other and whispered. They were confused by the fact that the large table at which they sat was bare. There was no tablecloth, or flowers, and definitely no food.

Connelly spoke above the murmurs of the crowd, "Welcome one and all! Welcome!" The guests became quiet and he continued, "I have many surprises for you this evening and since our guest of honor has not arrived yet . . ."

As he was speaking, Connelly noticed that everyone was staring past him with astonishment on their faces. He turned and was shocked to see Governor Bradley standing behind him. He recovered quickly. "So nice of you to pop in on us, Governor."

Everyone laughed. Connelly continued, "Please, let's welcome our guest, shall we?"

Connelly started to applaud and was soon joined by each of the people gathered there.

Connelly said, "Governor Bradley will address us after dinner. For now, however, sit back down and I will set the table."

When everyone was seated, including Governor Bradley, Connelly snapped his fingers. The room became dark as pitch and he smiled as he heard women scream and men jumping up out of their chairs.

The lights were not off for more than thirty seconds and yet when they came back on, the table looked much different. The light that now shone came from fifteen lighted candelabrums, which had suddenly appeared out of the darkness. As their eyes adjusted to the dimmer light, the guests began to realize that the entire table was set, from its tablecloth to the bowls of fruit and hot rolls, which lined the center of the table. In front of each person was a dinner plate, a bread plate, a beautifully presented salad plate, silver ware, glasses of water and wine. Everything was of the finest china and crystal, including the salt and pepper shakers.

This time it was Governor Bradley's to lead the applause.

Connelly beamed with pride and gave the signal for the chef and his servers to bring in the first course of the meal.

Floating unseen above the human heads was another banquet, which was already in full swing. Cono was entertaining Tumult and a few of his officers. The demons were gorging themselves from tables laden with rotting carcasses and swill which dripped from their chins as they talked to each other.

Tumult got up to speak, pounding on the table for quiet. He got it instantly, except for one little demon, who was so engrossed in what he was saying that he hadn't heard the request.

Without hesitation, Tumult pulled his dagger from its sheath, flipped it so that he was now holding the blade, and threw it with such speed and accuracy, that the demon puffed out of existence before he could get the next word out of his mouth.

Tumult now had everyone's undivided attention.

"I want to thank Cono and Lt. Poe for their faithful service and their hospitality. I know that it's been hard serving here in Covenant, the center of the enemy territory, but we'll soon claim this last stronghold for our lord. These bleeding-heart Christians, floating around on their idealistic clouds, will soon give us real blood."

There was thunderous applause from all gathered.

Cono now stood and said, "A toast to the successful

conclusion of our battle plans and to our leader who will bring us honor and glory!"

They all raised their glasses and drank the blood of their latest victims from the pit.

The human guests had now had their fill of food, dessert, and wine. After the table was cleared, Connelly dismissed the French servers with a wave. He and Anderson distributed a generous supply of cocaine, marijuana, and LSD, encouraging everyone to enjoy themselves. Soon it would be time to participate in the special ceremony for which they had all come. Everyone greedily sucked the white powder up their noses and then they sat back, lit their joints, and listened, as Governor Bradley got up to speak.

Bradley began, "Welcome . . ."

Tumult dug his claws deep into Bradley's spine and from that moment on, Bradley spoke only the lies which Tumult had spoken to his own men.

Tumult was the power behind all of Bradley's tricks.

The lesser demons took their positions next to their human hosts. Tumult had his puppet, Bradley, speak the sacred mantra, which, though it meant nothing, captivated the humans regardless.

As he spoke the last word of the mantra, there was a terrible clap of thunder, and all two hundred humans in the room disappeared in a great cloud of bright red smoke.

* * *

Mandy had been at the temple door greeting people since ten o' clock as ordered. She had attempted to make the new coven members as comfortable as possible. They were always a little self-conscious about removing their clothing in front of people. The rules stated that all participants had to be in the pure and holy state of nakedness.

People undressed quietly, folding their clothes and placing them in the baskets provided. They entered the temple and stood on the soft mats talking quietly, while they waited for the service to begin. There were entire families present from the father on down to babies feeding at the breast.

When the last member had entered the temple, Mandy securely locked the door. She had expected Connelly and Anderson to bring their guests in through the secret basement door and enter from under the altar which would rise impressively from the floor opening, a door leading up from the basement. She was not prepared for what actually occurred.

The torches lining the walls went out and then seconds later flared to life again. Mandy was shocked to see two hundred formally-attired people standing on the raised platform around the altar. These people looked as surprised as the people in the temple were. The two hundred soon recovered, undressed and joined the others on the floor.

Before Anderson put his clothes in his own basket, he reached into his pants pocket and pushed the remote button which turned on the secret camera. Everything would now be captured on tape and could be used later to blackmail their important guests, as needed.

Tumult watched as Cono took possession of Connelly. He was surprised at how admirably Cono was performing.

Connelly stood before the assembly wearing his violet robe which hung open in the front. Bradley, who was seated behind him, wore the exact same robe, except that his bore the powerful image of Satan on the back.

Connelly spoke, "As the Grand Master of the temple, it is my pleasure to call this meeting to order. We will begin by purifying the temple." Taking that as their cue, each member present began to urinate on the hosts which Anderson had spread on the floor.

Tumult and his demons rolled with laughter as the humans defiled themselves and sealed their fate.

Connelly spoke again, "Let us pray. Lord Lucifer, accept the fragrance of our offering as we purify this temple and make it a holy place in which to offer our sacrifice."

Now Connelly took the censer and lit the charcoal and sprinkled a generous amount of marijuana onto the heat. The sweet smelling smoke hovered around the altar. He went to each of the four corners, bowed, and then swung the censer over the altar. Then he took the razor sharp, ceremonial knife and cut the palm of his hand, allowing the blood to flow upon the altar.

"Oh, Prince of Darkness, we are ready to offer you a human soul."

He signaled Anderson to bring in the sacrifice.

Anderson led the woman toward the altar from a secret side room. Dr. White recognized the woman first, as Becky, the prostitute that Connelly had used to entrap him. For the first time, however, he realized that the baby that was to be taken out of her belly was his own child. He felt only a brief pang of guilt.

Becky had been on the altar many times, she liked being the center of attention. All she normally had to do was lie on the cold stone altar, allow Connelly to kill a dog, a cat, or a baby on her belly as he copulated with her and then she was free to enjoy an evening of wanton sex and drugs.

Tonight was different, though. She was nine months pregnant and her child would be taken tonight and then sacrificed tomorrow night. They had assured her that Dr. White would knock her out before cutting her open, taking the baby, and then closing her back up.

They had also assured her that he would use a bikini incision, so it wouldn't show. Becky was very proud of her looks and didn't want them ruined.

Connelly gently helped Becky climb onto the altar and lie back. She was tied down in a spread-eagle posture and then Connelly announced, "The sacrifice will now be conducted by Governor Bradley!" Connelly turned back to Becky and stuffed a rag into her mouth and secured it in place with another rag tied around her mouth and head. He leaned in close and whispered, "I'm sorry Becky, but this was Bradley's idea."

The hair on the back of Becky's neck stood on end as she watched Bradley approach her. He took the ceremonial knife and starting at the neck of the black, sheer lace, ceremonial gown which Becky wore, the governor sliced it from top to bottom. The blade was even colder against Becky's skin than the air that rushed into the opening of the garment. Bradley took the knife and cut his palm, just as Connelly had done, allowing the warm blood to flow freely over Becky's large, exposed stomach. He made the sign of the upside-down cross on Becky's stomach. As the blood ran down her side it caused a maddening itch which her bound hands could not scratch.

Bradley took the book of shadows and read, "Lord of Darkness, we have prepared this virgin her entire life for this moment. She has been made holy through fornication, molestation, incest, cannibalism, adultery and now, torture."

Bradley motioned to Dr. White to come forward and begin. Her eyes wide with terror, Becky saw the doctor's shaking hand grasp the hilt of the ceremonial knife. *My God*, she thought, *it's not supposed to be this way! This isn't happening! God help me, what is happening, what is he doing, what have I done?* Becky's fear caused a choking mass of bile to rise from her stomach and she vomited violently. Because of the rag stuffed in her mouth, the gorge began to fill her nose. She was drowning in her own fluids as Dr. White took the knife and made his incision.

White hot pain exploded in her mind. Before she lost consciousness she remembered a little song her mother had sung to her as a child. She began to sing it in her mind, "Jesus loves me this I know, for the Bible tells me so . . ." Becky cried out to the God she had never had the courage to believe in.

Demons looked up at the sudden flash of light as one very bold angel streaked into the temple and took Becky's soul as it left her abused human body. He hugged her to himself and left as swiftly as he had come.

Tumult stood stunned! What audacity the enemy had! Why would he want the filthy and most certainly damned soul of Becky, anyway. Tumult would never understand this Jesus.

It had been a much younger Tumult who had been waiting for the soul of a dying criminal tied to a cross next to Jesus. Much like this case, Jesus had forgiven him a split second before Tumult could take him. *Boy, that still frosts me!*

Tumult exploded in a rage whose fallout killed fifteen of his own men.

Dr. White saw Becky's bulging eyes and then saw the fluid running out of her nose. He grabbed at the gag and the fluid gushed out of her mouth, but it was too late. He turned to Bradley and said, "While I was getting the baby out, I'm afraid she drowned."

Bradley pushed White and the baby aside. He took the knife, cut out Becky's heart and drank the blood.

He then sprayed the audience with the blood from his mouth. He filled the chalices with her blood and cut pieces of her heart into bite-sized morsels, of which each member present would partake.

When this was finished, they gave their bodies and souls over to the demons.

Tumult was pleased with the results of the ceremony, despite the unwanted interruption of the angel. He watched as his demons took possession of the humans and laughed at all the unholy and demeaning things that they made them do. Parents defiled their own children, the humans spread human waste upon themselves, believing it would give them power. They became lower than animals.

True to his promise to promote Bradley to Ipsissimus, Tumult took complete possession of his soul, giving him total power over earthly things but damning him to an eternity of hell.

No one saw Mandy take the baby and slip out of the temple. Nor did they see her climb the ladder to the secret room, push open the door that Anderson had so carelessly left unlatched, remove the video tape, add a new one, and then leave the same way, covering the lock of the door with masking tape to keep the latch from working. She would normally have taken care of the baby until the night when it would then be sacrificed to Satan—so she was covered, in case she was stopped and questioned.

After she had finished dressing, she held the baby close to her and left the warehouse. She'd decided to call the baby Genesis, for he would be her new beginning. She didn't know how yet, but since the temple had robbed her of having children, she planned on keeping this one.

Grady, outside the warehouse, made note of the time that Mandy left. It was eleven-thirty and the night air was cold. He'd run out of coffee an hour ago and really needed some now. He wished he knew just exactly what it was these people were doing in there.

Warren, standing next to Grady said, "No, you wouldn't, Grady."

Tears streamed down Warren's face as he felt the evil oozing from the temple. He felt sorry for all of the poor souls being lost in there. Other than Becky, however, no one sought the help of their Savior, who even in this late hour would come and rescue their souls.

Aaron's voice penetrated Warren's sorrow, "I wish we could just go in there and fight them, but we have our orders."

Warren nodded, "We will pray, Aaron, for the Lord knows what He is doing."

They prayed together, "Most Holy God, our Creator, help these Christians to stand and fight this evil which infects the land. Give them the knowledge that these abominations are taking place and give them the courage to stop it. Fill them with your Spirit, Lord. Amen!"

The stench of the temple's vile acts mingled with the sweet aroma of prayer and rose before the throne of God.

A Voice thundered across heaven, "We will help these brave souls . . ."

Chapter 15
Code Blue

Aaron and Warren watched closely as the last of the lost souls left the warehouse. The humans looked dazed and shaken and maybe, just a little afraid. Connelly and Anderson had left in their limousine immediately after the service was complete. Bradley had just winked out of existence, to who knows where.

As this pathetic exodus from the temple continued, no one spoke or even looked at another coven member—the guilt, shame and fear were just too great for words. The demons had departed the human bodies in the same harsh way that they had entered them, leaving these people feeling empty and alone. The children would suppress the horrible memories that their parents inflicted upon them, but they would never be the same again.

Warren and Aaron watched in disgust as the drunken demons flew all around the warehouse and through the people, mocking and jeering them.

Grady was shocked at the condition of the people that emerged from the warehouse. When they had entered the temple last night, they had been talking, smiling, laughing, and seemed very excited. Now they were morose, some nearly comatose like walking zombies obviously crashing after a drug-induced high.

Grady zipped his jacket up a little further as a chill wind blew dust devils in a high twisting dance around the warehouse. He was tired; he desperately needed to go home and get some sleep. The last of the previous night's participants had exited the warehouse half an hour ago, at the ungodly hour of 5:00 A.M. and Grady rose stiffly to do the same.

Just then a van pulled up and stopped at the warehouse, and Grady hid himself again before he could be seen. He saw Mr. Cromwell get out and go to the back of the van. "Cromwell Crematory" was written on the back door. Mr. Cromwell took a collapsible cart from the back of the van and then, using his own key, entered the warehouse.

A few minutes later he rolled the cart back outside. It held a large, black body bag, which, unfortunately, looked occupied. Cromwell slid the cart and its suspicious contents into the back of the van, closed and locked the door and climbed back into the driver's seat.

As the van pulled away, Grady, his fatigue forgotten, made a bee-line for his own vehicle, and set out to tail the van.

Warren left with Grady. Aaron watched them leave, knowing that Cromwell, like so many times before, would already have the great furnace of the crematory white-hot in preparation of his arrival.

Aaron decided to assume human form and walk among the citizens of Covenant for a while this morning. He appeared as a young man wearing sweats and tennis shoes. Aaron began to jog, and the cool morning air washed over his face. The city was beginning to stir with other joggers, people on bicycles, and early commuters trying to beat the rush hour traffic.

As Aaron approached the city's central park, the first rays of sunlight streaked across the dew-laden grass and flowers, creating prisms of a dazzling color. Aaron was reminded of the brilliance of Jesus' light that could dispel the darkness of evil.

Aaron would normally have taken time to savor the beauty of the morning, but this morning he was just too angry. He was angry at what the enemy had done to the humans last night, and even angrier at what they had planned for this morning.

He was frustrated that his orders prevented him from interfering. He preferred active involvement. He was created for service, to God first and, as the Lord willed, to the human race. This time the Lord had ordered him to stand by while the enemy attacked Covenant and the man he had been assigned to protect.

Aaron sat down on a park bench which faced the rising sun as it peeked out from behind the New Hope Memorial Hospital. He remembered the fierce battle that they had fought and won over this building and now he had left it defenseless. He shuddered at the thought.

The birds filling the trees in the park began to sing their morning songs oblivious to the affairs of man. Aaron decided to enjoy God's gift to him and listened to the chorus. The air was fresh and filled with the fragrance of the flowers waking to the morning's sun.

In the distance, Aaron could hear church bells ringing and, more and more distinctly, the sound of voices raised in song.

Yes, he definitely heard singing! As he watched, the four roads leading into Covenant Square were simultaneously filled with people, marching in small groups of only ten people, as required by the court order, and singing at the top of their lungs!

Slowly, the marchers converged on the hospital and surrounded the large platform which had been built there.

Rev. Smith was the first of ten ministers and priests from the city's various denominations to climb the stairs to the platform. As he stepped up to the microphone, silence washed over the crowd in a wave that moved from the front to the back.

He began to pray, "Jesus, our Lord and Savior, bless our efforts this day. Our friend, Joshua, lies in this hospital, in critical condition, because of the violence of the enemy. Lord, we place Joshua into Your protective arms and ask that You raise him up and bless us again with his presence..." As Rev. Smith and the massive crowd continued in intercessory prayer for Joshua's recovery, Aaron changed back into angelic form and entered Joshua's room.

* * *

Dr. White felt a little better than he had when he'd woke up on the cold concrete platform in the temple this morning, though his stomach was still burning, his mouth was filled with the dry metallic taste of blood, and he needed a shave. He had slipped into the doctor's dressing area unseen and had thrown his soiled clothes away. He took a hot shower, shaved, and brushed his teeth, twice, and then took a strong dose of medicine for his headache.

When he was done making himself presentable, he slipped into the hall and went directly to the medicine storage cabinet. He looked both ways and, not seeing anyone, unlocked the cabinet, and took out the syringe and a vial of penicillin. He filled the syringe and slipped it into his pocket and then proceeded to ICU.

When Chad entered Joshua's ICU room, Nurse Audrey Blake looked up from recording Joshua's morning vital signs and smiled.

"His pulse is a little stronger today, Doctor, but his blood pressure is still too low."

Chad took the chart from Audrey and pretending to be interested said, "Thanks, Audrey."

Indicating the police officer guarding Joshua's door, he said, "Could you be sure that officer gets a cup of coffee, he looks a little sleepy. I'll be here for a few minutes, anyway."

"Of course, Doctor." She stopped and placed her hand on his arm and said, "He'll pull through, you'll see."

Chad answered, "I know he will. He's always been strong."

The nurse had mistaken Chad's pallor and shaking hands for concern, instead of what it really was—fear—fear that he might get caught injecting Joshua with the penicillin that had been so clearly marked on the chart as an allergen.

Nurse Blake had unknowingly made it easier for him. She took the officer by the arm and led him out, shutting the door behind her. Chad took a deep breath, and as he removed the protective cap on the needle of the syringe, he whispered to Joshua, "I hope you enjoy heaven as much as you said you would, because I'm going to help you get there. Then, maybe, I can get my life back." He inserted the needle directly into Joshua's arm and pushed the plunger all the way down. He yanked the needle out and stood there to watch. He watched as Joshua's cardiac reading fluttered. He smiled when Joshua's heart rate became erratic. He snickered when the reading flat-lined.

Aaron wept.

He contacted Beriack to tell him that it was accomplished.

He had watched Dr. White carry out his evil plan and had not been permitted to stop him. He stood by while the evil twins, Jealousy and Envy, mocked him.

"Whatsa matter, you pansy? Lost your nerve? Aren't you afraid we'll turn you into a pin cushion again?"

Aaron had finally had enough. He drew his sword and waved it threateningly at the twins who quickly scrambled behind Chad White's body. Aaron brought himself under control just in time to watch the doctor push the plunger home.

Beriack placed a hand on Chief Wilson's shoulder and gave him a strong suggestion to look in on Joshua.

Wilson was talking to Nurse Blake, who always seemed happy and friendly, when he got an urgent feeling that he should check on Joshua. She had told him that Dr. White was in Joshua's room right now, so he headed that way to see if White could give him an update on Joshua's prognosis.

As he opened the door he saw an animal standing over Joshua's body. Its form seemed to be that of Dr. White but its eyes were full of hate and its features were locked in a snarl. He saw the empty syringe and fear gripped his heart.

Chad turned to face the intruder. When he saw that it was Wilson, he brandished the syringe and charged, yelling, "Nooo!"

Nurse Blake had just poured herself a cup of coffee and sat down at her station to catch up on some paper work. She heard someone yell, "Nooo!" and then the buzzers on her board went crazy.

The noise was from Joshua's heart monitors and life support units. It had started with a flurry of beeps and settled into one steady tone. Nurse Blake slammed her hand down on the Code Blue Warning button and ran for the crash cart.

Chapter 16
Dr. White Is Apprehended

"And ye shall serve the Lord your God, and he shall bless thy bread, and thy water; and I will take sickness away from the midst of thee."

Exodus 23:25 (KJV)

Joshua and Patricia were laying on a rocky ledge of a mountain, rolling around with side-splitting laughter, rather precariously close to the edge of a sheer nine-hundred foot drop. They were holding their sides, tears streaming from their eyes as their happy sounds echoed into the valley below.

Moments before, Joshua had wondered out loud just how long it would take to drop that far. At the time they were sitting with their feet dangling over the edge of the cliff and looking far into the valley.

Patricia said, "Only one way to find out!" and gave Joshua a shove. He had fallen head first into the thin air, and dropped toward the floor of the valley below.

He panicked and screamed, trying desperately to grab for something to hold on to, but there was nothing.

Suddenly Patricia was dropping next to him.

"What's up?"

Joshua looked at her with wide-eyed terror. "Patty! Help!"

"Have you forgotten where you are? We can fly here! Just think about flying."

Then Patty banked to the left and flew away from him.

Joshua yelled, "Oh no, you don't!"

Suddenly Joshua banked right and flew in dizzying circles until he could figure out how to stop turning.

Before long they were chasing each other all over the sky.

Now they were back on their perch, wrestling and tickling, until they finally fell on their backs exhausted.

Patty rolled over on her stomach to look over the ledge. Joshua rested his chin against Patty's right shoulder and looked at the beautiful rainbow colors that stretched out before them in the valley below. He could smell Patty's familiar fragrance; he had really missed smelling her perfume, and feeling her soft skin against his. He took a moment just to look at her profile. He had almost forgotten just how beautiful she really was. The sunlight reflected the golden glints in her shining hair that brushed against his face in the cool breeze. Her blue eyes—well, a man could get lost in eyes like hers—they were full of such peace and love, and wisdom.

He felt very peaceful and full of love himself. He had never felt this wonderful while he was on earth. To finally be here in heaven and to see God's glory everywhere was quite an experience.

His reverie was interrupted when Patty whispered in his ear, "I've been hearing some very disturbing things about you."

He turned toward her with a concerned look on his face.

"What do you mean?"

"Well, it's been eleven years since I died, and during that entire time you haven't so much as dated another woman."

She smiled at Joshua's red face and the nervous little smile he got whenever she hit a nerve. "Look Patty! I just figured I'd never find anyone as good as you, and ... "

She covered his mouth with her hand.

"Don't use those excuses on me, Joshua White! I know you too well. You're a lonely man. You need a woman in your life down there and I expect you to get one!"

"Patty, I just couldn't! I mean, you're my life partner, I ... I ... "

"Sweetheart, I understand. I love you for your faithfulness to me; you are a wonderful man. But you need a companion, something I can't be anymore. It wouldn't mean you love me any less, and it certainly would not lessen my love for you."

"Honey, can we not talk about this right now? It feels a little weird talking to my wife about dating!"

Patty smiled. "Okay. Just so you know that you have my permission." She gave him a swift kiss on the cheek and then a little tug on the ear. "Hey, I'll race you to the ocean!"

Joshua jumped to his feet. "You mean, you'll follow me to the ocean!" and took off running.

* * *

Nurse Blake pressed the hospital intercom. "Code Blue! ICU Stat! I repeat, Code Blue! ICU Stat!"

She grabbed the crash cart and ran into Joshua's room.

She pulled up short. "What in heaven's name?"

Chief Wilson was handcuffing Dr. White to the railing of Joshua's bed. Dr. White's nose and upper lip were swollen and bleeding. There was a spent syringe on the floor at the doctor's feet.

Dr. Turner ran into the room. He yelled, "Vitals, nurse, let's hurry here."

Nurse Blake snapped out of it and went to work.

Wilson told Dr. Turner, "Dr. White here had just given Joshua some kind of shot when I came in."

Dr. Turner asked Chad, "What did you give him, Chad?"

Chad didn't look up.

Wilson grabbed Chad by the coat and shook him, "He asked you a question, Doctor. What did you give him?"

Chad looked up and, in a barely audible voice said, "I gave him a full syringe of penicillin. He's always been allergic to penicillin."

At the moment the Code Blue buzzer stopped and the long, shrill beep of the heart monitor cut through the room. Dr. Turner ripped Joshua's hospital gown away from his chest. Nurse Blake handed him a syringe which had an extra long needle on the end of it. Turner drove the syringe into Joshua's chest and pushed the stopper home. He took the needle out and threw the hypo on the cart. He grabbed the paddles that Nurse Blake had prepared for him and placed them on Joshua's chest.

"Clear!"

He pushed the button. There was a zapping noise and Joshua's body rose from the bed and then flopped back down, as the electric current surged through him.

"Still a straight line, doctor!"

Turner yelled, "Again!"

When the instrument was recharged, Nurse Blake nodded.

"Clear!"

Joshua's body convulsed again.

"Nothing, sir."

"It's just too late. I am afraid he's gone."

Wilson yelled, "It can't be too late! You have to save him!"

He grabbed Dr. Turner's lab coat and shook him.

Dr. Turner gripped the hands holding his coat. "Chief! I can't. He's gone. I'm sorry."

Turner gently loosened the police chief's grip and covered Joshua's face with the sheet. He gave the time of death to the nurse and reached over to turn off the heart monitor. Wilson stopped him.

"Leave it on for awhile and let Dr. White hear what he's done to his brother."

Nurse Blake burst into tears and ran from the room. She bumped into a lady who stopped her and said, "What's the matter, Nurse!"

Without thinking Nurse Blake blurted out, "Dr. White has just killed Joshua!"

Suddenly, realizing what she had just said, she covered her mouth and with a sob, ran for the ladies' room.

Marla Brinkle could not believe her luck. She peeked through the open door and saw Dr. White sitting on the floor, handcuffed to Joshua's bed; saw the body covered by a sheet and heard the incessant beep of the heart monitor. That was enough confirmation for her.

* * *

Cono had lost over a thousand men trying to sever Joshua's lifeline. As soon as a demon touched the lifeline, he was extinguished.

Just for fun, Cono assigned a particularly repulsive imp to the task. He would enjoy watching the little creep fry. He watched as his guards dragged the kicking, screaming little coward toward the lifeline and then yelled to his guards, "Throw the cry baby to his death!"

One guard grabbed the creature's feet and the other grabbed his hands and they swung him back and forth. With each swing, they built up momentum and at just the right moment, let him go.

The demon shrieked as he neared the lifeline. He could feel the searing heat of its power as he passed into it and then, suddenly, it was gone.

Cono jumped up. "What did he do!"

The little demon recovered, drew himself up to his full height and said proudly, "I did what over a thousand of your strongest men couldn't do. I killed Joshua!"

Cono was delighted despite the fact that it had to have been this idiot who had done it.

He could now report to Tumult, that he, Cono, had personally killed Joshua. With that in mind, Cono slit the throat of the strutting little nuisance who was busy bragging about his accomplishment.

* * *

Television programming all over the country was interrupted by a special news update. Marla's attractive face appeared on the screen.

Ellen White had just tuned in to watch a talk show while she washed dishes. She looked up when she heard the announcement and listened as Marla Brinkle began her broadcast.

"This is Marla Brinkle with an update from New Hope Memorial Hospital in Covenant where it has just been discovered that Dr. Chad White, the doctor who so valiantly saved his brother's life, has allegedly taken that same life. I don't know yet how he did it, but reliable medical staff sources have informed this reporter that he did indeed commit the act. I saw Officer Joshua White's dead body with my own eyes.

"This brings to a sad close the career of a fine police officer and close friend to many people here. I will be bringing you the official report as well as local reactions as soon as they are made available.

"This is Marla Brinkle reporting live from New Hope Memorial Hospital."

Ellen dropped the plate she had been drying and rushed to her car.

* * *

Patty took Joshua's hand as they walked along the beach of the most beautiful ocean Joshua had ever seen. Everything here was so clean and bright. The colors were deeper, more vibrant, and there was absolutely nothing to ruin the beauty of it. No sand ants, no crabs, or no snakes, no mosquitoes, no pop and beer cans, or soggy cigarette butts. It was wonderful.

Patty said, "Look, Joshua, the sunset is beautiful."

Joshua smiled as he put his arm around Patty's waist and they watched the sun quickly sink into the ocean.

Suddenly, the ground tilted below his feet and the world that Joshua and Patty had been enjoying all day exploded and evaporated into a flare of searing white light.

* * *

The word had spread quickly through the crowd. People got angry. Most were angry at Dr. White. Some were angry at God. The ones angry at God got interviewed while other reactions were overlooked.

Rev. Smith, who was fighting his own grief, stepped to the microphone and asked for silence. After many tries, it was finally quiet enough for him to speak.

He prayed, "Lord Jesus, You are our Creator and Savior. We are going to miss our brother, but we trust in Your will for his life. We know that Your knowledge is much higher than ours and we will bow to Your wisdom. Please send us the Holy Spirit to comfort us and to lead us into Your will . . . "

As Rev. Smith led the prayer, Marla, having gotten enough footage of the negative reactions, left for the station where she could do some real damage to the Christians' cause.

* * *

Chief Wilson wanted to wring the life out of Dr. White, but he could hear a small voice within him saying, "You must forgive him, Chief, for he is a victim of Satan's lies. Don't kill him, love him."

The chief looked at the pitiful figure of Dr. White, who was sitting on the floor shaking uncontrollably.

Chad was afraid. Afraid of what the law would do. More afraid of what Connelly would do. Maybe even afraid for his soul. He felt empty and alone and he didn't know what had possessed him to do these things.

The twins laughed as they left Dr. White's wretched body behind. They had done their jobs well. Not only had they killed Joshua, but they had sealed Dr. White's fate too. White was no longer needed, so they left him, alone and empty, to face the consequences of his crime alone.

Rev. Smith had come up to Joshua's room after turning the prayer service over to the other ministers, and was now praying over the corpse of Joshua.

Dr. White is Apprehended

He had just begun when the door burst open and Grady ran in pulling Mandy, holding a little baby, along with him. He slammed and locked the door.

When Dr. White looked up and saw Mandy and the baby, he fainted dead away.

Grady, out of breath as much from excitement as from running, launched into an explanation. When he finished, Chief Wilson looked at Mandy and said, "Mandy, I can't condone what you've done, but I will thank you for coming forward with the tape. It's the evidence we've been looking for."

Grady spoke up again, "That's not all, Chief. I stopped Mr. Cromwell this morning and we have Becky's body in custody as well. We have the murder and the murderer on tape and we have the body from the tape. We have Governor Bradley cold. All because Mandy here decided to trust us after all."

The chief ordered a VCR to be brought to Joshua's room so they could view the tape. As they waited, the men prayed, asking Jesus to tell them what to do.

* * *

"Joshua, it is time."

"I don't want to leave You, Lord. I want to stay here forever."

"You will return to Us one day, but for now, you have a job to do."

"I'm afraid."

"Yes, I know. Remember, you serve the one true God—the King of Heaven and Earth. There is no power above Ours."

"I will, Lord. Help me."

"We are with you always."

* * *

Ellen had, for the first time in her life, broken every traffic law in the books on her way to the hospital. She careened into the parking lot, nearly hitting a TV news van.

Without even turning the car off, she jumped out and ran into the hospital.

She burst into Joshua's room just in time to see her own husband take a knife and slice Becky open on the Temple video tape.

Before anyone could reach her, she slumped to the floor.

* * *

No one saw Governor Bradley appear on the platform; everyone had their heads bowed in prayer. He got their attention by shoving Father Powell off the platform right in the middle of his prayer.

The governor stepped up to the microphone and nodded to his men, who fired their automatic weapons just inches above the shocked heads of the crowd.

* * *

It was Grady's face that Ellen saw first as she came around. She sat up slowly and asked, "What's going on? Who was that poor woman?" Ellen pointed to the television, which had been mercifully turned off.

Wilson crouched down next to her. "I'm sorry you had to find out about this the way you did. It's going to take some explaining, but it goes something like this . . . "

Marla Brinkle was already at the news office writing the report she would give when the governor finished his speech. Since everything had already been rehearsed with Governor Bradley, she could accurately report this event before the other network reporters even got to a phone to call it in.

Dr. White is Apprehended

Marla's cameraman called and connected the live link, so that it would appear that Marla was still at the scene.

Governor Bradley, now live on the News Channel, as well as other stations that tapped in on the live network feed, looked at the shocked and angry mob of five thousand people.

"Citizens of Covenant! I have come to offer you one last chance to give up this belief in a God that is obviously so uncaring. Let me tell you how sorry I was to hear about your friend, Joshua White; may he rest in peace. But he filled your heads with this nonsense and now even his own God has ignored your pleas to save him.

"I have come to bring peace between all religions—Christian, Satanist, Muslim, Buddhist, Atheist, Jew—peace to all people, regardless of creed. All you have to do is remove the offending stone tablets in the park and avoid any public mention of the name of Jesus, and we can have peace between us. You no longer have to blow up buildings or kill innocent abortion doctors—just come over to our side."

The crowd protested just as Governor Bradley had predicted. A single gun shot rang out over the uproar of the crowd. A spot of blood appeared on Governor Bradley's chest and he fell to the ground. His bodyguards quickly surrounded him and rushed him into the hospital. Police grabbed the assassin who yelled as he was dragged from the scene, "We Christians will kill anyone who tries to get in our way. You will all believe in God or die!"

Chapter 17

A Miracle for the President

The President of the United States, Roberta Place, sat at her desk in the Oval Office, and watched the television screen in disbelief. She admired this man, Governor Bradley, who had at one time been her friend as well as her lover. He had been so supportive of her when her husband was murdered in a botched robbery attempt shortly after her election. He had worked hard on the Brice Bill, convincing her of its merit.

Now she had just watched him get shot down on national television.

Her reverie was broken when she felt someone rubbing her shoulders. She looked back and saw the familiar face of Dr. Lawrence, her family physician. The doctor had just completed the second full battery of tests on Roberta's son, Patrick. He was nine-years old and had not been feeling well lately, suffering terrible headaches during the day and terrifying nightmares at night, which kept both he and his mother awake.

Dr. Lawrence spoke, "I'm sorry, Roberta, but the results are the same and have been verified. Your son will die within six months from this brain tumor."

* * *

Marla's face appeared on all the televisions as she reported, "Governor Bradley has been rushed to a special wing of the hospital where he can be protected from the radical Christian terrorists. The police and the national guard will soon be called in to control the mob."

She stopped and watched one of her side screens which showed a small group of people coming out of the hospital. She spoke into her phone and told her cameraman, "Zoom in on this. I'll do a voice-over."

Aaron, Warren, Beriack, and Oath had fulfilled all of their duties in this part of God's plan. They now waited to witness the great work that their Creator was about to perform, right in front of millions of television viewers.

* * *

President Place wiped the tears from her eyes and watched her television screen as a small group of people pushed a hospital cart onto the raised platform in front of the hospital. Two police officers, a woman holding a child and two doctors accompanied the cart; one in hand-cuffs, a woman holding his arm as though supporting him. On the cart was a sheet-covered body. One of the officers, the local police chief, stepped up to the microphone and spoke.

"Brothers and sisters in Christ, we must have a prayer service and funeral for our friend, Joshua, right here and now. I don't know how long we have before they'll come to disperse us."

Rev. Smith stepped up to the microphone. "Lord Jesus Christ! We stand before You today a stricken people. Stricken by the assassination of our brother,

Joshua, who did nothing but love people and work for what was right and just in the world. Stricken by the attack by Governor Bradley who would wipe Christianity from the face of the earth.

"Now, we Christians will be blamed for this shooting incident, just as Christians were blamed by Nero for the burning of Rome.

"We are a weary people, Lord, who turn to You as our only hope. We are surrounded by the enemy at every turn and we don't know where to turn. Holy Spirit, comfort us, strengthen us, give us wisdom . . ."

As Marla Brinkle listened to Rev. Smith's prayer, she thought about how much she hated Christians and their foolish talk of a God.

When she was fourteen she had been raped by her uncle. When she told her parents, she had been beaten for lying. When she told her pastor, all he had told her was to pray to God for help and pray for her uncle's salvation. The pastor wouldn't go with her to the police for that was her parent's place. Her parents told the pastor that Marla had a tendency to make up stories, so he dropped the whole matter. Marla's uncle continued to rape her until she was eighteen years old and could move away.

No, she had no love for these Christians or their God.

"Camera One, cut the picture. No one wants to listen to this drivel."

"Whatever you say, Marla."

The picture remained on the air.

"I told you to stop filming, you moron!"

"I did! I don't know why we're still on."

Marla ran from her office and headed back to the hospital.

*   *   *

Governor Bradley was laughing as they carried him into the special wing which he had prearranged. His assassination had been perfectly planned, perfectly timed, and perfectly executed. He had doctors who would pronounce him dead, and then at the right moment, he would miraculously come back to life, and win over thousands of ignorant souls. He would have all the power and the answers that people seek out. He would proclaim Satanism as the new state religion and all other religions would be outlawed as blasphemy. It was a great plan and Marla had carried out her part very well indeed. She would be well rewarded. He smiled and continued his self-congratulations.

* * *

When Marla arrived, she saw the astonished look on the Christian's faces. As she stepped out of her car, she felt the ground shake and heard the deep rumble that was building far below them. She saw the storm clouds rolling in and heard the crashing thunder. Terrible flashes of lightning streaked across the sky. She hated thunderstorms.

Suddenly her fear turned to terror as she saw four angels standing next to Joshua's lifeless body.

President Place jumped to her feet when she saw the angels appear on her screen. As she and the rest of the country watched, these beautiful beings surrounded Joshua's corpse, one at his head and feet and one on either side of his body. They extended their luminous wings over the lifeless form and bolts of searing white light came forth. Lightning flashed in the sky, thunder crashed and rolled, the ground pitched and heaved, and in the midst of this, Joshua White's lifeless body suddenly sat up. The sheet fell from his face and he took a deep, shuddering breath.

A Miracle for the President

And then, Joshua smiled.

Joshua was shocked to find himself outside, on a platform, in front of thousands of people, and then it hit him. He had just interrupted his own funeral. That thought brought a smile to his face.

He swung his feet over the side of the gurney, stood up, and stretched.

He looked over at Grady. "What's the matter, Grady? See a ghost?"

Grady didn't answer; instead he stared, dumbfounded.

"Earth to Grady. Hey, could you get me something to cover this draft I'm feeling in the back of this gown? And could somebody please get me a cup of coffee."

Dr. Turner scrambled out of his lab coat and handed it to Joshua. Joshua put the coat on and thanked the nurse who hurried up to him with a cup of coffee. He took a sip and sighed like he was tasting ambrosia. The fact that he was alive and well finally started to penetrate the shocked stupor that had overwhelmed the watching throng.

As Joshua walked up to the microphone, he was greeted by a thunderous applause.

The President of the United States was also applauding in the privacy of her Oval Office. Tears flowed down her cheeks as she realized the miracle she had just witnessed.

"Oh, my God," she wept, "My God, Look at that! I don't believe it! He's alive! My God, He's alive! You're alive!"

She thought with sadness of her son, Patrick. But her thoughts quickly turned to joy and peace when she realized that when he died, Patrick would live again with the Lord.

"It's all true," she whispered. "I know the truth."

"I know the truth!" she was shouting now. "Lord, I believe Your truth!"

Then suddenly, she heard her name being called. The TV screen! It was this man, Joshua White, from Covenant—he was looking straight at her through the television!

"Roberta, listen to me. The Lord told me to tell you that your son, Patrick, has just been healed of his brain tumor. You are going to have him around for a long time yet.

"He also wanted me to remind you of your great responsibility to the country that you lead. God has given you the leadership of this country because He knows that deep in your heart, a faith in Him is growing and maturing. The United States of America was founded by a Christian people, for Christian people, so that they would have a place to worship their God with no persecution from the government. Now that very government has broken all ties with the Almighty God, Who gave it all of its power in the first place.

"The United States is to stand not only for freedom, but also for Godliness and truth. There are those in the government who have systematically sold their souls to the highest bidder and the result has been a lost generation with no anchor.

"You, President Place, are being asked to get us back on track. You must repent of your sins and turn back to the God that created not only our country, but the entire universe and so much more. With humility, Madam President, seek out the council of the Holy Spirit and allow Him to guide you through your assigned task.

"It won't be easy, for there will be certain enemies who will try to stop you, but you must remain faithful to the task. What I tell you is true, Madam President, just as my being brought back to life is true.

"You must stop this Brice Bill. It will send our country into a civil war, the likes of which has never been seen before. Innocent people will be killed and countless souls will be damned to hell for their lack of faith.

"Now, Madam President, call Dr. Lawrence and run those tests again. Remove all doubt and then use your renewed faith to rebuild this country's moral foundation. Let's run our government according to the Holy Scriptures and the Spirit who wrote it."

When he was finished, Roberta turned off the set and picked up the phone. She heard Dr. Lawrence say, "I heard! The tests have already begun."

Joshua now faced the crowd and said, "Everything I just told the President goes for us as well. We must unite in our cause. We must once again begin to believe in the power of God. He has not changed from what you read in Scriptures. He still has the power to heal the body and the power to save the soul. When we pray, we must know that the God of all creation is listening and carrying out His will through our lives. We must open ourselves to the Holy Spirit and we must believe in the power that He brings into our lives.

"Our faith has been polluted by the enemy. We no longer believe in a God of power.

"We mouth platitudes instead of prayers.

"It's no wonder so many of our youth turn to witchcraft and the occult. Those people believe in their power.

"We are at war, people! The angels you saw earlier are just a few of the legions of angels that work with you everyday. They protect you from harm, they carry your prayers to Jesus, and they carry His answers back to you. They are fearless warriors who stand between the enemy and the faithful.

"I am here to tell you that God is alive! He is mighty! He is just! He is Lord and King over all! But God will only come into your life if you repent of your sins and commit yourself to the saving grace of Jesus Christ, who came and lived, and died, and then rose from the dead for you. It is through his saving grace that you are born into the kingdom of God.

"Pray for peace, for faith, and a renewed belief in the power of the Most High God."

With that said, Joshua stepped back from the microphone, and then collapsed from the exhaustion of his ordeal. He was rushed back to his recently vacated hospital room.

During Joshua's speech, Marla had tried everything in her power to get him off the air, but as her engineer, Stan Boner, tried to tell her, none of the equipment would respond. She yanked all the wires and even covered the camera. Nothing worked. She finally knocked the camera over in an attempt to break it, but still, Joshua's glowing face and passionate words were broadcast across the airwaves.

She had stood there watching Joshua, with hatred seeping from every pore of her body.

Governor Bradley smashed his television set.

"Marla must have talked about my plans. This Joshua beat me at my own game. I don't know how he did it, but he took my death to life idea and got his in first. This ruins everything. Now I have no alternative, but to use force.

"Marla Brinkle, you'll pay for your loose tongue!"

Chapter 18

Convert and Murder

Dr. White sat, handcuffed again to Joshua's bed, exhausted and afraid. He was afraid of what Connelly would do when he found out that Joshua was not only alive, but that he was now a national hero. This wouldn't sit well with Governor Bradley either. These were dangerous men to cross.

Right now, though, he had to figure out how to get out of this mess. He should have had a plan, an alternate strategy in the event that he'd failed. He'd been so intent on getting rid of Joshua, so focused on that one thing, that he hadn't even conceived of failure.

"Let's go, White. You got some explaining to do." Chief Wilson had a firm grip on Chad's left arm, unlocked the cuff from the bed, pulled both of Chad's arms behind his back and re-cuffed him.

"Where are you taking me?"

"We're gonna take a little ride downtown. I thought you'd like to visit what's left of my office. I'm sure you can tell me something about that little gift in my desk, too."

"I don't know what you're talking about."

"Save it, White. We'll have plenty of time to chat at the station."

Wilson commenced reading Dr. White his Miranda rights.

Suddenly Chad felt a hand on his right arm.

"Hold on a minute, Chief."

Chad turned and looked into the tear-filled eyes of his brother.

"Chad, I love you and I forgive you for your part in this whole affair. Please repent from your sins before it is too late. While I was in heaven, Mom and Dad wanted me to ask you for your forgiveness toward them. They remember how they unintentionally put all that pressure on you by comparing us all the time. They said that pressure is what led to all this hatred and envy.

"Chad, in the name of Jesus Christ, let all the anger go. Let the hatred go. Cast off the demons that have been tormenting you for years."

"I don't want to hear your mealy-mouthed babble, Joshua. Man, you must really think I'm a push-over. I certainly don't believe that you went to heaven and talked to Mom and Dad. And you know what else? I don't need or want your stinking forgiveness!

"Ellen was shocked at Chad's vehemence. "Chad! How dare you!"

Joshua spoke up. "That's okay, Ellen. I can handle it. You don't really mean any of that, Chad. Deep down, inside your heart, you need forgiveness, you need acceptance, you need love, and most of all, brother, you need Jesus Christ."

"Don't say that name!"

"I will say that name, Chad. I will say the name of Jesus over and over again as I bring you before the throne of God every morning, noon, and night in my prayers, for as long as it takes to break Satan's hold on you."

"Stop it!"

"Jesus' name and His blood are more powerful than the chains that bind you. Right now, I plead the blood of Jesus over you, Chad, and command the forces of hell to loose their hold on you! Speak the name of Jesus, Chad, call upon His name."

"I can't!"

"You can, Chad! In the name of Jesus, you can speak that name."

"Stop, Joshua. You're hurting me!"

"Not you, Chad, I would never hurt you. But I will fight—with the last ounce of strength within me—I will fight and defeat the demons that enslave you. In the name of Jesus, by the power of His shed blood, speak His name, Chad. Cry out to the only One who can save you."

Jealousy and Envy had been ordered back to their post to prevent Chad from spilling his guts about the temple and Governor Bradley's plans.

Now they shrieked in pain as the name of Jesus washed over them, piercing their ears like shards of broken glass. Desperately, they tried to dig their poison talons deeper into Chad's brain, but the merciless pummeling of that wretched name was tearing at their thick, knotted skin and burning their yellow, bulbous eyes.

With agonizing screams, the twins pulled their talons out of Chad's brain and groped at their streaming eyes and ears. As soon as the tortured twin demons had loosened their hold, Aaron swung his flaming sword, and severed their grotesque heads from their squat little bodies.

Suddenly, Chad doubled over and with painful heaves, vomited violently. Wilson tried his best to hold him, but since Chad's hands were cuffed behind his back, he was practically dead weight. Wilson lowered Chad to his knees.

Joshua crawled out of his hospital bed and kneeled next to his brother, oblivious to the bile that trailed down the front of Chad's shirt onto the floor. He bowed his head and prayed for his brother. Ellen fell to her knees beside her husband and wept.

Chad spoke in a ragged whisper.

"What have I done? My God! What made me do such an awful thing?"

"It was the demons that controlled you, Chad, that made you do these things."

"But I've murdered innocent people—babies, women—Joshua, I tried to kill you!"

"Yes, Chad, you did all of those things. But Jesus gave His life so that you could be forgiven for these sins, and anything else you have done against the kingdom of God."

"It's not possible, Joshua. If you only knew all the horrible, evil things I've done. God could never forgive me, or love me."

"It is possible, Chad. The Bible says that 'neither death, nor life, nor angels, nor principalities, nor powers, nor things present, nor things to come, nor height, nor depth, not any other creature, shall be able to separate us from the love of God, which is in Christ Jesus our Lord.' Did you hear me, Chad? Nothing at all can separate you from the love of God!"

"If I could just believe that."

"You can believe it. It's true. God cannot lie. Satan has lied to you and deceived you for years. Satan can't tell the truth. He is the father of lies. But Jesus is the Way, the Truth, and the Life, and He is the only way to the Father God."

"Help me, Joshua. I know I don't deserve your help . . . or your forgiveness, but I need both. Please Joshua, I'm begging you, help me."

"I will."

The brothers who had never done anything together in their entire life, together with Ellen and Chief Wilson, bowed their heads and prayed.

Aaron hovered over the kneeling brothers and lifted their prayers of repentance, dedication and praise before the throne of God. In the spirit realm, Aaron could hear the choirs of heaven rejoicing in song as the sweet fragrance of a penitent sinner filled the air.

With a flash of light, another angel joined Aaron, and after saluting his lieutenant, took his position next to Chad.

"Welcome, Liberty."

"Thank you, sir. It has been a long time coming. It's good to finally be here."

"Sadly, it will only be for a short time."

"Yes sir, I know."

Asst. Chief Anderson shoved his way between the small crowd surrounding Joshua and Chad. He had a vacant, almost hollow, look in his eyes.

When he saw Mandy he yelled, "I want my tape back, Mandy."

Mandy stepped forward and spat out, "I already gave them to the chief and you're going down for all your evil acts."

Anderson raised his gun and shot Mandy in the chest at point blank range, and then turned and fired twice at Joshua.

Aaron drew his sword and easily deflected the bullet aimed at Mandy. He brought the sword down and around in a wide arc to protect Joshua from the two bullets that were speeding toward him, but suddenly,

Chad jumped up, and threw himself in front of his brother, wrapping his arms tightly around him.

The bullets ripped into Chad's exposed back and drove deep into his heart. He was dead before anyone even realized what he had done.

Liberty's assignment had indeed been a short one, and he now bent down and lifted Chad's soul out of his dead body and flew off with him to heaven.

Ellen's screams echoed off the hospital walls.

Chief Wilson fired three shots into Anderson's chest. The force of the bullets knocked Anderson on his back and he dropped his weapon. Wilson and Grady quickly restrained and handcuffed him.

Anderson's bullet-proof vest had saved his life, but it didn't stop the bullets from shattering four of his ribs.

Joshua's breath had been knocked out of him from the impact of the bullets striking his brother's body, but Joshua didn't notice it. He was watching the sky as Liberty carried his brother to the waiting arms of Jesus.

Anderson felt like a caged animal and the pain in his ribs and head was unbearable. To his horror, he saw the most hideous creature that he could have ever imagined coming out of his own chest.

The demon, Lt Poe in his true form, screeched at Anderson, "You fool! You are of no use to us at all anymore. I should leave you to rot in some jail cell while I take the pleasure of tormenting you for the rest of your miserable, useless life. However, I'm not about to lose my investment in you."

Lt. Poe plunged his talons deep into Anderson's black heart and with wicked enjoyment, tore it apart.

Anderson screamed in pain, his body convulsing as his heart exploded within his chest.

Poe grabbed the anguished soul of his victim, and drug it deep into the abyss.

As emergency room doctors rushed Anderson toward a trauma room, Joshua lovingly cradled his brother's body in his arms and spoke quietly to those who remained in his room.

"It is very important that you all believe what I've been telling you. We are in a spiritual war and your souls are the battleground. We are not fighting against flesh and blood, but against the evil one and his minions. Satan is bringing this battle to a deadly finish and I'm afraid that you may begin to see things that you would rather not see."

He bowed his head and silently prayed for strength.

Chapter 19
A Defector's Help

After submitting to an examination by various specialists, Joshua was released and met Wilson, Grady and Mandy in the hospital coffee shop.

"Jesus told me that Theodore Connelly is possessed by a demon named Cono. Connelly not only sells drugs but is the highest ranking warlock around, second only to Governor Bradley. Bradley is possessed too, by a demon named Tumult. Tumult has given Bradley power over the years until he'll now do anything the demon tells him to. We'll have to proceed with caution and prayer, but we must move quickly.

"Mandy, I'm glad you're with us. The Lord has a task for you. He wants you to take Genesis and go back to the temple tonight as planned. Governor Bradley will be anxious to sacrifice him, because he needs to save face with his people and he believes the sacrifice will give him the spiritual power he needs to defeat us."

Mandy held Genesis tight and shook her head vigorously. Joshua understood her hesitation, but he explained, "Only you can pull this off, Mandy. We need another film of tonight's meeting. Be assured, we won't let anything happen to him, or you."

Joshua motioned them all closer and whispered in a conspiratorial tone, "Here is what you must do, Mandy..."

When Mandy left to prepare herself for the night's work, Joshua turned to Grady.

"Grady, do you know Marla Brinkle?"

Grady said with disgust, "Yeah, I know her, but I wish I didn't. She's done more harm than Bradley!"

Joshua waved him to silence. "We don't have time, Grady! I need to speak to her before it's too late. If you don't find her quickly, it will mean that Bradley already has her. Find her Grady."

Grady left in search of the reporter.

Joshua continued talking with the chief.

"Look, Chief, I don't mean to be bossy here, but we need people we can trust on this raid tonight. Pick our best men and bring them to me later this afternoon. Don't tell them what it's about—demons have ears, too."

*   *   *

Marla Brinkle was very confused by the events that had just taken place. Governor Bradley had assured her that this Joshua person was a fake, just like all the other Christians she had ever met. Bradley had told her that there was no real power in Christianity, only old rituals and superstitions.

She was walking toward her car when she heard her name being called. She turned to see a police officer waving his arms and calling her name. She stopped to wait for him.

Suddenly Governor Bradley appeared behind her.

"We must talk, Marla. I need to know just what you told the enemy this afternoon. Joshua took my trick and made himself a hero. You'll have to pay for your blunder."

As Marla screamed, both she and Governor Bradley disappeared, leaving a shocked and angry Grady behind.

A Defector's Help

Marla was very dizzy after her transportation to the Connelly mansion. They had appeared in Connelly's den. Connelly looked up as if he had been expecting them.

Bradley turned Marla around and gently caressed her cheek and then slapped her hard in the face, knocking her to the floor. He stood over her glaring and then without a word, he took out a syringe, uncovered the needle, and then jabbed it into Marla's arm. She pulled back as if she had been shot and rubbed her sore arm.

As the world began to turn fuzzy and distorted she heard Bradley's last words to her with dread, "Tonight, my love, tonight, I will take you places and do things that you have never dreamed of. Then, I will sacrifice you to my lord Satan along with the boy child. My power will be limitless and I will then be ready to do battle against these pests that call themselves Christians."

Darkness engulfed Marla and she felt herself becoming once again the abused little girl hiding in the back of her dark closet, trying to stay out of the reach of her uncle's unwanted attention. Connelly bent down and ran his hand through Marla's hair, but Bradley grabbed his hand and said, "There's no time for that. We must go and prepare for the service tonight. I also have a few phone calls to make to a certain General."

Blade had been assigned to Marla Brinkle when she was a child, and now he was dispatched on a job that brought him great pleasure. After years of crippling hate and pain, Marla Brinkle was soon to be reborn in the Spirit.

He disappeared into the shadows just as Cono and Tumult entered the room.

Tumult stopped and sniffed the air, "I swear I can smell a stinkin' angel in here."

Cono also sniffed, but he could detect nothing.

"No angel is going to get through my sentries!"

"Have them double their efforts, anyway. I don't want anything to happen to this soul," Tumult ordered.

Each demon drooled over the still form of Marla Brinkle and dreamed of the moment when they could devour her precious soul.

* * *

Mandy sat in her car and watched Genesis sleeping peacefully on the seat beside her. She dried her tears, took a deep breath, and tried to get her courage up.

"Mandy Miller, you have to pull this off for Genesis' sake, if for no one else."

Genesis stirred and she lost herself in his peaceful, innocent face.

She had done exactly as Joshua had told her to do. She had parked two blocks away from the warehouse. Now it was time to meet the people Joshua had described to her.

She got out of the car and then bent over to take Genesis out. He was wrapped in a pretty blue blanket, which she pulled snugly around him against the cool evening breeze blowing around the buildings.

Just then, three men approached her. They were very tall and powerfully built. All three wore blue jeans, white T-shirts, and black slip-on canvas shoes.

The man in the middle had a look of authority about him, and it was he that spoke to Mandy first.

"Mandy, my name is Capt. Worl, and this," he pointed to the man on his left, "is Lt Devok, he'll be protecting Genesis. And this is Side, he'll be covering you. Now, as Joshua explained to you, we'll be just out of sight, but close enough to know what's going on at all times. I know that this is a real test of faith for you,

A Defector's Help

but you must trust me. Everything is riding on you tonight. You must play your part perfectly, so as not to bring suspicion upon you, and in turn upon us."

Capt. Worl put his hand on Mandy's shoulder and looked deep into her eyes and said, "Are you ready? Can you pull it off?"

Mandy was nervous for herself, and terrified for Genesis, but she answered, "Yes, Captain. I want to help end the wickedness done by these people and make this city safe for Genesis."

Capt. Worl smiled reassuringly. "Good girl. Let's do it, then."

Mandy turned and looked in the direction of the warehouse. She turned back to make another comment to Capt. Worl, but he and the other two men had apparently already gone to their posts without her notice.

She hugged Genesis close to her heart as she began to walk toward the warehouse. Remarkably, her nervousness and fear lifted and she felt a sudden surge of confidence and courage that had not been there just moments before. She really felt, for the first time since she said she would do this, that she could actually pull it off.

Just to be sure, she began to pray.

As she turned the corner, Mandy saw a group of people already gathering to get into the temple. She looked at her watch as she picked up her pace.

It was now 7:30; she was right on time, which meant that these people were a lot earlier than usual. This angered Mandy—it meant that these people were eager to see the day-old baby's murder. She quickly hid her feelings behind a mask of indifference.

As Mandy entered the crowd, she said, "Good evening, everyone. If you'll let me get to the door, I'll let you in and we can go right to the chapel."

The people parted for her and they all exchanged smiles. Once inside, everyone began to crowd around Mandy as she uncovered Genesis. They all wanted to hold the child who would bring them favor with their lord, so Genesis was passed around from one to another. It was all Mandy could do not to scream at them to give him back, but she kept quiet, smiling indulgently.

Mrs. Fulton, a very high ranking person in the coven, handed Genesis back to Mandy and asked, "You didn't get too attached to him, did you, dear?"

Mandy felt a sudden knot in her stomach as she looked into those suspicious eyes, and it took her a moment to answer.

"Oh, I'm sorry Alice, I didn't know what you meant for a moment. Of course, I didn't. I did make sure Gen . . . uh . . . . the child was well taken care of though."

Alice Fulton, didn't seem to notice Mandy's slip about the child's name. Mandy made a mental note not to make that mistake again.

She smiled at Mrs. Fulton and then said to the other people milling about, "Shall we enter the temple? Then, please, go to the main chapel and prepare yourselves for this evening's events." Mandy and Genesis led the others into the temple and they crossed over the point of no return.

Chief Wilson took the police officers who had been hand-picked by Joshua and deployed them at strategic locations around the warehouse that housed the sinister temple. The officers wore night-raid dress—a black jump suit, dull black boots, and black ball caps. They had also painted their faces black. They were armed with assault rifles, and 9mm service semi-automatic Berettas. He glanced at his watch; it was 7:00. *All we have to do now is wait.*

Wilson's thoughts were interrupted by the first arrivals outside of the warehouse. From his hiding place, he could still easily identify each person, and was shocked when the first person to arrive was Rev. Perkins, the pastor of a church in Covenant. Next to arrive was the local pharmacist, Gunther Barker. Wilson had gone to school with Barker and still lived on the same street. *There goes the neighborhood*, he thought, and also made a mental note to dump his blood pressure prescription down the toilet.

By the time Mandy arrived, the chief was pretty ticked off at the citizens of Covenant. People that he would never have dreamed were involved in the occult were piling out of the steady stream of cars, like a clown-act from hell. There were also many others that he didn't recognize, *probably out of town visitors*.

As he watched Mandy take the people into the warehouse, he prayed for the success of the mission. *Please, God, protect Mandy and the child from harm.*

He always got nervous when he had undercover operatives working on a case. This was the first time he had used a one-day-old civilian, and, God-willing, the last time too.

At exactly 8:00, Connelly's limousine pulled up and deposited Connelly and Bradley at the front door of the warehouse. Wilson looked over at his man, Robins, and was satisfied to see that he was getting pictures of everyone that arrived.

His blood ran cold when he saw the motionless form of Marla Brinkle being carried into the building.

It was all he could do not to rush them right then and there. He pacified himself by rechecking the warrants he had in his pocket—one was an arrest warrant for Connelly and the other a search warrant for the entire warehouse complex and its contents. He was still waiting for the FBI agent who was bringing the Federal warrant for the governor's arrest.

The FBI had been very interested in the copy of the tape that Wilson had sent to them. He had been a little nervous about bringing them in; he had no idea who was with Bradley and who wasn't. Joshua had called one of his friends in the FBI and after talking with him at length, he'd felt assured that this guy could be trusted. *I guess we'll soon find out.*

Grady watched from the secret room as the coven members gathered. He couldn't help blushing as he watched their naked forms. He was especially embarrassed when he saw Mandy enter, lay Genesis down gently, and proceed to disrobe also.

He turned away and checked to make sure that the new tape was in the video recorder and running, looking up just as Connelly and Bradley entered the temple. Suddenly, he was filled with rage as he saw the still form of Marla Brinkle being placed on the altar.

Connelly looked down and smiled as Marla, who was tied, spread-eagle, on the altar, started to come around.

"Marla, dear, so happy you could join us."

Tumult had seen the police officers surrounding the building and he laughed at their efforts. *My army will have no problem dealing with these bozos.*

Marla woke up with a splitting headache. *Bradley must have drugged me.* She tried to rub her throbbing brow, but found that she was bound hand and foot. When she opened her eyes, her anger instantly turned to horror.

"Are we comfy, Marla?"

"What's going on? Why am I tied up? Where's my clothes?"

A Defector's Help

"Questions, questions! Always the reporter, right Marla?"

"What are you going to do to me?"

"All in due time. You'll see, we won't keep you in the dark for long. Trust me, you'll have a front row seat!"

Connelly laughed hideously at his little joke.

Bradley had been watching Connelly and Marla from his chair behind the altar. Now he stepped up to her and spoke charmingly as ever.

"Did you have a nice nap, my dear?"

Marla shot back, "No! I did not! You can't do this, untie me, you deviant!"

Bradley held a chalice in one hand and a paintbrush in the other. He now dipped the brush into the chalice and said, "But Marla, you are a very lucky girl. Tonight, you get to be our holy altar, upon which we plan to offer up the boy child to our lord of darkness."

As he spoke, he had begun to paint strange symbols on her body, with what appeared to be blood. She felt the cold sticky substance and the prickly feeling of the brush and she fought off the urge to vomit. She closed her eyes again to avoid having to watch what Bradley was doing.

Bradley took wicked pleasure in describing his actions in full detail.

"I am using the sacred blood of last night's sacrifice to paint these holy symbols . . . "

Marla felt the sour bile rising in her throat and before she could stop herself, she vomited on herself and Bradley.

Bradley laughed, " Are you all right? Yes, I see that you're getting some color back now. Bradley quickly gagged Marla and then continued to explain what was going to happen to her as though he was describing how to plant a tree.

"Connelly is the celebrant tonight, so he will get to sacrifice the little one on your stomach. Then after he copulates with you, he will cut your heart out and bless the assembly with your blood. If only you hadn't informed the enemy of my wonderful plan. I had such hopes for you. Oh well, the best laid plans and all that."

Marla shook her head violently. Her mind screamed, *No, I didn't say anything, it wasn't me. I didn't know about all this.* She was terrified; Bradley was completely mad. She closed her eyes and tried desperately to remember how to pray.

Mandy held Genesis closer to her bare chest. She was hoping against hope that Bradley and Connelly would both fall over dead from a heart attack. Instead, Bradley gave her the signal that meant to bring on the sacrifice.

Bradley turned to Connelly and said for all to hear, "Theodore Connelly, I turn this sacrifice over to your trained care. What you do here tonight will make us the most powerful warlocks in the United States. Nothing and no one will stand in our way."

Grady had watched the horror unfold from his hiding place with tears of frustration and anger running down his cheeks. True to his assignment as mapped out by Joshua, he had remained at his post, taping the whole sordid scene.

As the video camera continued to run, Mandy handed Genesis over to Connelly. This was Grady's signal to let Chief Wilson and the others into the building.

Grady climbed down the ladder and carefully made his way to the front of the warehouse.

Wilson signaled for his men to follow him, as Grady led them into the building. They crept quietly up to the hidden temple door.

Grady punched in the code that Mandy had given him, but didn't hit the engage button. Instead he waited with his finger on the button until he would hear the faint beep in his ear phone.

Marla's eyes widened in disbelief as Mandy brought a tiny baby boy up to the altar and laid it on Marla's stomach. He felt warm on her skin. The baby let out a short cry, his arms and legs flailing in protest at being unwrapped and laid thus, but he soon found his thumb and started sucking fiercely on it.

Marla watched as Connelly walked up to the foot of the altar, disrobed, and began to pray.

"Father of darkness, we are gathered to complete our offering to you. We give ourselves without reservation to you, my lord. Accept the humble offering of this child born in sin, and this faithless woman that we have stolen from the other side. Give to us, your faithful servants, the full power we deserve. We will use this power to further your cause, oh lord. I now offer to you, Satan, Prince of Darkness, the ultimate gift of two human souls."

As Connelly spoke, he picked up the ceremonial knife and placed it against the throat of the innocent child.

Marla tried to scream, but her attempt only allowed the gag to work its way further into her throat. Tears ran down her face as she watched in helpless horror.

Mandy's heart skipped a beat as she reached for the small radio that she had hidden in the basket that held her clothes. To her dismay she couldn't find the radio and thoughts of betrayal crept into her brain. She was very close to full-blown panic when her hand finally brushed against the radio. She pushed what she prayed was the right button.

Grady and Wilson were beginning to get worried. It was already 8:50. They thought they would have been called in by now.

Grady was about to return to the secret room to take a peek when he heard the long-awaited beep. He pushed the engage button and the door unlocked. Grady pushed on the door as hard as he could and he and the others rushed in.

"Freeze! What the..."

The scene that met them was so unbelievably horrifying it couldn't be real. Grotesque creatures, unspeakably hideous, were poised like gargoyles all around the room, in every corner, on every shoulder.

Grady whispered to no one in particular, "I don't think we're in Kansas anymore, Toto!"

Suddenly, the terrifying apparitions started shrieking and hissing and flying about the room as an army of massive and beautiful beings entered the room, flooding it with light.

Marla was struggling, trying to knock the baby off of her stomach in an attempt to save his life. She stopped when she saw that the knife had cut the baby's skin. He began to cry.

Suddenly when she thought that she was as terrified as she could get, she saw a noxious yellow vapor coming out of Connelly's mouth. The vapor took form—it had red eyes and a mouth full of sharp teeth that were set in rotting black gums. The look this creature gave her made her skin crawl.

The demon raised his long arms above his head and cried, "Spawn of Satan, arise and do battle."

When he said this the assembled crowd began to convulse with pain and screamed as one hideous demon after another oozed from the faithful followers.

Suddenly, a streak of light flashed like lightning and Marla watched in amazement as the grotesque creature above Connelly was gone in a billowing cloud of red smoke, leaving behind its noxious odor. The lightning flash took on the form of the most glorious man she had ever seen. Armed with a flaming sword, he whirled about, and ran Connelly through as he lunged for Marla and the child.

Mandy came running over and frantically began untying Marla.

Bradley watched in disbelief as his magnificent plans were being torn from his grasp. He jumped up and grabbed the ceremonial knife, from where it had fallen on the floor next to Connelly's body. He ran over to where Mandy was still trying to untie Marla. He pushed her out of the way and raised the knife over his head.

"I'll see you in hell for this, Marla!"

Grady aimed his 9mm Beretta right at Bradley's chest and fired. Bradley threw himself behind the altar. As he hit the floor, a monstrous demon rose out of him and drew a curved, blood-red sword.

Capt. Worl, Lt. Devok and Blade attacked Tumult in unison. Tumult blocked, then parried, then attacked with all his might. Worl countered with a double backhand swing and cut off the end of Tumult's nose.

Tumult screamed so fiercely that everyone in the room stopped and looked at him—demons, angels, and humans alike.

He held his bleeding nose with one hand and grabbing Bradley by the scruff of the neck with the other, yelled, "Retreat! We'll get them tomorrow!"

He then vanished, taking Bradley with him. Like a massive cloud of locusts, the demons made their retreat, leaving their human hosts to whatever fate might await them.

Chapter 20
Witch or Christian

As Mandy fell, she had pulled Genesis close to her chest, which acted as a cushion and saved Genesis from what would have been a fatal fall. Falling on her back with the added weight of Genesis' body on her chest had knocked the air out of Mandy as well as giving her a large painful knot on the back of her head.

She was dazed for a moment but when her vision cleared, she saw the large, ugly demon grab Bradley and disappear. With great effort, Mandy struggled to get up while still holding Genesis close to her. She staggered over to the altar and untied Marla Brinkle.

"Get dressed, quickly," Mandy said, pointing to where Marla's clothing still laid in a pile on the floor.

Marla, moving as if she were sleepwalking, offered no resistance as Mandy led her into the small bathroom just to the right of the altar.

"You okay?"

Marla only nodded.

Mandy closed the door and left to retrieve her own clothing.

Marla dropped her clothes on the floor, dropped to her knees by the toilet bowl, and retched miserably until her stomach and throat burned. Trying desperately to control the dry, rasping heaves that followed the vomiting, she pulled herself to her feet and rinsed her face and mouth with cold water.

She began to pray to the God that she had so long ago deserted, but was interrupted by a knock at the door. It was Grady.

Marla hurriedly pulled on her clothes. She opened the door and when she saw the attractive, young police officer, she instinctively started to fix her hair.

"Officer O'Leary! Excuse me, I look terrible."

"Never mind that, are you okay?"

"I'm still alive, but I really don't understand what just happened in there. I think they drugged me. You won't believe what I thought I saw in there."

"No, you weren't drugged, except maybe when they first brought you here. I saw the demons also, and they are for real. Joshua knew that you'd have questions and he asked if you'd come and see him. Are you up to it?"

Marla blushed, "I don't know if I can face him. He tried to warn me, but I threw him out of my office. That almost got me killed. He must think I'm such a fool."

Grady gently took her arm and led her toward the door.

"I think you'll find Joshua a very forgiving person. He understands human weakness better than anyone I know. He needs you, Marla; he needs your voice, and I think you'll now agree that there is something to warn people about."

Marla nodded and allowed Grady to lead her outside.

In the temple's torchlight, the occultists had looked fearless and evil. Now, however, Wilson noticed that they looked like frightened and embarrassed children.

He surprised himself by feeling compassion for them. Their misguided souls and lives were suddenly left empty, with no direction at all. As the lights in the warehouse were turned on, the occultists were startled out of their stupor. Realizing their nakedness, some tried in vain to cover themselves, others frantically searched through the scattered baskets for their clothing.

Wilson knew from his years of experience dealing with criminals, that these people would be in for a hard night. They would sit in their jail cell and all the horror and shame of what they had done would come crashing in on them. Surely, some of them would think that they had gone insane.

Any punishment the laws of the land would mete out would not erase their horrifying act from their tortured hearts and minds. They would need God's help to ultimately overcome their shame and guilt. Wilson decided he would arrange for the area ministers to meet with each one of these deceived servants of Satan.

Joshua had spent the evening on his knees praying for Wilson, Grady, and Mandy and everyone else involved in the raid on the Temple. As he lifted his voice in prayer he felt a dark and smothering presence filling the bedroom where he knelt. When he opened his eyes he saw an angel of the Lord wrestling with a huge and hideous apparition that could only be a demon from the abyss.

Tumult had Aaron bent backward over the dresser that was next to Joshua's bed. His massive claws were around Aaron's throat. He dug his claws deep into the angel's throat as he tightened his furious grip.

"You spineless servant of this worthless man, I'll tear you apart and feed you to the damned."

Prompted by the Holy Spirit, Joshua spoke boldly to the suffocating presence.

"In the name of Jesus Christ, I bind you demon of Satan, and command you to cease your attack.

"Lord God, strengthen Your holy angels with the power of the blood of Jesus Christ."

Tumult suddenly let Aaron go, and Aaron fell to the floor. Tumult flew straight for Joshua, drawing his sword with a raging scream.

"I'll rip you to shreds, Christian!"

Joshua spoke again as he felt the darkness start to engulf him.

"I plead the blood of Jesus Christ over this room, over each window and doorpost, over the roof and foundation. In the name of Jesus, demon of hell, I render you powerless to do harm here. I am covered by the blood of Jesus!"

Tumult stopped just inches from Joshua's face and fell on the floor writhing and shrieking in pain. Aaron drew his flaming sword and struck a mighty blow to Tumult's chest.

"Be gone, Tumult. The name of Jesus has made you powerless here."

Tumult rose, spewing vicious curses at Aaron and Joshua.

"I have Bradley, you, and your puny little Christian. You have not seen the last of me or my master."

He left the room in a stinking billow of red smoke.

Grady glanced at Marla as he drove her to Joshua's house. She looked over at him and smiled timidly.

"I've had better days, Officer."

"Hey, call me Grady."

"Okay, Grady. That's a nice name. Irish, right."

"What was your first clue?"

"Well, maybe the red hair."

Grady blushed furiously, thankful for the darkness that hid it.

"My dad has red hair, too. I guess it's a family curse."

"Oh no! That's not what I meant! I like it, really I do."

"Yeah?"

"Sure. Sometimes when I say things, they don't come out like I meant them to."

"Me, too. Most of the time, probably."

"Were you scared tonight too, Grady?"

"Scared? Man, was I ever! I've never seen anything like that—the sacrifice and the people with that look of bloodlust in their eyes."

"You said you saw the demon too, right? You weren't just saying that so I wouldn't think I was going crazy?"

"I saw it all right!"

"Did it scare you?"

"At first, yeah it did. But then, well, y'know, I know that God is more powerful than any demon. He's more powerful than Satan himself! And since I'm a Christian, I knew that God would protect me and that He has given us the ability to battle demons like that one."

"You really believe all that?"

"Yeah, I really believe it. You don't?"

"I don't know what to believe. I thought God didn't exist. Of course, I didn't believe in the devil or demons either. Now . . ."

"Kinda shatters all your walls, doesn't it?"

"What do you mean, walls?"

"Y'know. Those thick walls you build around your heart and mind that keep you from seeing things the way they really are. You start looking at everything logically, like nothing that can't be explained is ever real."

"I'm a reporter. I am paid to deal in facts."

"Is that what you've been doing, dealing in facts?"

Marla hesitated, then looked away.

"Listen, Marla. I don't know why you said what you did on TV. That's between you and God, not you and me. But you need to look at things with new eyes now.

You need God to open your eyes. The only way He can do that is if you open your heart to Him."

Marla turned back to Grady, tears glistening in her eyes.

"Well, we're here. C'mon Marla, let's go see Joshua. I know he'll be glad to help you see clearly. We both will."

"Thank you, Grady."

Taking her hand, Grady helped Marla out of the car, silently praying for God's guidance where she was concerned.

Joshua answered Grady's knock on his door with a smile and a rough bear hug.

"Whoa Josh, you're crushing me!"

Grady laughed good-naturedly, giving Joshua a light punch in the arm.

"Praise God that you're both okay!" Joshua smiled warmly at Marla.

"Thank you, Officer White. That's very kind of you . . . considering . . . "

"Hey, none of that. I believe God has brought you here right now to help us, and I'm thankful He kept you safe so you can fulfill the plan He has for your life."

"You think God pays any attention to what I do?"

"Jesus said that the Father knows whenever a sparrow falls and knows the number of hairs on your head!"

"After what happened tonight, there's probably a few more gray hairs for Him to count!" Marla said with a wry smile.

Joshua chuckled, "I'm sure we'll all have a few more gray hairs by the time this battle is won."

"What do you need from me?"

"Then you'll help us?"

"I think that I'm safer being on your side than being one of the bad guys."

"You're always safer being on the Lord's side, Marla."

Joshua and Marla spent the next few minutes discussing her part in his plan.

Meanwhile, Wilson and the other officers had been busy booking the forlorn and abandoned occultists for complicity and corruption of minors since some parents had involved their children in the occult ceremony.

Joshua arrived as the last of the offenders was read his rights and placed under arrest.

He looked with sadness and compassion at the frightened prisoners who were sitting on the floor shackled to the railing along the wall. With tear-filled eyes, he began to speak.

"My friends!" Again a little louder, "My friends, please look at me and listen, for I have good news for you."

He not only got their attention, but also that of Chief Wilson and the other officers, who couldn't wait to find out how to get good news out of all this.

Joshua continued, "My friends, you are now free from the evil influences and slavery of the demons that have controlled your thoughts and actions for so long. Now is the time to repent and to turn to the Lord Jesus Christ. He will forgive you, all of you, no matter what you have done. Jesus died on the Cross, making Himself a sacrifice, pleasing to God, for the reparation of our sins. His sacrifice of love is the only sacrifice that can change your life, change your heart, and free you from the chains that enslave you to the evil one.

"Satan fills your heart and minds with hate, anger, lust, greed, murder, and every other dark and deadly emotion and thought. Jesus came to give you abundant life—a life overflowing with His peace and His love. He will give you a peace that surpasses your natural understanding and a love that is greater than any earthly love you have ever felt.

"All you need to do right now is repent of your sins and confess that Jesus is Lord and He will forgive you and fill you with this peace. Do you want that?"

Joshua waited expectantly for their replies. Some of the shackled prisoners had started weeping while Joshua spoke, a few had stared at the floor or turned their heads as though they weren't listening. Joshua bowed his head and quietly prayed for the Holy Spirit to speak to the hardened hearts of the prisoners.

Soon, even those who had seemingly turned away from Joshua's impassioned words began to weep. The penitent pleas of the occultists brought tears to the eyes of Wilson and the other officers. Some of the prisoners fell to their faces under the force of the convicting power of the Holy Spirit, sobbing contrite words and pleas for mercy from God.

Joshua's prayers continued fervently as he watched the moving of the Spirit. Prompted by the Lord, He raised his voice.

"Please repeat this after me. I reject Satan and all of his evil deeds. I reject his darkness and I embrace the light of Christ. I confess that Jesus is Lord of my life. I ask you, Jesus, to forgive me for all of my sins. Cleanse me from all unrighteousness. Fill me with Your Holy Spirit." As the voices of more than two hundred prisoners, and even the police officers present, repeated Joshua's words, the temple began to rumble and shake. The banners on the walls were torn in half and then burst into flame. The altar of sacrifice split in two and then crumbled into a pile of rubble.

The temple floor, with its symbols of evil, pitched and rolled, causing the prisoners and officers to hold on for dear life as a web of cracks and fissures wove its way beneath their feet. A howling wind filled the entire area and swept through the temple, shattering the remaining demonic idols against the floor.

The ones who had refused to repent did so now, and they too received the Holy Spirit. The next two hours were spent praising God, and singing, and sharing testimony.

Chief Wilson had already given orders to his officers to get all the names, addresses, and phone numbers of all the people here and then he let them go home. He told them that they would be notified as to court dates and times by mail.

Chapter 21

The Trouble With Tapes

Marla closed her eyes and wept bitterly as she said, "Please Grady turn it off. That poor woman! How could Dr. White and Governor Bradley do that to another human being? I mean, to butcher someone alive!"

Marla shivered and Grady put a protective arm around her.

Before he had left the temple, he had gone to the secret room and retrieved the tape from the video recorder. Now he and Marla were sitting at the police station watching the tape from the previous evening as well as the new tape.

Marla continued softly with her face buried in Grady's chest, "Grady, that could have happened to me tonight, if you and the others hadn't come and saved me."

Grady answered, "I wish I could take the credit for it, Marla, but you'll have to thank Josh."

Marla sat up and gave Grady a questioning look.

"Josh planned the entire raid and told me to find you and bring you to him. That's what I was doing earlier today when I tried to flag you down in front of the hospital. You should have seen the faces that Bradley was making behind your back. I knew from his expression that he was going to kill you, but then you just vanished. What happened to you, then."

Marla thought for a moment. "It's hard to say, Grady. I felt light-headed and then all of a sudden we were in Connelly's den. I felt weak, tired, and a little scared. Governor Bradley gave me a shot, which knocked me out. I awoke in that awful place . . . "

The blood drained from Marla's already pale face.

"I'm sorry, Grady, but I can't talk about this right now. I just can't believe that people can do things like that to each other."

Grady nodded, "I know what you mean. Josh told us earlier that these witches are under the direct control of powerful demons whose total purpose is to defile the human body and steal the human soul."

Marla remarked a little sharper than she had intended, "So Officer White is saying that these vile human beings are themselves victims?"

"Yeah, that about sums it up."

Marla looked as if she was about to say something else when Chief Wilson walked into the room along with Joshua.

Joshua asked, "Did you get the tapes, Grady?"

"Yeah, I did, and I showed them to Marla, just like you said."

Joshua turned to Marla. "What do you think, can we use these?"

"I want to help, Officer White, but I'll need to get these to the Capitol if I'm to convince my boss to air them."

Joshua thought about it for a moment and then decided, "All right, but I want Grady to go with you for protection. If you leave now, you should be able to get there by 9 o'clock in the morning. Marla, would that give you enough time to get this on the noon news?"

"That should be fine."

Joshua reached out and grasped Marla's hand.

"God bless you, Marla. I'll be praying for you and Grady."

Tears welled up in Marla's brown eyes. She let them fall unchecked down her cheeks as she said, "I don't deserve God's blessing, but I appreciate your prayers."

She and Grady left the station.

They had decided to take Marla's car, so Grady went over to his own car and pulled out a large book. Grady opened it up and put the two tapes into the cut out portion of the book.

Marla exclaimed, "Grady, you cut up a Bible?"

Grady laughed, "No, silly! See! It's only the cover of my family Bible. The book was a dictionary. It hides the tapes quite well, don't you think?"

Marla nodded and they got in her car. She leaned down and put another set of the tapes under the driver's seat. They had decided that she would drive so that Grady could keep a better watch.

As they pulled out onto the road, Grady asked, "Will your boss run this story, Marla?"

Marla thought for a moment, and then answered, "I really don't know, Grady. He's always taken pleasure in twisting the truth around to make Christians look bad. He's also a good friend of Governor Bradley and supported his election campaign. He won't be thrilled to find out that Bradley is a murderer."

Marla was turning onto the highway which led to the interstate when suddenly her heart skipped a beat. On both sides of the highway, there were military vehicles parked as far as you could see. Grady read "National Guard" on the side of one of the vehicles. There were several soldiers in the road and they were stopping vehicles and questioning the occupants.

Marla's heart was in her stomach as they pulled up to the barricade which blocked their progress.

As Marla came to a stop a soldier came up to the car and asked to see her driver's license. A second soldier came over to Grady's side and ordered him out of the car. Grady reached for his back pocket to pull out his badge when the soldier hit him in the stomach and roughly ordered him not to move again. The guard took Grady's wallet out of his back pocket and looked at his badge and ID card.

He yelled to the other guard, "Charlie, this is the one the boss told us to bring. Ask the cute chick where the tapes are?"

Marla's guard leaned into the car through the open door and reached over Marla and took the Bible from between the seats. He yelled, "Hey, Bob, all I found was this here Bible."

"You, idiot, they ain't gonna have it in plain sight! Search the broad, see if it's on her."

Charlie liked that suggestion and as he reached for Marla, Grady attacked his guard. The guard was expecting it, however, and the butt end of his machine gun found Grady's nose, breaking it. Grady went down, his blood spurting out onto the highway.

Marla frantically reached under the seat, grabbed the tapes, and shoved them at the guard. "Here take the tapes, just don't hurt Grady anymore."

Marla shivered as Charlie put his hand on her shoulder and said, "Get out of the car, pretty lady."

Grady yelled, "Drive off! Get out of here!"

The guard, Bob, brought his club down on Grady's head and Grady slipped into oblivion.

Marla floored the accelerator. Charlie screamed in pain as he was knocked to the ground and Marla crushed his legs beneath her speeding tires. Bob rushed to Charlie's side.

"That was very careless, Charlie, and you know how the general hates carelessness."

He picked up the two video tapes laying next to Charlie.

"I'll just take these and make sure the general gets them. We can't afford any more stupid mistakes."

Charlie fainted from his pain and loss of blood.

Bob motioned to a couple of guards.

"Roll Charlie here into a ditch and make sure he don't crawl outta it."

He pointed to Grady.

"Then put this joker in the half-track."

One of the guards asked, "What about the woman? Should we take care of her?"

"No. We got what we was looking for, just take care of Charlie like I told you."

As the half-track pulled away, the sound of a short burst of machine-gun fire could be heard, piercing the early morning air.

Tears blurred Marla's vision as she checked the rearview mirror to see if she was being followed. Frantically, she prayed and asked God to protect Grady. She felt guilty about leaving him, but was more determined than ever to get these tapes to her boss and make him air them.

* * *

Joshua and Chief Wilson looked at each other in total disbelief as they pulled up to the police station. Rev. Smith and the other ministers and priests who had participated in the prayer vigil for Joshua at the hospital, were laying face down with their hands cuffed behind their backs on the grassy area in front of the station house.

There was a tank parked in the street directly in front of the station, its large cannon aimed at the area where the clergy were imprisoned.

This is the last scene that either Joshua or the chief expected to see in America, but nevertheless, here it was.

As they quickly got out of the car, two National Guard soldiers ran up to them, ordered them to the ground and relieved them of their service revolvers. When the chief objected, one of the soldiers hit him in the head with the butt of his rifle.

Joshua heard the chief groan as he fought his way back to consciousness.

"Lay still, Chief, these men mean business."

Wilson heard Joshua as if he were a long way off.

"What's going on? Why has the National Guard taken over the station? What are they doing with the clergy?"

"I don't know. We're not close enough for me to catch what they're saying to each other."

"Who's doing all that talking I can hear?"

"That's the ministers and priests—they're praying!"

"Good idea!"

Wilson remained motionless—it eased the pounding in his head—until he heard the half-track pull up.

The guards jerked Wilson and Joshua to their feet and half-dragged them toward the half-track. As they approached the half-track, they saw the motionless form of Grady being thrown out of it onto the ground. His body hit the ground with a sickening thud.

Wilson yelled, "Hey, that's one of my men!"

"We're collecting what belongs to us, Chief Wilson."

Wilson and Joshua turned and saw a military man standing behind them. On his head, he wore green helmet which had a large white star in the middle of it. On his chest were three rows of ribbons and several medals. He wore field gear and had a 45 cal. pistol strapped to his hip. The man's boots were mirror black. He rubbed his forefinger across his neatly trimmed mustache.

"Gentlemen, allow me to introduce myself. I am General Frietegg of the National Guard, at your service. I am here to assist you, Chief Wilson, in quelling these riots."

Wilson opened his mouth to object, but the general held up his hand.

"No, don't thank me, Chief, that's what we're here for."

He took Wilson's arm.

"Now, here's how the schedule will go. At 11:00 tomorrow morning, my troops will blow up the churches and the Christian schools, since you'll no longer need them. Between now and then, I expect all Christians to register at the city hall and then go home and wait for further instructions. After the city has been purged of the Christian blight, we will summon you to a meeting where your fate will be made known to you.

"From this moment on, martial law has been declared and an 8:00 P.M. curfew is in effect. Anyone, including police officers, found in the streets during curfew, will be shot."

Joshua spoke up, "The press won't let you get away with this. I don't think the citizens of the United States will allow this to go unpunished."

The general laughed lightly. "As for the press, they were told that if they left immediately then none of them would get shot, accidentally of course, in the riots. The local networks agreed to air, as written, the reports that we send them. So you see, the citizens of the United States will only see what I want them to see, which will be some very radical and unruly Christians, who, turning violent had to be shot."

Joshua spoke again, "I don't believe that you have the authority to just go around shooting people at your whim. We've been free citizens too long to just buckle under to your empty threats."

"You know, Officer White, Governor Bradley thought you might say that. I don't want to leave any doubt in your mind about either my intention, or the scope of my authority."

The General pulled out his 45 cal. pistol, aimed it at the chief's head and pulled the trigger twice.

Joshua's anguished scream had no effect on General Frietegg. Without another word, he simply turned around and walked back to his Jeep. He smiled to himself as Joshua's tortured cries surrounded him like a serenade of agony.

Chapter 22
Casualty of War

Capt. Worl did not always understand his orders but he always obeyed them. Shortly before General Frietegg arrived, Worl had been ordered to refrain from interfering with anything that would happen next, that order extended to all angels present.

When General Frietegg drew his revolver, however, it was all that Worl could do not to swoop down and knock it out of his hand, but he didn't. Beriack stood by and watched as Chief Wilson was shot in cold blood.

Capt. Worl, his wings fully extended, circled overhead, watching reverently as Beriack took charge of Andrew Wilson's soul and whisked him off to Paradise. He watched with sadness as Joshua crumpled to the ground to hold the chief's bleeding head against his chest. Joshua was rocking back and forth, much as Job had done so long ago, forlorn and forsaken, a man who, by all outward signs had been abandoned by God.

Capt. Worl sent a message to Lt. Aaron, who then placed his hand on Joshua's shoulder and whispered, "Pray, Joshua. Pray!"

Joshua jerked his head toward heaven and yelled, "My friend is gone! All is lost!" He bowed his head again and wept bitterly.

Aaron said softly, but firmly, "Pray, Joshua, for God's plan to be accomplished. Give your sadness to

God. Don't try to understand. Trust what God asks of you now. Trust Him with all your heart, for nothing is impossible with God. Pray for wisdom, Joshua, and for peace."

Capt. Worl watched as this hopeless figure of a man transformed before his eyes. With the whispered urgings from Aaron and Joshua's memories of his own recent death and resurrection flooding back upon his grief, hope returned slowly to this man of God.

Joshua slid out from under the chief's head and laid it gently on the ground. He got onto his knees and looking toward heaven, began to pray, "Yes, Lord, I do believe! Forgive me for my lack of faith, Jesus. Despite all that has happened, I want to do Your will. I will trust You to work and to do Your will. Help me to see past the circumstances, help me to see You only.

"Thank you, Jesus, for this victory. I will trust Your wisdom."

* * *

General Frietegg pulled up to Connelly's mansion in his jeep. He was to meet with Bradley to plan tomorrow's operation. As he reached for the door bell, the door swung open and Frietegg gasped in surprise.

Standing before him was a man he could hardly recognize as Governor Bradley. The governor's hair stood straight out, and his face was extremely pale. His eyes were dark circles set deeply into their sockets. His lips were stretched across his teeth in a grotesque grimace-like smile.

Bradley spoke in a deep, distorted voice that turned Frietegg's blood to ice.

"Ah, General Frietegg, do come in, I've been expecting you."

Bradley stepped aside to let the general enter, but Frietegg hesitated a little too long. An unseen force picked him up and threw him into the house. He hit the floor rolling and was back on his feet, with his revolver drawn. He aimed at the governor, but before he could fire, the gun was ripped from his grasp and thrown across the room.

As Frietegg stood there with his mouth gaping open, Governor Bradley explained, "You can't hesitate and expect to win this war tomorrow. There are more forces working here than you realize, and I want to explain to you what is going on. Please sit down. Would you like a drink?" Bradley indicated a chair as he walked across to the bar and mixed the general a double. As he put the drink into Frietegg's shaking hands, he continued in the same disembodied voice, "We were having a nice little child sacrifice last night, when we were raided by the police, and those confounded angels. The police shot my body guards and a few of my other men and many of our demon forces were lost. My spirit guide, Tumult, got me out of there, but they killed Connelly. This was supposed to be an easy mission; intimidate the Christians into submission, and then usher in the New Age Agenda.

"Instead, the Christians are far from intimidated, they're fighting back with prayer and fasting and open revolt. Nothing has gone right yet!

"We kill Joshua White and he comes back to life and brings his traitorous brother, Dr. Chad White, over to the enemy camp before we can eliminate him. Not only does Joshua White come back to life, but he does it on national television, causing millions to doubt, in seconds, what it took us years to make them believe."

Bradley stopped suddenly. "Why do you have a smirk on your face? This is a disaster, not a comedy!"

Frietegg smiled, for he was getting into his element.

"Your worries are over, Bradley. I've brought Joshua White and the other Christians to their knees. I paid a little visit to Covenant today and put some fear into those sheep. I informed them that tomorrow we're going to march on Covenant and blow up their churches and schools. I also told them that you'll let them know at that time what their own fate will be."

"And they believed you?"

"In order to convince them that we're serious, I shot Police Chief Wilson in the head. He is, of course, dead. When I left, Joshua White was a broken man. We won't have anymore trouble out of them, I assure you."

"Well done, General! I tell you what, let's have another drink and we'll discuss the plans for tomorrow's attack."

"Wait, sir, I have more good news." Frietegg reached into his field jacket and pulled out two tapes and handed them to Bradley. "I believe you wanted these back?"

Bradley accepted the tapes, but then had a second thought. "And the girl, what happened to the girl?"

"She got away, I'm afraid, but not before we got those."

Bradley's face twisted in that grimacing smile again. "Yes, this is good. This is very good. It would have been nice to have the girl back. I had plans for her, but she's not important anymore." He put his arm around the general's shoulders. "Come, we have work to do."

The two men took their refreshed drinks into Connelly's den to study their maps and lay out their attack plan.

* * *

Marla Brinkle sat on the hood of her car, furious with herself for missing her noon deadline. She had let Officer White and Grady down.

She rubbed the big toe on her right foot which she had used to kick her flat tire in frustration.

"That was really bright, Marla Brinkle! Kicking the tire really helped, didn't it?" She stopped for a moment and then shook her head, saying, "Now, I'm talking to myself. This isn't getting me anywhere."

She hopped off of the car, groaning as her toe hit the pavement. She limped back to the trunk again, hoping that somehow a spare tire had materialized. Her car was provided by the television station so it had never occurred to her to check for a spare. She had never used the trunk, preferring to carry luggage or groceries in the back seat.

With renewed frustration, she began to pray.

"Well, Jesus, you know I'm more used to making fun of you than I am asking for your help, but here goes. I'm broken down in the middle of nowhere. I was supposed to deliver these tapes by noon today and here it is already . . . " She looked at her watch, "1:30. I've been sitting here for hours. I'm thirsty and hungry. On top of that, no one will stop to help. Please help me, Lord. I really need help!"

Marla returned to her post on top of the car's hood.

In the distance, she heard the rumble of a large engine and thought that it must be a truck. She looked toward the sound that came from the direction she'd been heading but, whatever it was, it was still beyond the hill that rose up in front of her. What she eventually saw on top that hill brought fear crawling up her spine.

She whispered, "Great, Jesus, I pray for help and You send this!"

Marla had been counting since the first motorcycles topped the hill and she was up to thirty already, with more coming. The first biker pulled over to the side of the road, just across from her. The big man held up his hand and all the bikes, more than fifty now, pulled over to the same side of the road. As the echo of the engines died out, the big man got off his bike, stretched, and then lumbered toward her.

Marla knew she had a deer in the headlights look on her face. She couldn't move.

The man wore blue jeans, a white T-shirt, and a denim vest with a number of symbols on it. He was heavily tattooed. His hair was long and black and pulled back in a pony tail. His beard was full to the point of shaggy.

His deep voice boomed, "Need help, lady?"

When she didn't answer, he continued, "Look, you shouldn't be out here by yourself, it's dangerous. Let's see what we can do."

Marla jumped as the man raised his hand. She just knew he was going to hit her and then, who knows? Instead, he gave a hand signal, and three men, just as large as he was, came running up.

Without a word, the brawny leader went to the trunk of her car, peeled back the carpet and removed a false panel. He took the tire out of its hiding place and handed it to one man and the jack handle to another. Oddly, he didn't remove the rest of the jack from the trunk.

One man popped the hub cap while the other loosened the lug nuts. Then the leader and the third man picked the car up while the other two men put the new tire on and re-tightened the lug nuts. When they put the car down, the man with the jack handle finished tightening the nuts.

The leader picked up the flat tire and placed it in the trunk along with the jack handle and then closed the trunk, saying as he did so, "Lady, soon as you can, you best get that plugged. These small donut tires ain't good for too many miles, and you got to drive slower with them, too." Marla, who was still terrified, said, "H-How much do I owe you?"

The big man just looked at her and smiled. The men with him laughed and Marla felt a wave of nausea in her stomach.

One of the men who'd been standing by the driver's door reached into the car and said, "Look a Bible!", but his smile turned into confusion as he opened it. Without a word, the man handed it to the leader. He took the tapes out of the Bible/dictionary and held them up, with a questioning look at Marla.

Then it hit Marla and she lost what little remained of her composure, "Oh my God, he sent you. Governor Bradley sent you to get me and the tapes!"

Tears ran down her cheeks and when the big man reached toward her, Marla screamed. The nausea that had threatened just moments before, overcame her, and she slipped, gratefully, into darkness.

When Marla opened her eyes she saw only the darkening sky. Then, as she came around, the fear started to well up in her again. Suddenly, she realized that her head was propped up on a saddle bag from one of the bikes. Her clothes and dignity were intact, and a woman was bathing her forehead with a damp cloth.

"My name is Lydia, honey. You just lay still there until you come out of this all the way."

"What happened to me?"

Lydia shrugged her shoulders and said, "You tell us, lady. My man there, Killer, was just helping you out and all of a sudden you started screaming and talking about the governor and tapes and who knows what? We figured afterward, you know, after you fainted, that we musta scared you pretty bad. We forget how mean we look when we're all together like this. Anyways, here's what my man was gonna hand you, when you lost it."

Lydia handed Marla a card which read, "I owe a favor to a person in need." The bottom of the card had

A DARKNESS OVER COVENANT

the initials J.W. written on it. The card was new, but something caught her eye. Then she had it. She sat up so suddenly that she almost knocked Lydia over.

Lydia exclaimed, "You ain't gonna lose it again, are ya?"

Marla smiled, "No, I'm sorry, I have to ask a question."

She turned to the big man who was sitting on his bike, eating beans out of a can.

"Did Lydia say that your name is Killer?"

He answered through a mouth full of beans. "That's right, Killer, at your service."

"Do you know this man with the initials J.W., like it says on this card?"

The man put the can of beans down, all attention now, and nodded.

Marla, getting excited now, practically yelled, "Is it Joshua White from Covenant?"

Killer yelled back, "Yeah, what about him! Listen lady, what's your name, anyway?"

"Oh, I'm sorry, I'm Marla Brinkle of the News Channel. I'm a reporter and boy, have I got a story to tell you!"

It took some time but she explained all that had happened to her over the last couple of days. Killer, along with everyone else in their group who had crowded around, listened intently. When she was finished, Killer related to Marla how Joshua had saved him from his destructive lifestyle and helped rid him of his demons. After he had served his time, he had started this Christian motorcycle gang.

"We travel around the country doin' what good we can, on our summer vacations, holidays, and weekends. When Officer White and I last saw each other, he handed me that card, put his initials on it and told me to do something nice for someone else as payment for his good deed to me. I liked that idea so much that I had copies made up, with Officer White's initials on 'em. When people ask me what the J.W. stands for, I tell 'em my story."

Killer stood up. "Well, it sounds to me like my friend is in trouble and needs our help."

Looking around him, he asked, "Whaddya say? Should we go and do what we can?"

The other bikers rose to their feet and cheered. They all knew Officer White through Killer's stories about him and wanted to help him. Everyone gathered into small groups and joined hands. Marla, who was no longer afraid, held Killer's hand on one side and Lydia's hand on the other and joined in as they prayed for guidance for their mission.

* * *

The National Guard herded the handcuffed clergymen into the police station holding cells. Once their cuffs were removed and the guards had closed and locked the cells, the ministers and priests joined hands, each within their own cell groups, and continued the vigil of prayer that had begun first at the hospital and then on the lawn of the police station.

Joshua watched in silence as the mortuary attendant took away the body of his friend and superior officer, Police Chief Wilson. The ambulance attendants lifted Grady onto a gurney.

"He'll be okay, Officer White, it's looks like a severe concussion."

Joshua thanked the attendant and watched both vehicles pull away.

"Tell me what to do now, Lord. I need Your guidance more than ever."

He continued in prayer as he started the long walk to his own home.

Chapter 23
The Battle of Covenant

Governor Bradley climbed into his jeep with General Frietegg. Frietegg commented that Bradley looked more normal this morning, but Bradley didn't want to find out what he meant, so he let it drop without comment.

Bradley was thinking that even with all the setbacks, his plans were about to be fulfilled. He was going to really enjoy watching all those schools and churches burn.

As if reading his mind, General Frietegg asked, "Bradley, why do you want to blow up their schools, anyway. I mean, they're all public schools, aren't they?"

Bradley answered impatiently, "Yes, their schools are public, but they've refused to take God out of the schools. They've refused to take the Ten Commandments out of the schools. They even have the audacity to teach against abortion and contraceptives. The schools must go and be replaced with my schools."

That thought brought a smile to Bradley's face. He could feel his confidence returning. He was a very powerful man, and the thought swelled his chest and widened his smile.

He looked in the rear view mirror at the impressive display of firepower and troop strength that followed his jeep; five tanks and five hundred men loaded in troop carriers.

He said to the general, "What those tanks don't destroy, those troops will."

Both men laughed, but the general stopped suddenly, and gave the signal to listen. At first Bradley couldn't hear anything, but then faintly he heard . . . music? No, not just regular music—*I know that tune . . . Amazing Grace!*

He turned to the general. "I hate that song."

The general nodded in agreement as he kept his eyes on the horizon. Bradley followed the general's gaze and was shocked at what he saw coming down the road.

Bradley whispered to the general, "People as far as you can see. Who are they?"

The general grabbed his field glasses. "It's those blasted Christians—hundreds of them. That fool, Joshua White, is leading the pack!"

"It looks like he's got some of the local cops with him, too."

"They're all fools, dead fools!"

Frietegg gave a signal and the tanks moved ahead followed by the troop transports. The soldiers jumped out of the transports and took up positions between and in front of the tanks. Some knelt and some laid down, but all guns were pointed at the marching Christians. The general pulled up to a position just to the right of his line of defense and stood up in the jeep. He observed the approaching entourage through his field glasses again. He couldn't believe his eyes, they had no weapons! Even the police officers were unarmed!

He turned to the governor and asked, "Do you want me to take them out?"

Bradley considered it. He pointed at the crowd and said, "Wait a minute, what's that?"

Frietegg looked through the field glasses and said, "It's White. He's coming alone. I could have one of my men take him down as he approaches, He . . . "

"No!", Bradley yelled, "That's already been tried and it didn't work. Let's hear what he has to say first and then you can kill him."

Joshua looked back over his shoulder as he approached the tanks, and he saw the huge semi-circle that his friends were forming behind him. They held their Bibles and continued to sing "Amazing Grace."

In front of him was a line of five tanks with approximately five hundred soldiers filling in the gaps between them. To his left was a jeep in which he could see the figures of General Frietegg and Governor Bradley, so he changed direction and walked toward them. He didn't miss the fact that every weapon there was trained on him, changing direction with him.

As he approached the jeep, he prayed, "Lord, this is Your mission and Your message. Please help me. I want these men to repent and claim Jesus as their Lord and Savior, even after all they've done. Lord, I'm afraid, but here I am. I am willing to do whatever You require of me." Joshua spoke as the Spirit prompted him, "General, Governor, we meet again."

The general smiled maliciously. "The pleasure is all yours."

Bradley was more pleasant. "Well, Officer White, you certainly are persistent, I'll give you that." Making a sweeping motion with his hand, he asked, "But why this? What can you possibly accomplish with these bodies and books? Are you stalling for time to save your churches? Do you think we won't just roll right over you and then destroy your city, anyway? Come on White, speak up!"

Joshua smiled. "I'm very glad you asked me all those questions, because the Lord has sent me here with many answers. First of all, these bodies and books are all we need to fight against you and your evil forces. Do you see this Bible I hold? This is not a shield—it's a sword. It is a mightier weapon than you could ever imagine. Your tanks and your weapons mean nothing to God. The evil spirits that infest your souls are no match for the power found in this Book and in the name of Jesus Christ."

Joshua opened his Bible. "Gentlemen, I will read the answer to you out of this Book. This is from Ephesians 6:12, 'For we wrestle not against flesh or blood but against principalities, against powers, against the rulers of the darkness of this world, against spiritual wickedness in high places.'

"You see, Governor, our battle isn't with you but with the evil one who controls you."

"I am well aware of who has aided me in my rise to power. Do you think I sat idly by, waiting for this power to come to me? Ha! I searched for the master, and he heard my ambitions and helped me to plan my takeover of this miserable city, full of dimwitted Christians!"

"Your bargain with Satan will cost you your soul, Governor Bradley. You may have found the power you coveted, but we are here now. Armed with the power of the blood of Jesus, the sword of the Word of God, and shielded by our faith, we will crush you and your master in the name of Jesus!"

"Well-spoken, White! But, alas, your threatening words are spoken in vain. Your piddling powers will gain you nothing."

With those derisive words spoken by the governor, General Frietegg pulled out his 45 cal. pistol, took careful aim at Joshua and pulled the trigger.

There was a loud click, but that was all.

Joshua said, "Aren't you tired of settling things with a gun?"

In answer, Frietegg jumped out of the jeep, grabbed a rifle from one of his men and fired at Joshua again.

Again, there was only a click. Again and again, the general pulled the trigger, but the rifle continued to misfire.

Frustrated, General Frietegg yelled out, "First company! Fire!"

The general's front-line troop raised their weapons and fired upon Joshua. Instead of the thundering sound of rapid-fire rifles, they heard the same clicking noise that had followed the general's attempts.

Frantically, Frietegg ordered that all weapons be checked.

Joshua shook his head, locked eyes with Governor Bradley and said, "I bear a message for you from Jesus Christ. He has instructed me to read Isaiah 37:33-36 to you."

He took a deep breath and began to read, in a loud voice, from the Holy Scriptures. "Therefore, thus saith the Lord concerning the King of Assyria: He shall not reach this city, nor shoot an arrow at it, nor come before it with a shield, nor cast a siegeworks against it. He shall return by the same way he came, without entering the city, says the Lord. I will shield and save this city for my own sake, and for the sake of my servant David. The angel of the Lord went forth and struck down one hundred and eighty-five thousand in the Assyrian camp. Early the next morning, there they were, all the corpses of the dead."

Joshua closed his Bible and said, "So the Lord has spoken yet again, about His city, Covenant. You, Governor, are the evil king who must repent and be saved, or turn and go back the way you came and leave us in peace. If not, you will perish, just as the Assyrians did."

General Frietegg had heard enough. He pulled a sharp field knife out of his boot and lunged at Joshua. Joshua side-stepped the attack and wielding the stick which held the white flag like a staff, he knocked the knife out of the general's hand, breaking his wrist. Frietegg fell to the ground screaming in pain.

Joshua looked at Governor Bradley, still in the jeep,

"Well, Governor, will you repent, turn from your wickedness, and confess Jesus as Lord."

Bradley grabbed the radio and ordered all soldier's to fix bayonets.

Joshua raised his Bible in the air and waved it. In one great wave the Christians and police officers knelt and raised their voices in prayer. Joshua turned in his Bible to Psalm 91 and began to read aloud again, his voice booming above the others.

"He who dwells in the shelter of the Most High will abide in the shadow of the Almighty. I will say to the Lord, My refuge and my fortress, My God in whom I trust!"

The soldiers advanced upon Joshua and the praying Christians, hatred and murder in their eyes.

"He will cover you with His pinions, and under His wings you may seek refuge; His faithfulness is a shield and bulwark."

The voices of the Christians rose in even more fervent prayer and praise to the Lord.

"You will not be afraid of the terror by night, or the arrow that flies by day."

Suddenly, the advancing soldiers stopped and one by one began screaming in pain, dropping their weapons which had suddenly turned to red hot molten metal.

"A thousand may fall at your side, and ten thousand at your right hand; but it shall not approach you." General Frietegg, holding his broken wrist, got to his feet and ran toward Joshua again, hurling venomous curses. Suddenly, he stopped and clutched at his throat, his eyes bulging painfully. He fell to the ground again, still clutching and clawing at his throat and, finally, ceased to struggle as death overcame him.

"You will only look on with your eyes, and see the recompense of the wicked. For you have made the Lord, my refuge, Even the Most High, your dwelling place."

Governor Bradley looked on in horror, as one by one the soldiers deserted their posts and either fell to the ground screaming and cursing in pain or stumbled off to find relief for the seared and blistering skin on their hands.

Joshua closed his Bible and began to pray aloud for God's will to be done and for the salvation of the wounded soldiers.

* * *

Capt. Worl, his faithful guards, Left and Right, Lt. Aaron and the army of angels that accompanied the praying believers, valiantly fought the horde of demons that advanced upon them in sync with the advancing soldiers.

Fortified by the sincere and fervent prayer of the Christians kneeling behind Joshua, the angels steadily held the upper hand, banishing demon after demon to the abyss with a swing of their flaming swords.

Tumult watched in frustration as his evil army was being whittled down to nothing.

Loosing his grasp on the head and shoulders of Governor Bradley, he unsheathed his curved sword and with a bellow of rage, headed straight for Capt. Worl.

"I should have killed you, Worl, at the foot of your Master's cross, when you were all ordered not to interfere."

Signaling Left and Right to stand aside, Worl faced Tumult. "You will not hinder the work of the Mighty God this time either, Tumult. This time, I will certainly send you back to your master!"

Aaron dispatched another demon and then turned and watched as his commander battled the mighty Tumult who had been their principal nemesis for eons. Hovering over Joshua, he lightly touched his shoulder and whispered, "Pray for power, Joshua. Plead the blood of Jesus. Ask God to strengthen His warriors."

Joshua felt a prompting in his spirit and began to intercede in prayer, coming against the forces of evil with the blood of Jesus and asking God to gird His army with strength.

Tumult raged on, striking blow after blow against the captain of the angelic army. Confident of victory, he began to laugh, taunting Worl as he pummeled him with his bloody sword.

"You can't win, you sniveling fool. You are nothing but an irritating gnat, and I am going to take great pleasure in ripping your wings from your measly broken body."

Though he felt strength and power flowing back into his body, Worl continued to fight as though his strength was spent. He feebly swung his sword at the raging demon, but Tumult ducked, kicking out as he did so and knocking Worl to his back.

Tumult straddled Worl's body and raised his sword high over his head.

"Covenant is mine!"

With a mighty cry of victory, Tumult made to plunge the sword into Worl's chest.

"The earth is mine, says the Lord!" quoted Worl and raised his sword, burying it deep within Tumult's chest. The sword exploded into a million dazzling shards of lightning, and with a mighty clap of thunder and a bloodcurdling shriek, Tumult disappeared from earth, reappearing before the enraged Prince of Darkness himself!

With renewed strength and fervor, the army of angels fought on, sending the remaining demon warriors on their journey back to the abyss.

Governor Bradley huddled in the general's jeep, impotent with fear. All of his former bravado and arrogance had left him. As he struggled to regain his composure, he could not help himself from playing out his future in his mind. He realized that somehow these namby-pamby Christians had managed to subdue all of his forces, both physical and spiritual. He was a broken man.

Not one to accept defeat lightly, nor allow himself to be subjected to ridicule or any other form of degradation, Bradley reached into the inside pocket of his suit coat, pulled out his own snub-nosed revolver, and placing it in his mouth, pulled the trigger. His was the only gun that worked properly on this day.

Startled by the sudden sound of gunfire, Joshua and the kneeling Christians stopped their prayers and looked up. Joshua ran toward the jeep, hoping to find that the governor had miraculously missed his target. Looking at Bradley's mutilated body, he spoke quietly, quoting Psalm 37:12-15,

"The wicked plots against the righteous, and gnashes at him with his teeth. The Lord laughs at him; for He sees his day is coming. The wicked have drawn the sword and bent their bow, to cast down the afflicted and the needy, to slay those who are upright in conduct. Their sword will enter their own heart, and their bows will be broken."

Chapter 24
The State of the Union

Capt. Worl stood aside as Governor Bradley held the small gun in his mouth and ended his life. As his scarred and twisted soul rose out of his body, he held his hands out pleadingly to the angel captain.

"Please, you must help me. I didn't know."

Capt. Worl spoke without emotion, "You did know, Governor Bradley. You heard the gospel and rejected it, choosing instead to follow the Fallen One. But I am not your judge, Christ is. I cannot help you."

As Bradley's pitiful pleas continued, a demon escort rose from the abyss, and engulfed the governor in their foul-smelling blanket of darkness. As his pleas turned to cries of despair and terror, Bradley was drawn down into the abyss, to meet the one he had chosen to serve.

Joshua turned away from the jeep that held the governor's body and started back toward the multitude of believer's who now stood to their feet and began praising and worshiping the Lord. The biker's revved their engines and formed a circle around the Christians, lifting their own free hands into the air with shouts of praise and thanksgiving for their victory.

Suddenly the sound of a helicopter was heard overhead, and the rejoicing crowd was illuminated by the search lights of Airforce One.

After waiting for the crowd to scramble out of its way, the Presidential helicopter landed safely and two Secret Service Agents climbed down, followed by President Roberta Place and two other Secret Service Agents.

Waving a greeting at the surrounding crowd, she approached Joshua.

Extending her hand, the President said, "Looks like I may have missed the boat here."

Smiling, Joshua shook her hand, saying, "I don't think this would have been much of a pleasure cruise."

Observing the damaged weapons and the soldiers who still lay in agony by them, she replied, "No, there is no pleasure in battle, even when you are victorious. And were you victorious, Mr. White?"

"Please, Madam President, call me Joshua. And yes, the Lord was victorious today."

"Governor Bradley?"

"He's dead, Madam President, by his own hand."

"I see. Well, let's clean up this mess, shall we?"

"If I may, I would like to have the Christians minister to the soldiers before they are taken away. Perhaps there are some who desire salvation after what has happened."

"Certainly! That is very compassionate of you, Joshua."

"Our Father is a God of compassion."

Remembering her own son's miraculous healing, she smiled in agreement, tears welling up in her eyes.

Joshua excused himself and together with a large number of volunteers, began to kneel and pray with the soldiers.

*   *   *

Joshua handed the President another piece of pizza and laughed when the Secret Service agent went for his gun, out of reflex.

"These guys never relax, do they?"

Roberta smiled and answered, "I'm glad they don't, especially now. I'm afraid that there are going to be a lot of people who won't like the new me, but that's a small price to pay for all the Lord's done for me."

Joshua smiled at Roberta and said, "Well, there will always be a hot pizza and common folk around here for you to visit."

He motioned to the Secret Service agent to be ready and he reached out and touched Roberta's hand. Her hand was cold to the touch, indicating the kind of stress she was under, but he held it in both of his, and looking into her eyes said, "I mean it, Madam President, anytime at all that you need a fellow Christian to talk to, I am always available to you. If you need anything at all to help you in the task that lays before you, don't hesitate to send for me. We are all in this together."

Joshua saw the tears well up in her eyes and he said in a cheery voice, releasing her hand after a friendly pat, "By the way, why are you here? I mean, what made you come to Covenant at the exact time that you did? No one knew about the battle but us."

Roberta perked up, "Oh, it's the most wonderful thing. I got a phone call from a wonderful reporter named Marla Brinkle and . . . " She stopped when everybody in the room burst out laughing. With a confused look that clearly said she didn't get the joke, Roberta asked, "You know her?"

Joshua, still chortling, said, "Yes, we do. It's just that we're not used to the word wonderful being used to describe Marla Brinkle . . . "

"Oh, really. I find that hard to believe."

"You see, Marla was against us at first, and leveled some pretty wild accusations at Christians in general. Anyway, now she's on a mission to get some important tapes to the News Station, at the capital. But, please go on with your explanation."

"Ms. Brinkle called me from a cellular phone. She said she was calling from a motorcycle and she was with a man named "Killer". She congratulated me on my son's recovery, and I thanked her and asked how I could help her.

"She said that the man who had spoken to me over the television about my son's healing—you, Joshua— that you were in trouble. She said that the whole city of Covenant was in trouble, that Governor Bradley planned to roll into Covenant with his tanks, and blow up the churches and schools.

"While I was speaking to her, my secretary came in and handed me a box on which was written, 'To President Place from Marla Brinkle'. The secretary assured me that it was secure. When I opened the box, it contained two video tapes. I told her that I had received her package and asked what was on the tapes. She said they were copies of the tapes showing Governor Bradley and Theodore Connelly performing ritual sacrifices during Black Mass observances.

"I hung up the phone and put one of the tapes into the machine. I couldn't believe what I was seeing! It suddenly became very clear to me what Governor Bradley's hidden agenda had been all these years. I knew that I had been duped—used by this madman— and I felt sick and dirty. But more than that, I was angry!

"I called my Chief of Staff and told him to get that National Guard unit to pull back from Covenant until I could arrive and assess the situation and I ordered my helicopter prepared. I then called Marla Brinkle back and told her that I was heading to Covenant by air. She told me that she was at the station trying to get the equipment to work. She said it should be on by six tonight. Which, . . . " Looking at her watch, "is right about now."

Joshua motioned for Joe to turn the television on, while the President finished her story.

"Anyway, she said that 'Killer' would get her safely back to Covenant."

As if on cue, the fifty motorcyclists that had rescued Marla Brinkle and then aided the Christians in their battle against Bradley and Frietegg poured into Covenant's Square, followed closely by Marla's car, two TV vans, and a convoy of reporters. The windows of the pizza parlor shook from the roar of the engines. Everyone in the pizza parlor stood up and watched in awe at the stirring display of bikes.

Joshua smiled as he recalled first meeting Harold Barber, or "Killer" as his biker friends called him. He led the others out the door of the pizzeria and walked over to Killer. They hugged roughly, pounding each other on the back, and then clasped hands. Joshua introduced him to the President.

"Pleased to meet ya, Ma'am."

"The pleasure is all mine, uh, Killer. As I understand, we owe you a debt of gratitude."

"Nah, I didn't do nothin' 'cept what the Lord woulda wanted me to do."

"Well then, I will be sure to thank Him for using you then."

"That would be just fine, Ma'am."

Marla scrambled out of her car and ran over to Joshua, Killer, and the President. Before she could even come to a standstill, she was blurting out the story of how Killer had saved her and arranged for the tapes to get to Washington, via one of his runners, and finally how he had escorted her to the Capitol and then back to the News Channel. She further explained how, try as she might, she couldn't get the equipment to work. When she returned to Covenant, the control boards had suddenly come back on line, and they were preparing to run both tapes, edited for modesty.

"Mine." Marla pointed out.

Now the truth would be known as the whole nation and perhaps the world was shown just what had happened in Covenant, and perhaps in many other places as well.

When Marla took a breath, Roberta gave her a hug and said, waving a hand to take in the gang, "I see what you mean about a safe escort. Did you have any trouble?"

Marla was about to answer when sirens ripped the air with their shrill cries and tires screeched as several State Police Cars fish-tailed around the corner and entered the square, nearly hitting the long line of the motorcycles.

The troopers jumped out, carrying shot guns and others had their 9mm's already drawn as they rushed toward Joshua, Killer, Marla, and President Place. Joshua and the other officers pulled their own weapons. The Secret Service Agents surrounded the President, their weapons also drawn.

As the troopers entered the secured area they were quickly surrounded and disarmed. The trooper in charge, Sgt. Hunkers, yelled, "You can't do that, we have a warrant for Marla Brinkle's arrest. It's ordered by the governor himself and he expects us to bring her in. I will . . . "

President Place, yelled, startling everyone, "That'll be all, Sargeant! Governor Bradley is dead and as President of the United States I am declaring a state of emergency until I can determine the good guys from the bad guys!"

The trooper looked small and scared as he stood on his tip toes, held by the scruff of the neck by a towering Secret Agent.

The troopers were ordered to leave and they reluctantly complied, mumbling useless threats as they left.

President Place, who was in her command mode now, continued, "Marla, I think you were interested in an interview with me, is that right?"

"Yes Ma'am! If we could go over to the trucks and get ready, they should be finished showing the tapes soon and it will be time for our live feed." Before the two women left, Marla pulled Joshua aside and asked about Grady.

"Grady's in the hospital with a concussion. He'll be okay—that hard Irish head of his can take quite a beating."

"And Chief Wilson? Did he get everything he needed at the temple?"

"Yeah, he did. The general put a couple of bullets in him though. Chief Wilson has gone to be with the Lord."

Tears fell from Marla's eyes as she thought about her confrontation with the chief at the hospital.

"I wish I had told him how sorry I am about the trouble I've caused."

"Hey, don't even think that way. The chief was a good and righteous man—he wouldn't have held anything against you. Trust me."

Marla smiled gratefully at Joshua and then excused herself to conduct her interview with the President.

The engineer gave Marla the two minute warning and they moved to a spot in front of the huge stone replica of the Ten Commandments that stood in the city square.

Marla's assistant counted, "three, two, one," and pointed at her to begin. "This is Marla Brinkle, action news reporter, with a live report from the Covenant City Park. With me is President Roberta Place..."

* * *

Phillip Huggens, Vice President of the United States of America, sat in Roberta's chair in the Oval Office, dreaming of how it would one day be his chair, his office.

He jumped out of the chair when the President's face appeared on the television screen. He stood there looking for all the world, like a little boy caught with his hand in the cookie jar. He went over and turned the set down, irritated at himself for being so jumpy. If he was to pull this off, he would have to be a lot cooler and wait for the right moment.

Huggens listened as Marla continued her report, "... a story of good vs. evil. Over the next few weeks and months, I will bring you a full accounting of the events that led up to the activities you saw depicted in the tapes, which were just aired. Those tapes are real. I am an eyewitness to one of the atrocities you saw.

For now, however, as I said earlier, we are privileged to have President Place with us today. The President has asked to address the nation and we feel it is important that you listen. Madam President..."

Marla stepped aside and the smiling face of President Place filled the screen again. Huggens sat back down in Roberta's chair to watch.

"Good evening, my fellow Americans and may God bless you all. I want to thank the Lord Jesus Christ for saving my son's life and then saving my own soul. I would also like to thank Joshua White and all the citizens of Covenant, for standing up for Jesus, even when the world in its madness had turned away from Him. Yes, I believe only madness could cause us not to see how loved we are by God.

Huggens stood up and yelped, "What!" and then fell back into the chair as if in shock.

The President continued, "I have seen and heard of many wonderful miracles occurring right here in Covenant. I myself have received Jesus Christ into my life, along with the Holy Spirit, who guides and comforts me. I make a public promise to all the citizens of the United States and the world beyond it, that I will do everything in my power to right the wrongs that have been done in our country in recent years. Up to now, I have been part of the problem. As of today, I will fight for solutions, with all the powers of this office.

"Our policies have produced a Godless generation of lost souls, who have no guidance or purpose. In the weeks and months ahead I would ask every Christian citizen to pray that the Lord alone will guide me in how to best handle this problem.

"To you non-believers, I pray that you will open your hearts and hear the Word of God and turn from your sin. Joshua White shared this Scripture with me..."

Roberta opened her Bible to the page she had marked in 2 Chronicles 7:14 and began to read.

"If My people who are called by My name humble themselves and pray, and seek My face and turn from their wicked ways, then I will hear from heaven, will forgive their sin, and will heal their land."

She closed the Bible and bowed her head for a moment before continuing to speak.

"Before my fellow Americans, and before my God, I publicly denounce Satan and his demons and I ask forgiveness for my many sins. I accept Jesus Christ as my Savior and ask Him to be Lord of my life.

"I invite all of you who are watching right now, to join me in this prayer of repentance. Repent of your sins before it is too late.

"God bless you all and God bless America!"

When the camera turned back to Marla Brinkle it found her on her knees with tears streaming down her face as she accepted Jesus into her life, repenting of her own sins. The camera man cleared his throat noisily and Marla wiped her eyes hurriedly, but remained on her knees as she said, "We will continue to interrupt regular programming with updates as more information about the conspiracy in Covenant becomes available. This is Marla Brinkle reporting live from the scene of the battle. Good evening."

The world of Vice President Huggens had just turned inside out. He sat open mouthed and numb as he watched the celebration on the Oval Office's television set. He thought longingly of all his plans, despairing at how they had just gone up in smoke.

The phone ringing snapped him out of his self-pitying reverie.

"Yeah! What do you want! I..."

The dark, cold voice on the other end of the phone said, "Shut up and listen! She must die! I don't care how you get it done, but you will do it."

Nervously, Huggens asked, "But, how? I mean, she's guarded night and day. She..."

"I'm sure a man in your position has ways of getting things done, right? I don't care how, just do it! Understand?"

Yes, he understood all too well. Either she died or he did.

Huggens said, "OK, I'll see to it, but it'll take some planning and that'll take time."

There was a soft click as the phone caller hung up the phone without responding. Huggens' hand was shaking as he returned the phone to its cradle.

* * *

Capt. Worl knelt before Jesus Christ in an attitude of reverent worship.

Jesus spoke to His faithful captain.

"Capt. Worl, I don't know when I shall return to the earth, but I feel my time grows short. With the battle of Covenant, we have drawn the line in the sand and the humans must choose whom they will serve now before the time is past.

"Our next battle will be to save the entire United States of America, not just Covenant. I am putting you in charge of all the angelic forces assigned to the United States and I want you to put Aaron in charge of all the angelic forces we have in Covenant. I am counting on you and all of our forces to be ready to help My people in their coming crisis. Of course, the Holy Spirit is with them to guide and comfort and empower them. With the help of the heavenly host, they will overcome Satan and his forces.

"Worl, go and serve, with My blessing."

Capt. Worl rose in a flurry of translucent wings and turned toward earth. He would seek Christians willing to live and die for their Lord and Savior Jesus Christ, and together they would defeat Satan.